# THE GRASPING ROOT

*Also by Margaret Pinard*

*The Keening* (Book 1 of *Remnants*)

*Dulci's Legacy*

*Memory's Hostage*

# THE GRASPING ROOT

Book 2 of *Remnants*

## MARGARET PINARD

Taste Life Twice Publishing

# PART ONE

# Chapter 1

THE HOUSE STOOD its ground. The solid log structure was a dark spot against the thick layer of snow, surrounded by dark trees reaching up into the inky night. The early spring quiet did not penetrate indoors, where needles clacked and small coughs joined the fire's crackle. The MacLean family sat snugly in the warmth of their fire.

There was plenty of wood to be had on their property, enough so that they would not perish of cold even in this wild Nova Scotian forest where they'd put down stakes. But food was harder to come by and they'd had a hard winter foraging and hunting to keep all five bodies and souls together.

If the oppression of hunger hadn't been enough, there was the new absence of their father to adjust to. His dramatic return home last autumn, when he had collapsed at their boardinghouse rooms in town unable to say a word, had been followed quickly by his death. They were left with little clue about how he'd received his multiple bruises and internal injuries or why he'd been the target of such violence.

As newcomers to the province, the scene had excited much comment. Many a housewife had clamored for details in the street. The MacLeans were content to retreat to the hills where such gossip could not hurt them. However, soon they would need to go to town for seed and supplies. It was time to clear the land for their first spring crops. Then they could cart the logs they'd felled over the winter down to the mill for cash.

The MacLeans may not have had experience felling trees before that winter, fisherfolk and crofters as they were, but they found their rhythm. The red spruce and white pine that lay in the snow would be their only source of income for supplies to last them through the starving times of late spring. The glacial cold that had kept them in its grip all winter was relinquishing its hold just in time for them to make the trip to the mill.

Muirne sat on the trestle bench with her back to the table, face to the firelight. A mending pile of ragged wool socks, her duty as the eldest daughter of the family, lay in her lap. Muirne occasionally glanced up at the lean faces of the others in the firelight. They were ranged around the cabin, each absorbed in different thoughts or pursuits. Neil sat on the stack of old plaids they kept for insulation, gazing into the fire. Mam sat next to Muirne on the bench, spinning rough fleece onto a spindle.

Sheena and Alisdair were comparing foot sizes, with Sheena taking turns to tickle the toes of the youngest. Muirne took a moment to bask in the companionable quiet, so different from the charged, tense atmosphere of earlier in the winter, when she'd had to pretend she couldn't hear her mother weeping beside her in bed.

Her thoughts were interrupted when Mam put down her spindle. Her mother looked so much older than she had only a year ago. Her hair was still an ashy blonde but gray had crept in. Lines around her mouth and eyes bore testimony to the many painful emotions that had been etched on that face.

Mam shared with her a mute look of peaceful surrender. Surrender, because how else to greet the decisions of the Almighty? Peaceful, because—well, they had survived the winter, hadn't they? Muirne smiled slightly and her mother shifted her eyes to her eldest child.

Mam said, "Haven't had a storm for near two weeks now."

Neil continued staring into the fire as if he hadn't heard.

"Neil."

"Yes, Mama." Finally he looked away from the fire. Muirne busied her hands with the darning needle again but strained her ears to hear her mother's quiet voice.

"No storms for a while. I think it's settling down. Might be time to get the logs ready."

"Aye. I'll be checking the streams in the morning. See whether it'd be easier to slide them down that way or fashion a sled to go over the snow. I've some parts laid by that might do."

"Ah. That sounds well, then."

A moment of scrambling on the floor as Alisdair grabbed for Sheena's foot. She evaded him by tucking them under herself. Grumbles of 'Not fair!' and giggles punctuated the stillness. Her mother spoke softly again.

"Were you planning on writing another letter?"

When there was no answer, Muirne sneaked another look at Neil. He'd lost his vacant expression and his cheeks were even flatter.

"I--I hadn't thought about it."

"Hadn't ye?" Mam shot him a skeptical glance. "Who's tellin' tales now?"

"All right, I haven't decided yet, then."

"Do you still have feelings for the lass?" she asked, so

softly that Muirne felt it more than heard it.

Neil ducked his head. Fidgeted with his hands. Muirne looked up again to see him appealing to Mam with his eyes. "Aye. I still wish she would join me."

"Then write her again. The Atlantic Ocean is not an impossible barrier." Mam took up her spindle and recommenced her spinning. Muirne felt her heart stretch at her mother's encouraging Neil when things still seemed so precarious. It never hurt to hope, though. Did it?

"We should have a thanksgiving prayer tomorrow," Muirne heard herself say. Her family looked over, surprised. "We have made it through our first winter here. The first load of logs will get us started and we'll have wheat sprouting before we know it." Her words came faster as she warmed to her own idea.

"A fair thing to do," Mam agreed. "Early, before Neil starts on the sled tomorrow. And we'll mark the celebration with breakfast afterwards: acorn mash!"

Smiles and groans greeted this announcement. They'd been eating acorn mash since the oats ran out. It was time-consuming to boil and soak the acorns, but at least the white oak grove where they could still be found wasn't too long of a trudge. The next morning after prayers, Muirne picked up her wooden spoon and contemplated the sandy brown mush. The hope of something better seasoned her appetite, and Muirne felt satisfied.

The trees they had felled first lay in the interval below the house: that land would be the best for their first crop of oats. While the long spruce logs lay curing, there were the roots to dig out. The borrowed tools from last autumn were brought out again and put to use. That early spring of 1824, they subsisted on the meanest diet as they worked: foraged weeds from the riverbanks, eggs from the chickens who'd survived the long winter inside the house with them, and scant meat from the hares and foxes Sheena and Alisdair managed to trap. Their cheek-bones all showed and the boys' hipbones jutted out of trousers that hung low. They needed multiple layers of wool jerseys to keep warm. Neil and Muirne had taken Alisdair out on the not-so-bad days with them, not to help saw into the great trunks, but to help gather daily firewood. Sometimes it seemed like they were forever sizing and collecting sticks of wood. But Muirne was grateful for every minute in that warm cabin when the elements howled outside.

Muirne had received two letters from her beau Mr. Turner over the winter, and they had broken up the pattern of family interaction like a staff to an icy pond. Everyone got to inspect the letters, which were dissected for their handwriting, grammar, and spelling. Neil used them as teaching tools. When Muirne had acquiesced to Mr. Turner's—Edward's—correspondence, she told him that they would be examined like this. It saved her from burning with quite as much self-consciousness as she might if he had been more sentimental.

The first one had been very formal, full of condolences, hopes, propriety. The second was more like his own voice: teasing and wry, with snippets of medical college life and gossip from Halifax, a town which they had never visited. Peeks into his life, outside their closed world, were welcome distractions from the silence. Muirne felt his words bolster her when the drudgery and abstinence of the cabin became oppressive. She had begun to hope he would offer for her in the spring, and enjoyed private moments of heady anticipation.

When the small, flat intervale was mostly cleared, a picked-clean pile of tree branches stood high enough to make any settler proud. When the air finally started to dry out in late April, it was time. Their gangly group moved off the ridge through the snow early in the morning, quickly descending into one of the many small valleys. Muirne immediately shivered without the sun that was just starting to lighten the bottoms of clouds to the southeast. It would be as good as gone while they rambled through the low valleys. Along with Neil and their mother, she helped pull the sled with ropes. Sheena and Alisdair walked alongside it, each resting a hand on the rough logs. Brisk air brought spots of pink to everyone's cheeks.

They were all glad of the thaw: an excuse for getting out of the cabin, meeting neighbors, and going to town. It had been right to stay home during winter; the family had turned in on itself to cope with losing Gillan. *I hate those expanses of silence that aren't really silent. I will be glad to get work underway and not be so mournful, so hemmed in by the weather.*

They hadn't talked aloud about Gillan since the funeral in Pictou. She spoke of him in her prayers each night but neither her mother nor Neil had volunteered their thoughts on the mystery—why someone would beat their father so mercilessly without any provocation. For whom in all the Canadian provinces would he know? And who would hate him fiercely enough to beat him and leave him for dead in the wilderness? She tried to mirror

Neil's and Mam's respectful silence, burying her hurt and bewilderment deep, but avoiding it only made her more fearful of their adopted country.

No news had come yet about the perpetrator of the crime, but with the roads opening again, there was more hope of the murderer's apprehension. Muirne knew her mother waited for news of an investigation. An anxious line appeared between her brows whenever Muirne returned from the postbox or Tom the postman could be heard passing by. Wouldn't someone have tried to figure out what had happened? Meantime, she watched Neil struggle to take their father's place. She waited for Edward to come back and make her his wife. She wished for someone to tell them all would be well again.

# Chapter 2

As THEY PULLED their way down the slope, Neil caught sight of a column of smoke to their left.

"I bet that's the Frasers' cabin," Neil said. "You know, the ones that brought around the moosewood tea and wool for winter clothes?"

Alisdair glanced up, screwing up his face to see, and let loose an explosive sigh.

"We're only that far along? I thought we were halfway to town," he said.

A brief smile went round at such a hopeful estimate. Neil regarded the angle of the sun and suggested a short rest. They agreed and found a place in a small dell. Sheena used a short stick from the forest path to draw in the snow that still lay on the ground. Neil came over to take a look, stretching the sore spots in his back.

"Not bad," he said. He pointed to one of her marks. "That's backward, though. Says 'Eb' instead of 'Ed'." Muirne glanced up from her seat on the edge of a log.

"What's that you're spelling, Sheena?" she asked.

"Nothing," she mumbled. Before Muirne could rise and regard what she'd scraped with her stick, Sheena had kicked her clogs through it and squatted close to Neil. Neil tried to hide a smile. Muirne settled back down with a suspicious glance at her young sister.

"Did you write that girl another letter, Neil?" Sheena asked him, wiping her clogs dry as best she could with

her knit gloves. *So she's worrying after both her siblings'*
*romantic attempts, is she? Good. Maybe then she'll stop moping.*

His eyebrows rose as he looked at his younger sister.
"Meddling in everyone's affairs, are we?" he teased. When
she raised her eyes, he patted his chest. "I did. It's safe by
my heart," he said in a conspiratorial tone.

Sheena's cheeks puffed up in a delighted grin. "You
know what I'm going to do when you get back with the
oat seed, Neil?" she asked, still in a voice for secrets.

"What, then?"

"Make a patch for the seeds from home, and guard it
very carefully, so we can have barley and oats *from home.*"

"Ah," was all Neil said. He remembered the parting in
Port Glasgow last spring, the gifts of earth and seeds
from Mull given to them by Gillan's sister Jenny. They
had sent word of their safe arrival last spring, then had to
write again in the autumn after Gillan's death.

Neil flexed his hands, relieving the cramp of holding
the ropes. He looked to his mother and sister. They nodded and took up the load again. By sundown, they had
reached a scattering of houses below the snowline.
Sheena was dispatched to the creek for water and the
party sat on the side of what had become a discernible
path. Sheena came back with a full bucket, careful not to
spill as she walked. They took turns dipping the tin cup
into the bucket for a drink.

The sawmill was only a mile away but they would
wait for new light to guide the logs across the flat land.
They used the shelter of the trees against the wind and
the weight of the leaves upon their blankets for added
warmth, little concerned with what the people in the
nearby houses might think of them. If the strangers had

no hospitality to offer them, Neil thought, they could keep their spiteful opinions to themselves.

The next day brought them the rewards they sought. Neil bargained as well as he could for a fair-enough lump sum from the miller, who would store the logs several weeks and then float them down the river to a bigger port when the ice melted. The miller told him about the men who would come soon to do the job of log wran- gling—canoeing alongside in the rapids and guiding the logs through tricky bends in the river's course. Not a job he'd fancy.

They entered the town of New Glasgow, lightened of their burden of timber but still lugging the sled, now piled with only their packs, which were nearly empty. Their first stop, even before the mercantile, was the New Glasgow post office, where a letter waited for them. The clerk handed it down to Alisdair, whose head just rose above the counter. The joy on his face was catching.

"Let's have a look at it then," Neil said, smiling de- spite his own disappointment.

Alisdair handed it up to him. Neil angled it so that his mother could see as he read the direction.

"It's from Aunt Jenny, all right," he said. "Maybe we'll wait 'til we get settled for the night before we all read it out?" Mam met his gaze and pursed her lips. She nodded. Better to save any emotional display for the privacy of their own family, rather than in plain view of the post office customers.

Neil folded and put it away, withdrawing as he did the other letter from his jacket pocket. Sheena saw him and smiled broadly up at her brother.

"That'll go on a ship back home, Neil?"

"I 'spect so, Sheena. Slowest form of post waits for the best weather. We'll hope for a reply before the snows close in on us again." Neil gave her a brief smile, then lapsed back into studied passivity. He knew it didn't fool Muirne. Her hand curled around his elbow for a brief moment and squeezed. It didn't do to hope, he thought. But hope he would. Perhaps losing Gillan meant he was owed something. Enough to have Letty answer his letters. Enough to have her change her mind and consent to be his wife. His first letter was unanswered after a year; this was his second. He prayed it would merit a response.

The drama of Neil's letter dispensed with, they continued to the mercantile and paid up their account in cash. Mr. Bracethwaite the owner smiled broadly and made chit-chat, putting out the welcome mat now that he knew his investment had not starved in the snows of their first winter.

The man was tall, with spindly legs and a bit of a rolling gait. He squinted a lot, as people came in, as if sizing them up. Neil was happy when he renewed their credit for the season without peering at their account for too long. He helped Neil find the farming items he needed. That little sketchbook of Canadian edible plants had done them well over the winter, for certain, but he hoped they wouldn't have to scrape so close to the bottom of the barrel next time.

# Chapter 3

THOSE MAJOR TASKS accomplished, they went to confer with their former landlady, now-friend, Mrs. Conaghey, in Pictou. They walked the mile across the bay, the ferry not yet operational, and returned to the large boarding-house by the water for the first time since Gillan's burial. Mrs. Conaghey ushered them into the back parlor. It was just as sparse and threadbare as they remembered it, a testament to the woman's own thrifty ways and generosity to others. Muirne had a funny feeling when she stepped onto the bare wood floors that she had cleaned as part of their room and board. Would they end up back here, or manage to keep the bit of independence they'd won hiding in the hills?

She sat for over half an hour, mostly listening, as these sessions usually turned out to be rather one-sided. She was glad along with the others to hear the news, however, and Mrs. Conaghey was only too gratified to pass it on. Neil grinned and she couldn't stop blushing as the large woman banged on about a former suitor of Muirne's.

"Oh, don't worry your nose about my James, my girl. He's already found himself another lass to moon over. My sister had better keep a close watch on him, is all I can say. When I think how he is settling down in that law office, and how fine a catch he will be, I just don't understand it..."

"But surely, your sister had someone in mind for

him?" Mam replied, looking up from the knitting she had brought along.

"Oh! Well, as to that, she's had several somebodies in mind, but young James can't seem to catch any young lady's eye! Now't wrong with him I can see, but there allus seems to be someone else earlier or quicker, or better set-up or I don't-know-what. Poor boy."

Eventually she got around to the subject of the town doctors. Muirne's ears perked up.

"And of course we'll see the typhus come from one of the next ships, now that old Dr. Skinner has seen fit to leave us for England. There's no call for it, as I see it, none! But he will go and leave us at such a time..."

"But isn't it his wish that some of his students who are about to set up their own practice stay behind so we won't be left without a medical man?" Muirne asked.

"That *might* have answered, my girl, but he's taking the advanced students *with* him, of course. They're to learn the very latest at the university in London. That's the whole purpose of the trip!"

"He's taking—oh!" Muirne burst out. She looked at her mother in panic before remembering to answer Mrs. Conaghey's comment. "I suppose that is the best way to learn." It was a feeble rejoinder, but the lady accepted it and charged robustly on.

"Well, all a question of timing, my dear. For those who sicken this summer while we are without immediate aid, it will not be the best way for them to learn. Sending to Halifax will do no good."

"No, indeed, ma'am," Muirne said faintly.

She left their visit feeling exhausted, although she had merely sat in a sturdy chair and sipped at tea—real tea from China, not moosewood tea that was made with striped maple twigs. Her mind was spinning. Her last letter from Edward had mentioned nothing of a journey to Britain. But he was one of the most promising students that Dr. Skinner had. Was he making other plans without her?

Neil went with Alisdair to collect their sacks of oat seed at the mercantile while the women sat in the shadow of a large oak by the south road. Muirne missed seeing him go, standing numbly by the packs and focusing on nothing. Sheena and Mam sat on the stack of folded plaids on the sled. Muirne had almost forgot their presence until Sheena spoke.

"What's wrong, Muirne?"

"Nothing, Sheena."

But something was wrong. Edward would almost certainly make one of the party to journey to England. So why hadn't he told her? Was he going to just disappear on them? Was her only hope for an anchor in the storm going to blow away and turn out to be a disappointment, too?

Mam abruptly turned toward her.

"He would have said if he was to leave for England, would he no'? It's a bloody long ways. He should not be going away without consulting you, or at the very least letting you know his plans—not if he expects you to be his wife."

The vehemence of the speech startled all three of them. Muirne swallowed.

"We're not engaged, Mam. I think—I thought it was going to be so—soon, but—we're not yet engaged; he need not worry about taking me into account in his decisions."

"You can defend him now, but you make sure you know the truth of it next time ye talk; that's all I'll say." Mam's mouth closed in a grim line. "I don't want you to be pullin' one way while yer husband pulls another, 'tis all."

Muirne went to where her mother sat, slumped on the sack of grain. She put out her hand; Mam clasped it. The look in her mother's eyes was no longer peaceful surrender. It was defiant desperation. Muirne felt the power of her mother's emotion: a fury, held in by the thinnest of barriers. Muirne thought of Gillan's rash decision to go off by himself and set it beside her mother's decision to remain with Neil to build the house. Pulling one way, and another. *Oh, Mam.* By the time the boys returned, her mother had composed herself. Sheena had retreated to the tree, her arms hugging her knees close.

# Chapter 4

ON THEIR RETURN route, the MacLeans took the first opportunity given them for something other than survival: they went a-visiting. Neil knew it was expected of them but chafed a little at the necessary social calls when he could be planting seed in the ground.

They had neither food nor drink nor woolen goods for gifts but still Mam managed to find something— water-reeds woven into a basket, or pine boughs turned into a wreath—so they would not arrive empty-handed. They were welcomed in turn by the Ogilvies, the Allmans, the Massons, the Frasers, and the MacGregors. The five families lived on tracts of land given to earlier settlers within a ten-mile radius, known as the Ochil Grant. They offered up what surplus they could to their newest neighbor. Neil thought the Ogilvies were none so pleasant—Lowlanders, they were—but their last stop, at the cabin nearest theirs, afforded them the Highland welcome they were used to.

"Well, sure, and let me look at the lot o' ye," said Mrs. MacGregor as they tramped in. Mr. MacGregor was some years her senior, and only partially attempted to rise from his chair by the fire, but the missus was all movement and fuss. The old man hadn't visited last winter, either, Neil remembered. *Must like bossing people about from here.* The thought gave him a chuckle as the man in question raised an arm and a son came running with a new cup of grog.

Mam stood closest to Mrs. MacGregor and motioned to each of the children to come forward. "You remember my eldest, Neil." He stepped forward and bowed slightly, smoothing the amusement from his face.

"Muirne, my eldest daughter." Her smile was somewhat resigned, this being the fifth time, but she curtseyed well.

"Sheena."

Sheena settled wary dark eyes on the older woman and executed a wobbly curtsy.

"I see we'll have to fatten you up, won't we?" interjected Mrs. MacGregor. "All that lovely dark hair—it'll go stringy if you can't get them enough fat to eat, Mrs. MacLean. But it's always hard the first winter, isn't it? We have just the thing for you—"

Before she could finish her sentence, Alisdair piped up, "But what about me?"

Mrs. MacGregor turned from where she was already moving to fetch something for Sheena and smiled down on the little tow-headed boy.

"And this is Alisdair," Mam said, smiling. "He was very disappointed to hear he had slept through you and your sons' visit for the New Year."

"Mr. Alisdair, I'm pleased to meet you as well. Can you bow as well as your brother now?"

Neil raised a brow at Alisdair, a challenge.

Alisdair executed the lowest bow a six-year-old could be expected to do without tumbling over and they all praised his efforts. The ice broken, the company fell in well together. One of their grown sons stopped by and added to the lively scene at the supper table.

"Married to a lovely lass out by French-fort last year, weren't you, Gerald, otherwise he'd've loved to have you as neighbors."

Mrs. MacGregor waggled an expressive eyebrow at Muirne. She blushed. Neil smiled at how easily his sister was riled by these types of comments.

Sheena, who'd been busily sipping a mug of cattail soup, plunked the cup down to hurriedly interject.

"But she's already got a beau, Mrs. MacGregor. He left us a little treehouse for his letters and everything—"

"*Will* you be *quiet*, Sheena," Muirne hissed.

"Well! That *is* good news, and who's to say you're not next, Miss Sheena? Girls around here do marry young." She shot the astonished girl a smile then reverted to her previous thought. "What good fortune, indeed. Of course I'm sure Neil has everything in hand—good lad—but another strong young man couldn't go amiss in managing your holding, being new and all—"

"Oh, but he's from—"

"*Sheena.*" It was their mother that time, in a note that brooked no argument. Mam shot her a look and Sheena dropped her gaze. Mam turned back to Mrs. MacGregor.

"While it would no doubt be a boon, we don't expect any help from that quarter quite yet. But Muirne and I are doing a fair enough job at being Neil's helpers."

Neil nodded his agreement.

"Well, and I don't mean to speak out of turn, but we do feel right sorry for ye, after losing yer hisband as ye did last autumn. If there's ever anything we can do—I can always call on Gerald or Tom to help you out for a spell."

The brittle ice swept over them just as they were feeling relaxed and welcomed. *They're kind sentiments.*

*Trying to help. Not their fault I can't do everything that's need-ful.* The pause stretched awkwardly until Mam broke it.

"Thank you, Mrs. MacGregor. We appreciate the offer." She paused for a moment before continuing in an altered tone. "Some of the other neighbors were not so kind in their attentions to this family matter. I appreciate your—kindness."

Mam faltered on the last word. Muirne put her arm around Mam's shoulders and rubbed her arms briskly. Alisdair fidgeted at the edge of the bench, glancing rapidly around at everyone's face. Neil saw he was about to ask an awkward question and cleared his throat.

"Thank you, Mrs.—Mr.—MacGregor, for your hospitality," he spoke quietly as he nodded at each of them. "It has been good to feel at home again."

Tentative smiles greeted his hearkening back to Scotland's ways, and the family soon retired to the makeshift beds provided them by the MacGregors.

# Chapter 5

AFTER A WEEK of visiting, their return home, laden with gifted foodstuffs and seed stores, was counted as a great fortune. Muirne, however, walked with her family into the front yard like a soldier asleep, eyes on feet, trudging along. She didn't even glance at the sweet little postbox as they passed it. Sitting on the lowest branch of the lone tree standing by the road, the rough-painted miniature house had been placed there by Edward. She didn't want to think about Ed right then; his abandonment was filling her whole being with confusion and hurt. When they reached their door, Sheena stood up from her own hunched tiredness, looking around as if she'd been in her own trance of fatigue. Muirne saw her abrupt movement out of the corner of her eye.

"Muirne!"

The cry held recrimination, disbelief. Muirne turned to her sister mutely, offering no excuse. Sheena tripped back down the road to the tree and tried to jump up to the height of the box but she couldn't reach it. Muirne's extra inches were just enough. Frustrated, Sheena looked for a handhold to climb the tree. Muirne bit her lip. There would be nothing there now, if Edward was already setting his sights on English ladies. True, he was not all that well-off but his position was much more assured than theirs, stranded here as they were without father or friend. Muirne scrunched her eyes tight. *No, that isn't true.*

*We've just met our neighbors, and there were some very agreeable people among them. I'm just overreacting.*

Neil yelled close by, making her flinch. "Sheena, come in now. I'll check it for ye in a wee while."

Sheena ran back up the hill and marched past her sister, eyes brimming.

"Sheena," Muirne coaxed, about to offer an apology. Sheena threw herself into Mam's box bed, a makeshift closet with mattress inside. Muirne sighed. *I'm not surprised that Sheena would side with Edward.*

"Let's just put the things away and plan out the field, aye? First things first," Mam murmured.

The tension dissipated, deprived of Sheena's indignation on Mr. Turner's behalf. Muirne took a deep breath. *I side with Edward, too—I just needed to think the worst before realizing I'm being a ridiculous wet blanket. See?* She felt better already.

Their discarded rucksacks formed an island of canvas and linen and dirt in the middle of the room. Muirne helped Mam root around on the back stoop, stowing supplies, then started beating the rugs that had been set out to air for the days they were away. She heard Alisdair inside on the floor, twirling the small top Mrs. MacGregor had given him. Neil disappeared down toward the new field.

Sheena took her place with the rug-beater outside and Muirne came back in, picking up an emptied sack to fold and put away. She stopped at sight of Neil and the letter he held. Her hand went to her front in a little fist. The corner of the cotton sack drooped.

Neil met her gaze and held out the letter. She draped the sack over the back of their one tall chair and plucked it from his hands. She strode right past him out the front door. She stopped immediately outside and squatted by the door. She gazed at the envelope. *This is my third letter from Edward.* Her heart teetered on the edge of a cliff: hopeful that he loved her, desperate that he love her, doubtful that he'd choose her, fearful lest he reject her— in this very letter. She ripped it open.

She read it over three times, trying to assure herself that the words she read were not something in a dream. They blurred and swam, and she at last closed them. She regained her composure listening to the voices of her family inside, who carried on without any notice of how her whole life had just shifted.

"Alisdair, here: start a fire for us," Neil called.

The rhythmic beating of the rag rugs subsided and Sheena rejoined the family inside.

"I believe we might do well to purchase a lamb on our next trip to town," Mam said.

Muirne opened her eyed. Lamb!

"It will be good to have some milk for making our own cheese. And if we get an older one, there will be our own wool. And there is the security—"

"Of course, Mam! A good idea, for the winter. We may as well start building a flock now," Neil said.

"Flock!" said Alisdair.

"Aye, they wasn't just dreams I was talkin' last year, ye know. We'll have to clear a deal of timber if we want to get off the debt lists, an' the prices still depressed."

"Will they never go back up?" Sheena asked.

"Not unless there's more war, dears, and we don't want to be wishin' that," said Mam.

After a moment's pause, there was some clacking

with the firestarter flint. After much clacking, an excited squawk.

"I'll go get some bigger sticks!" Alisdair said.

"I'm hungry," Sheena said.

"Well, my girl! You're in luck. Supper tonight is going to be a feast, for we've the goodwill of five families to feed us."

Muirne could hear some of the forced cheer in her mother's voice. She shifted and got up.

"The goodwill, and the nosy interfering," Neil said. "That's right! Now, will ye have kippers or potatoes or oysters this evening, ma'm'selle?"

Muirne entered in time to see his overture to Sheena.

"Can't we have them all at once?" Sheena asked.

Mam smiled and Neil let loose a chuckle.

Mam lugged the water to the big pot over the fire. She made a soup of their neighbors' gifts. Into this quiet, contented mood, Muirne went to her brother's side. She handed the letter to Neil then went to fall dramatically onto their other straw mattress. Mam started in asking her what was wrong but she just waved toward Neil. He cleared his throat and read it aloud.

*My dear Mrs. MacLean and Family,*

*I was much aggrieved to find you away from home on this visit. I came myself in the hope that I could bring you news which might cause you, I flatter myself, some dismay and yet some joy. However, after spending the night, I cannot afford to spend more time away from the school, and so must inform you in this letter, inadequate as it is to communicate my grief at parting from you for some time.*

*I will travel with Dr. Skinner on his voyage to England this* winter. There was some confusion about who was to accompany him this year. He makes the effort but rarely and many students jockeyed for the position purely for the status conveyed on those chosen.

However, he chose only six. These are all advanced students, that they might benefit the most from the experience of touring modern hospitals and observing London's new operating theaters. I am honored to be among those chosen and I hope this pleases your family as well. Any honor done me reflects well upon those who have bestowed their most valuable friendship.

We will be away for some months, departing on the Twenty-Ninth of July, and it is for this reason that I wished to speak especially to one of your family in particular. There are scant weeks until our departure but such is my surety of choice and ardor of suit that I cannot but hope that my offer of marriage for your lovely daughter Miss Muirne is accepted so that we might be wed before being parted for such a long period.

Please excuse the barefaced and beggarly manner in which I have proposed, and do not take it as an indication that this should be how I shall treat your daughter henceforth. I had no expectation of not finding you at home and am only thankful I had paper, ink, quill, and wax to effect even this meager attempt.

If I do not hear from you before I must make sail, I include my address below and will write to Miss MacLean from there as soon as possible. If you can send a message or come yourselves to New Glasgow, to Dr. Skinner's, you may make me the happiest of men. If not, at least let me to know if Miss MacLean would allow herself to be engaged to me, with marriage to follow upon my return after the winter storms abate.

Your ever faithful and devoted servant,
Edward Turner

# Chapter 6

"THIS IS GREAT news!"

Neil turned to Muirne. She was sitting up on the bed now, her eyes calm but her face flushed unevenly.

"Is it no'?" he probed.

She rose slowly. He saw the beginnings of her smile before she ran and jumped at him. Neil held her close and swung her around gleefully. She yelped in astonishment; he laughed all the harder. Sheena danced around them both.

"You'd never know it from all the fancy words he uses but it sounds as if he's asked you to marry him, Muirne— is that right, Neil?" Mam asked, with a teasing glint in her eye.

Neil nodded.

"That he has, and in as fine a manner as we may ever see in this house." He showed the letter to his mother who merely glanced at the fine script and sighed. She clasped Muirne's hand.

"All the nonsense about being shipped off to England —was it Mrs. Conaghey's mistake about the dates?"

"No, indeed, Mam," said Neil. "He's going."

"Yes, he's going, but only just found it out," Muirne pointed out. She was positively shaking with excitement and girlish pride.

"He wishes us to marry before he leaves. He was here to ask himself but had to leave before we came back.

Preparations for travel, no doubt. But he wishes me to hasten back to New Glasgow to give my answer and have the banns read."

"What, go right back?" Sheena asked, exasperated. "I wanted to get the seeds in for my—"

Neil turned to tease her. "Come now, Sheena, is that any way to receive such a handsome proposal? Would you like to read it?"

He glanced at Muirne. She blushed but nodded her permission. As Sheena sat down with the romantic epistle, mollified, Alisdair popped in with his arms full of three large branches.

"This should keep our fire going all night, enough for Sheena to have to get the ash bucket ready," he said. Sheena merely waved her hands at him to leave off while she was so entertainingly engrossed. The branches clattered down next to the hearth. Nobody moved toward the fire. Alisdair frowned at his older siblings but Neil found it hard not to laugh, when Alisdair looked so put out not to be the center of attention. Mam explained.

"Your sister has just had a proposal of marriage, Alisdair—isn't that wonderful news?"

Alisdair's jaw dropped open; his pale brows knit together. He looked from Muirne to Sheena, then back again. "But, but—I thought—isn't Muirne—?"

They all exploded into laughter then except Sheena. She made a face at Alisdair then went back to reading the letter.

Mam made an effort to stop laughing enough to explain. "Well, Sheena'll be getting her own addresses soon enough, Alisdair, but this one's for Muirne. It's our Mr. Turner, of course."

Mam turned to Muirne again. "What does he say about an answer and the ceremony and the minister and his family and—oh, surely he's said it all in a letter that long?"

Mam laughed again. It made Neil's blood course, to hear all this laughter. It made him realize how long and lonely the winter had been. It had seemed to go by quickly, but also at times, agonizingly slowly. He felt a twinge deep in his gut for how lost he had felt back in the throes of cold and hunger and hopelessness. Now they were making plans for a wedding! New life! Springtime! He welcomed it, but felt a resistance, a caution, as if afraid of what would happen if they enjoyed themselves.

"I am to meet him as soon as possible in New Glasgow but he does not mention a ceremony. Perhaps merely sending a messenger—?" Muirne's gaze shifted to Neil.

He drew himself up and placed his fists on his hips. "We've already been on the rounds the past week and a half and we need to get our bearings. Then we must get to sowing the oats! Why not go yourself? Stay with Mrs. Conaghey the night. Bring an escort." He clapped the back of Alisdair's head lightly.

"Are ye sure it'll be safe, Neil?" Mam asked.

"We surely didna have nae trouble. There's plenty of folk about, with the snows melting and spring coming on. Well, Alisdair? Will ye be a good escort?"

"'Course I will!"

"Well, then, let's settle in and get at least some work out of ye before the morning. Unless?" Neil cocked an eye at his sister. She bore the teasing tolerably well.

"No, no, we'll go in the morning," Muirne said. "I'm quite able to stand the suspense one night. Tonight we celebrate!"

Out came the washboard and the whetstone and the few metal tools they'd packed away while they travelled. They got through the chores of restocking the house in record time to allow for more song and merriment before the world quieted. The Allmans' wild huckleberry cordial quickly disappeared, in proportion to the volume of the songs they sang. Neil's rattling spoons and his mother's trilling tin whistle inspired more liveliness and high spirits than that unassuming cabin had ever seen.

"I want to stay to get my seeds in the ground but I also want to go with Muirne to meet Edward, since he's her fiancé now." Sheena was pining not being able to do everything at once. Neil helped her decide.

"You're staying."

Muirne and Alisdair left in the morning, freshly supplied with more of their mother's oatcakes and some twists of boiled greens and eggs. Neil brought Sheena down to the field with him for the morning. Neil's first attempt to break up the small field progressed slowly; Sheena's efforts to make furrows in the hard ground were barely noticeable. She was shaking with effort, though: he saw the sweat pouring down her brow as she hacked at the frozen patches with the blunt shovel.

"About time for dinner," he said. The words interrupted her concentration for a moment and she almost stumbled, so intent she'd been on flinging her weight at the ground.

"All right," she said. They came in the back of the cabin around noon. Neil wiped his forehead and dropped his rough gloves into a pile near the back door. Mam smiled as they entered.

"Well timed, as usual," she said. She rose from her seat with the mending and went to fetch the bowls for the stew simmering over the fire. They ate with less conversation than usual around the table, a giant split log speared on two trestles. When Neil finished, he raised his eyebrows at Sheena.

"You ready to try again? I have a different tool in mind for ye."

Sheena looked troubled. "Maybe tomorrow. My hands are a bit shaky still."

Neil felt a bit contrite. He should have stopped her sooner. "Aye. All right."

Sheena flexed her fingers gingerly and reached for a wooden box on the floor. She withdrew the small piece of blackboard from the Rev. Mr. Balwhidder and their remaining stub of chalk. She saw Neil watching and shrugged.

"I need some practice and I might as well do it while there's light through the window." She gestured toward their one window, more of a gap in logs than a proper window. Neil had made the opening at Muirne's request, dubious of its usefulness. But the wooden shutter and the cloths around it kept it snug, and he had to admit it was nice to let in the light when the day was fine outside.

"I need to get better at the writing bit, and some of the reading is impossible! Will you help me read Mr. Turner's letter after supper, Neil?"

"Aye, if you help me with the tools. Clean off the ones in the back, will ya? The hoe and *cas-chrom*. I knocked off the big clods but they could use a good scrub so the rust don't start."

"I will, in just a moment." She continued carefully with her "D's" until the end of the line. Neil stood and put his hands on his hips, letting loose a bounteous exhalation.

"Done!" she said. She flashed a mischievous, dark-eyed glance at Neil. "For the moment."

She whisked out the back door for the tools, cloths, and cleaning compound while Neil was still chuckling. *Resilient, that one. Finally.*

# Chapter 7

MUIRNE, BACK ON the blazed path with Alisdair, did not spare a thought for what Sheena might be getting up to. All her thoughts pressed forward to the town where she might live, to the medical men she might entertain, to Edward's family, whom she had yet to meet. Alisdair rescued them from getting lost twice by pointing out the markings on the trees.

The second time he did so, Alisdair rolled his eyes at her. She did deserve it.

"Head in the clouds," she thought she heard him say. Muirne was reminded how different his childhood was turning out from hers on the island: first in Glasgow, then in a boarding-house, now in the wilderness. No sense of home or family beyond their four cabin walls. The stark contrast between how well she understood her family and how little she knew about Edward's background now prompted a scary uncertainty. What were they like? Why had he not talked about them before? Were they cold, calculating people? She didn't actually know any English people. She shivered and pulled her shawl tighter.

When they regained the village outside Sawmill Brook, they made camp in the same clearing they had found the preceding journey. The layer of leaves was still needed to feel truly insulated from the cold air. The mental exertions of her day had completely worn Muirne out and she went to sleep that night immediately upon closing her eyes. The next day would bring her to a fiancé, if she could find him.

She and Alisdair went straightaway to Bracethwaite's Mercantile in the morning. The grocer looked puzzled to see them again so soon.

"We're looking for a Mr. Edward Turner," Muirne said.

"Oh yes. Mr. Turner is in the neighborhood. I believe he is currently with Dr. Skinner, in fact. Right down Williams Lane."

She and Alisdair thanked him and hurried along the side street to Dr. Skinner's.

When she knocked, the door was opened by the very man she sought. Edward's eyes lit up when he saw her. He stepped into the street and framed her face with his clean, spare hands. She felt his fingers hovering near her temples, felt his eyes bore into hers.

"Miss MacLean," he said. His voice, while steady, held something reverent in it. He opened his mouth to say more but was preempted by Alisdair at her side.

"And me, I'm her escort!"

"Ah! Mr. Alisdair. Well done." He stepped back and let his hands fall away from her face. "Your sister has arrived safely and you have discharged your duties well. But what is the purpose of your errand?" His eyes came back to rest on her face. "Can it be—?"

Muirne felt her heart expand with the deep breath she took. "We are here with a message and desire some more information, sir."

"Oh, do you, indeed?" A curtain passed over the reverence in his eyes. They became playful, soft. "Well, come in. Dr. Skinner would find this a most proper use of his sitting room."

He ushered the two of them inside then led the way to the parlor on their right. He stashed their rucksacks under the window and motioned for them both to sit. Muirne recognized Edward's graciousness in acting as their host and felt comparatively out of place and awkward. How could she possibly jump in to such an intimate topic?

Alisdair had chosen the largest armchair. His feet didn't touch the floor. Edward didn't laugh but turned to Muirne with a glint in his eye. She gazed back, appreciating his fine, broad shoulders, his well-brushed coat, the dark, buoyant curls on his head. He sat with one booted leg crossed in front of the other.

At last, he broke the silence. "May I hope that this visit means your mother gives her consent? Are we to marry as soon as possible? I figured things could be settled in less than the two months before——"

Muirne raised a hand.

"The information, sir, that we desire, is about the ceremony, the church, the minister, your family, your plans to——"

"Ahhh," Edward interrupted, with a slow nod of his head. "But after all that?"

"After all that—well, I believe my answer will be yes!" *How can he think otherwise? But I desire to know him better, not to let such an event as a six-month long voyage dictate when and how I agree!*

Edward smiled. At first it seemed too impersonal a smile for such a moment but then he dimpled, showing his teeth, and reached forward to kiss Muirne's hands.

"The twenty-ninth?" Muirne said, her question lifting

the end of the word.

"Yes, we sail on the twenty-ninth of July and there is much to do before then," Edward agreed. "As for the church, I would be happiest if your family chose someone they were comfortable with to officiate. If it were up to me, I would simply go to the Justice of the Peace, because, my dear—" here he leaned forward "—I am an atheist. I think you should know this now so it is not a secret between us. I decided to become an atheist and cast off the Church's teachings while at university in Halifax. After my studies in biology—but you are upset."

Muirne had scrunched up her brow at the word 'atheist,' but gave a start at 'cast off the Church.' Her clenched hand hovered in front of her ribs while she took a deep breath.

"You mean you've thrown off the protection of Holy Church? But—why?"

"I can explain it to you, at length, but not right at this moment. Will you stay in town tonight? There is much to say, to explain—"

He appeared a bit choked, perhaps thinking better of the suddenness of his announcement. *And no wonder. Not belong to the Church? Why that was worse than being a Catholic!* Muirne blinked and scrambled to answer his question.

"Yes, I had thought to ask Mrs. Conaghey—"

"Or you could stay here with the doctor. Dine with us here tonight and we can speak more afterward?"

"And Alisdair? Will there be room?" she asked.

"Certainly. He's got plenty of room here."

Muirne didn't like the evasiveness she heard in Edward's voice. He was trying to get away from her; he was nervous. Very well, so was she. No, not nervous. Terrified. She could definitely use some time to recover from his shocking statement. It couldn't be what she thought.

"All right," she said faintly.

"Excellent," Edward replied. "I have an errand to perform but dinner should be in an hour. You can stay here in the parlor or walk about the garden if you like. Dr. Skinner will likely be down in half an hour or so to serve drinks. I'll be back by then."

With a quick nod, he was gone. Muirne looked at Alisdair, with his feet still dangling. She widened her eyes to forestall tears and cleared her throat.

"Well. That was not what I expected."

# Chapter 8

MUIRNE'S MIND WAS in a whirl. Forget phantom parents. He didnae believe in God? What kind of a man was so kind and decent and didnae believe in God? Was he a Jew? No, they believed, just in a different God. She'd never even heard of *no* God. Dear Lord. Her hands were shaking in her lap. Alisdair looked at them. She saw he was confused and scared for her.

"Now, Alisdair," she said, making a show of dusting off his shoulders and straightening his non-existent lapels. "You heard what Mr. Turner said about being an atheist?"

He nodded.

"But you don't know what it means," she prompted. She didn't meet her brother's eyes.

"No."

"Well, neither did I, exactly, but I think I do now."

She furrowed her brow and let her hands rest on his shirt-front. She shook herself and looked him full in the face to impress upon him her instructions.

"The important thing is that we want to hold our tongues in front of the people at dinner. They're strangers. And Mr. Turner will tell us what he means later. He deserves a chance to explain himself, doesn't he?"

Her voice shook. She was *lying*. What was he already doing to her good principles?

"Aye," Alisdair said cautiously, as if he hoped it was

the right answer.

"All right, then. Let's be careful and hold our tongues while we're at dinner, yes?"

"Yes, Muirne." Alisdair chewed his lip and broke eye contact. He would be thinking about what Edward's words meant until allowed to ask later.

"And Alisdair," Muirne warned, "it may be that Mr. Turner and I would like to speak alone about personal things. But don't worry—" she forestalled his protest. "I will tell you all the things he tells me about the—the atheist bit—all right?"

Alisdair nodded, looking far from content.

"Let's walk in the garden, then," Muirne suggested. There was no servant nearby so they poked about in several rooms before finding a side door to the alley that led to the back. Behind the house was a sheltered gazebo, looking out to what would be a fine expanse of lawn once the snows melted. There was a grander entrance to the garden she could see now; apparently she had taken the servants' route. *Of course I did.*

Muirne walked the rock path toward the gazebo, Alisdair trailing behind. They stood, admiring the view of white ground and black trees before them. A silence cropped up—that charged sort of silent accusation that only young boys can keep up.

"Please, Alisdair. Just—I'm not sure where I stand now. We must both be very careful. I'm not at all sure that I can forgive someone…godlessness." She whispered the last word.

"But I will hear him out. I want to be fair. Maybe I don't understand what he means." Alisdair looked sympathetic. "I don't know what to do. I wish—but it is just us.

I will hear him out." She took a firm hold of herself, nodded at Alisdair, and walked slowly back into the house through the intended entrance. It wouldn't do to lay all her worries at the feet of her six-year-old brother.

The doctor came down to the parlor soon thereafter and offered them a drink. He was portly and balding, with a clipped black and white beard, and very gracious. He served Muirne a sherry: her first. It tasted sour but warmed her belly. When the other medical students began to gather, she felt flighty and nervous again. She strove to maintain her composure as one after another of the young men were introduced to her. Alisdair sat in a corner with a glass of milk. Finally Edward reappeared. He nodded and shook hands with some of the others, patting his coat pocket a time or two, and made his way over to Muirne.

They walked into the dining room, which was more splendid than any Muirne had seen. She didn't stop Alisdair from staring at the long polished table or the mullion windows because she was rather too enraptured herself.

"It's like a kirk," Alisdair breathed. The gentlemen snickered at that. Alisdair cringed, his head retreating into his jacket collar a little. Muirne shot her brother a secret smile to signal it was all right.

Throughout the long meal, Alisdair did tremendously well. She knew he would be hard-pressed not to burst out with his thoughts as he was accustomed to do at home, but she was relieved to see him comfortably quiet and observant for once. For her own part, Muirne struggled to follow the conversation between Dr. Skinner and his students. Besides her own swirling doubts and fears about Edward, the men were using words she'd never heard before. She concentrated on getting the fish on the slender fork to her mouth without dropping it.

"And in Edinburgh, it seems they've not even stopped at auscultation, but the physicians are now palpating patients——!"

"In their homes or in the operating theaters?"

"In their homes! At least the surgical operations are still out of bounds, but dear Lord, where does it stop?"

"Indeed," Edward said.

He smiled at Muirne to include her in the conversation.

"But perhaps we might pass on to a subject that is more enjoyable to our lovely guest. What is the talk of up on the ridge, Miss MacLean?"

Alisdair stifled a snort.

Muirne smiled her embarrassment at the question: the talk was of *him*, of course. But she carried on gamely.

"Well, I have heard Neil speaking of the oat crop. This will be our first spring planting here so that is all our thought at the moment."

"Ah, yes, the spring planting," ruminated Mr. Thurston, a student a little older than Mr. Turner. He had come over from Port Hawkesbury on Cape Breton Island. "My brother Ian will have another few weeks, I imagine, before he can till the soil. Is it just the oats, or were you planning on other crops? I don't think Turner mentioned where your family has land."

"Up the East River, Mr. Thurston, south of here. And we've only cleared a small patch. We will clear more as we plant. The oats will at least hold us through the next winter."

"Do you keep any animals then, Miss MacLean?" This

question came from Dr. Skinner. A woman in a mobcap came to clear their fish plates and slice the venison steak.

"We haven't any stock yet, Dr. Skinner." In her peripheral vision, she saw Alisdair's head twitch with indignation. "Just the chickens," she amended. "And we're hoping to buy a lamb toward the end of summer," she said, her smile broadening as she watched Alisdair get brighter and prouder in his seat.

"Well, it's soon enough, to be sure. You only arrived last year. And that tragedy with your father," Thurston clucked. "Quite a disruption to any plans one might have had."

Alisdair's good humor vanished instantly; he shrank into the chair.

Muirne didn't know whether to respond vehemently or to let the subject drop. She supposed the man meant no harm but she wanted them to know that her father's death was no mere disruption. It had plucked the heart out of them for many months. They were only now getting on their feet and now there were new—she glanced to Edward—disruptions. She could say none of this to the men present, though. She felt a bit like Alisdair must have felt all evening: tongue-tied.

Edward drew the gazes of the men at the table. "One assumes the authorities are looking for the figure responsible for Mr. MacLean's death. I don't think the case has been closed. Do you, sir?" He directed his question to his host, but it was Dr. Arkady who spoke.

"I am friends with the magistrate, and no, it has not been closed." Dr. Arkady said this and made a slight bow from his seat to Muirne. She acknowledged it gratefully, and shot a look of mingled frustration and appeal to

Edward.

"That is comforting news, I'm sure. None of us wants to live in a place where anyone can take up arms against his fellow for no reason—no law and order. I daresay it is a particular case for your friend the magistrate, Arkady?"

Dr. Arkady turned down the ends of his mouth, emphasizing the doughiness of his face. He was several years older than Edward and already in his own medical practice on the north side of Pictou. He had taken port before dinner, a behavior which had raised Dr. Skinner's eyebrows. Muirne imagined the habit might have something to do with his stoutness. He had come to impart some of his research questions to Dr. Skinner before his voyage.

"A particular case? I don't know about that, Turner. Seems like there are more people apt to be violent that settle the wild than in cities. Makes sense, wouldn't you say?" A general chorus of nods and assent went round the room.

Muirne wished to redirect the conversation as Edward had done but couldn't think how. One of the other doctors changed the subject, though, and she was given a reprieve from having their eyes on her. More words passed that she paid little attention to. She breathed shallowly and looked down at her plate, where the remains of her cheese course rested. She did not remember finishing her steak or nibbling on the two cheeses on her plate, but apparently she had. *Get a hold of yourself, girl. These are important men, Edward's colleagues.* But a part of her sizzled with indignation at the comment that settlers of the wilderness—folk like her family, forced out of their own homes—were more violent. How did these men come to be here, anyway?

When the men turned to talking of the magistrate and his friends in politics, she relaxed a little and tried to follow. Alisdair gradually ceased his mope and listened to the discussion with a dawning fascination. He had already wolfed down all his cheese.

At long last, the men withdrew to the front porch, where it was the older doctor's habit to have a pipe and observe the street before he retired. The woman with the mobcap returned to show Alisdair to the room she'd prepared for them. Edward guided Muirne to the parlor and seated her in the window seat, where they could be seen by the men outside. He sat opposite.

Muirne waited calmly for Edward to gather his thoughts. It was his turn to explain, to make sense out of this chaos he'd exposed her to. When he looked up, she did, too, expectantly.

# Chapter 9

"I'VE BEEN AN atheist for four years, Miss MacLean. When I first started medical study, my father was proud of my career choice. My parents live near here, out west."

Pinpricks of feeling moved uncomfortably at the bottom of Muirne's ribcage, contained but spoiling for an opportunity to escape. *Why did he not tell us of his family, if they are nothing to be ashamed of? Why did he not tell us of his religious scruples*—she generously called them—*and allow me to think of him as a marriage prospect? Marrying a godless —I'd as soon be able to marry a Native!*

"I informed my father of my choice to leave the Church, in my new belief that Nature is responsible for all of creation. I said I couldn't have faith in one Supreme Being made in our image, but neither of them understood. My father has all but cut off contact, though my mother still writes me letters. You know that bottle of brandy I had when your mother was attacked by wasps?"

Muirne nodded. She was nervously biting her inner cheek as she listened.

"It was my father's, given to me by my mother in secret via my godfather." He gave her a faint smile. "So, you see, things are not so straightforward within my family. I do hope to able to provide for you and our family by my own means, my own labors. That is what I wanted to explain to you, your mother, Neil—when I visited."

He finished his recitation and waited. She felt the

pinpricks being packed down into some hard, sharp substance in her belly. He was trying to assuage her concern over not being supported by his family. But what of his faith? His soul?

"Mr. Turner." She tried to keep her voice steady but it wanted to shake with indignation. "You said you wished me to choose the church for the wedding. How can you possibly think any minister would wed us if you do not believe in their doctrine?"

"I know it is dishonest to lie but I intended to speak with the minister and explain my situation. I don't see why my faith in the civil marriage wouldn't be equal to your faith in the religious one."

Muirne's brows drew together as she grasped for understanding of this reasoning. It seemed all wrong. She felt her legs tense to stand but noticed that one of the men smoking outside was watching them through the window. She restrained herself. She took a steadying breath, willing her mind to fight through the cloud of betrayal she couldn't help feeling. She raised her eyes to his, seeing once again the gentle acceptance that had drawn her to him. She took another shaky breath.

"If you don't believe in God, what do you believe our lives are for?"

"I don't believe they're 'for' anything. I think we're here by chance. That our lives are our own to do with as we will, including fighting for what is right, improving our minds, sharing our good fortune, and—happiness."

He stumbled on the last word. Muirne thought that all sounded fine but how could you know what was right when you threw out the Bible? When you didn't believe your priests or ministers? When you called the whole thing a sham, perpetuated for thousands of years? The enormity of his decision presented itself then and she gasped. How dare he?

"How do you dare think everyone else is wrong, and only you are right? What kind of monstrous pride—"

"It was not pride." Edward's voice hardened. "An event happened that suddenly changed everything." He took a deep breath, looking away from the window. "It was the death of my godfather's son. We were very close, as close as brothers. He died in a canoe accident, alone on his way to town. It made me conscious, more deeply conscious, of the accidental nature of our lives, of history. I returned to medicine after the funeral and undertook to examine every one of my beliefs—in the greater good, in a Supreme Being, so many things."

He looked back up at her. "It is not pride but humility. And I don't ask that you forsake your own beliefs. I wouldn't do that, Muirne."

Muirne could feel her heart softening again, but that hard, sharp feeling in her gut battled with her compassion. She nodded for him to go on.

"My family are Church of England, Muirne. I know your family are Church of Scotland. Even if I had remained in their faith, there may have been objections on those grounds. I know this is a lot to consider for one night. I hoped you would be more open to other ways of thinking than my family. Tell me, what have you to say to all this?"

Muirne gazed at him. He withstood her scrutiny with grace. She saw how an expression of forthrightness nobly concealed one of silent pleading, betrayed by the upward twitch of his brow. She suddenly gasped, unaware she had been holding her breath.

"I have little to say in this moment but that I value your honesty. I may wish you had told us earlier, but what's done is done. I believed I knew your values from your manners, your courtesies, your courage. I didn't know you were brought up Church of England." She was ticking off points as they came to her, unable to easily summarize or analyze her feelings after all she'd heard. Her speech slowed.

"I don't believe that worshipping in a different Church would have been as difficult as you think. At least, not as difficult as this, to accept. But you mean to make a good life for your family. You mean to minister to the sick of this country. You intend to raise your children to believe—what, exactly?"

He straightened then leaned forward, placing his forearms on his legs. "I would want them to reach a good level of education, to where they can choose for themselves what to believe. Until that time, I would have nothing against your instructing them in biblical teachings, which, I must say, have done no harm in how you turned out." A tentative smile.

"And in all other activities, you would just go along? Pretend?" Muirne asked. "Like a wolf in sheep's clothing, hiding in the pew before everyone? Won't you feel contempt? I must say I can't see it."

"My dear, I feel the highest respect for your family and the greatest love for you. I would not allow that to become contempt. No."

She scrunched up her forehead, uncertainty written in its lines. She couldn't ask Mam her opinion just now, nor Neil, but what would they say? Neil was no party man, to let a man's loyalties sway his opinion of his character. He would undoubtedly stand by a man who had proven himself hard working, loyal, and of good sense and good temper, as Mr. Turner had. But honesty? Was waiting until now the right choice? And Mam—what would she think? Edward seemed to be the perfect choice in every other way. He was vigorous, intelligent, well-connected, sensible. He did come with family problems but then so did she. She looked at the situation as unsentimentally as she could.

Edward would be a doctor. He would live in town. He would be able to help her family. She would be one less burden on their farm's limited capabilities. She knew him to be kind, sober, good-humored. Practically a gift from God. Her eyes widened. If Edward noticed the change, he didn't comment. He merely waited. The hard, sharp mass dispersed.

"I suppose we could plan to post the banns, then."

Edward leaned in further, placing one knee to the window side of her and pulling her in for a kiss.

When he let go, her lips tingled. She felt breathless and dizzy but blinked it away, ordering her thoughts into practicalities.

"We'll—I mean, I'll—talk to the minister tomorrow. I'll see about some new bleached muslin at Bracethwaite's before we leave. I'll tell my family, of course. I don't think we should tell anyone else. About your atheism, I mean. We wouldn't want others to form a bad opinion without having met you. When you start your practice…"

"That's exactly the right of it. The practice." He shook his head slowly. "Thank you, dear Muirne. You prove yourself to be exactly the woman I want to marry, each time I see you. Darling Muirne!" He caught her up in another kiss, one that wandered across her cheek and down her throat. "I will teach you not to be always so practical," he whispered in her ear, before detaching himself.

"You are right," he said. "Much of the future will depend on how we start out. We shall see what your minister says tomorrow. For now, I think I've kept you overlong." He glanced out the window, saw no shapes moving in the dark, and drew a sharp breath. "Indeed, yes, they've come in and must be waiting for me in the parlor. Forgive me, Miss MacLean. I must say good night now. Sleep well, my darling. I want so much to make you happy."

He touched her hand briefly; she thrilled at the simple touch as he disappeared through the door.

# Chapter 10

THE NEXT MORNING, Muirne woke feeling numb all over. A fogginess resided in her head. The shock of the evening's revelation and her capitulation to Edward left her feeling drained and apprehensive. She rose late. Alisdair was positively bouncing around their small room by the time she was dressed and ready to take leave of their host. The servant woman informed her Dr. Skinner had already left on an errand. She handed them rations for the road at his order, though, so Muirne figured she must not have embarrassed herself too badly last night.

They headed back to Bracethwaite's for material for a modest wedding dress. Muirne first calculated the quantity of cloth the dress would require—about three and a half yards at a minimum—and then tried to figure how much to spend out of their credit on the grocer's books. There were a few fabrics available and she ran her fingers through the bolts of all of them. Her hand caressed the silk longingly. Unbleached muslin was the cheapest. She sighed.

"Mr. Bracethwaite?"

"Ah, yes. Miss MacLean. What is it you need this time? Directions? Time? Market schedule? Oh, me! No, I was meant to set aside something for you." He waved her away from the bolts of cloth, making her drop the silk she was holding and stand back to give him access. She watched as he yanked the roll of silk out and laid it across the counter. Ducking underneath the pass-through, he came back up with shears.

"Oh, but that's not the fabric I need, sir. I want three and a half yards of this unbleached muslin, please."

"No, I have an order for eight yards of this creamy silk stuff. Sorry if it's nae to yer liking, but that's what the man said."

Her breath caught.

"Aye," said the grocer. "Mr. Turner was here earlier and bid me set it aside for you. Said you'd be along presently. All paid for. Just let me cut it out straight, then." He maneuvered around the counter to hold the silk taut and cut along its edge.

"I don't know what to say. Thank you, Mr. Bracethwaite."

She glanced down to see Alisdair watching with a stormy expression. *Ah, yes. He'll be needing a full accounting on the way home.*

"I'll take some ha'penny sweets as well, please." It wouldn't hurt to reward the boy for behaving so well. Sweeten him up before explaining what she'd done. He'd be her practice round before she had to destroy the illusions of everyone else waiting for her at home.

As they traveled back to the ridge that afternoon, Muirne relayed the story Edward had told about his friend's death. She spoke aloud her reasons for accepting him despite his 'faith in creation,' as he put it. Alisdair's eyes bugged as he took it in. He was quiet, listening as she unspooled her thoughts, a large butterscotch wedged in each side of his mouth.

"While he is at odds with his father, his mother still supports his career. I suppose I shall meet them at some point. They only live a few dozen miles to the west, he said. I shall judge their characters then. I wonder if his father is as kind as he is. He did not mention what his profession was. Apparently not medicine."

Alisdair didn't even complain about lugging the yards of silk cloth folded up in brown paper and looped over his back with rope. Muirne carried their camp blankets strapped to her own shoulders.

"He will be speaking to the minister about it this morning. He preferred to undertake the duty himself, in his own way. I fear the man's eyes will pop out of their sockets. I still can't imagine how one person can believe himself to be right, when thousands of years and millions of people say otherwise."

She paused in her rambling recital as they came to a more level path through the forest. The dappled shade held a chill and the ground was a muddle with all the snowmelt: the signs of spring. Alisdair spoke for the first time.

"Well, everyone believed that the humors were responsible for gout until they realized it was sugar in the blood."

Muirne looked at him in astonishment. "Where did you learn that?"

He shrugged. "One of the men told me about it after dinner. He was showing me the surgery equipment. He made it sound exciting but the saws and knives and such looked awful."

Muirne smiled. "How very interesting that you remember. We will have to get you down into a village school as soon as you get your letters down. You'll have to hurry or Sheena will beat you to it!"

"Ach, Sheena doesn't need school!"

Muirne tsked at him. "She needs to be able to read, right enough. It's the only way to defend yourself in this new system."

She thought immediately of her mother's unsuccessful attempt to defend them against the Laird's new plan back on Mull, then tried to shake that failure from her mind. Thoughts of Edward flooded back in.

"Edward knew a chaplain at the medical college this winter who was agreeable to debating his heathen views. This chaplain did debate with Edward, at length, but neither managed to convince the other he was wrong."

Muirne smiled but it was bittersweet. Scholars and clerics were all well and good, but what would she do when it came time to raise their children? If Edward stayed silent on all topics of religion, they would notice, especially after talking to their neighbors and schoolfellows. And would he go with them to kirk? If they lived in town, she would attend. Another support fell away from her hastily constructed future. Had she made the right choice?

"Is it the chaplain as will marry ye then?" Alisdair asked.

"Oh, no. He's in Halifax. I suggested Edward ask the Reverend Mr. Balwhidder, who met us at the shipyard, you remember? He seemed a decent sort. Even if his eyes do pop out, he'll listen to what Edward says. At least I hope he will."

"So we'll have to make *another* trip to New Glasgow? In how many weeks?" Alisdair was incredulous.

"It takes three weeks to read the banns, but we haven't even decided where it'll be. We've barely talked over the details of the ceremony. That part completely slipped my mind when he started in on all this *atheism*."

Muirne spat out the word, resenting it more strongly than she had any word before. Edward had bought her fabric for a dress. She supposed that meant he would make the other arrangements as well, but how awful to be in such a rush because of a silly ship departure!

"It makes the most sense to be married in New Glasgow, for there are fewer of us on the ridge than there are guests who would have to travel to attend us there."

"But where would you hold it? At the doctor's house? We've no house for all of us to stay in."

"True, but maybe he will find one for us before he leaves. Or maybe I'll just come back a married woman and stay at the cabin until he returns. I don't know! He'll have to decide for us."

New possibilities danced across her brain in quick succession, the likes of which Muirne had never imagined back in their snug blackhouse on Mull.

# Chapter 11

NEIL WAS BELOW in the new clearing attending to the furrows when he heard his mother's voice calling out in Gaelic.

"Neil, someone's here that shouldn't be! Come up!"

A stranger? Here? He clambered up the side of the hill, leaping over thick clumps of bear clover. His linen shirt was streaked with dirt and whipping in the wind as he pulled up to a halt by the front door of the cabin.

His mother stood in front of their closed door, her arms crossed tightly across her middle. The unwanted visitor was a stout man, well-clothed and well-shod, of about Gillan's years. He had longish black hair, ruddy complexion, beetling eyebrows, thin lips, and startling blue eyes. Neil saw a chestnut horse standing a dozen feet away, its neck dark with sweat. Neil looked from his mother's locked jaw to the stranger's reddened face. He tried a conciliatory tack first.

"Can we get some water for your horse, sir? Looks like it's had quite a journey up our hill." The blue eyes turned to glower at him. His mother spoke to him first, in Gaelic.

"I've already gone and offered him hospitality, Neil. He won't have it. Insults us instead." It was rude to speak a language a guest didn't know. Something must have already transpired to make her act so spitefully.

"What is it, Mam? Who's this?"

She switched back to English, glaring at the stranger. "Ask him yourself."

Neil drew himself up, collecting his calm. "I am Neil McLean. Who are you and what's your business?"

"My business? I'll tell you my damned—"

"Ah-ah," Mam interrupted. She held out a hand behind her as the front door banged open. Sheena came to stand at her mother's hip. "Please restrain your language around my children. And you haven't yet told us your name." She even left out the 'sir.'

"My *name* is George Turner. I live in *Colchester* County. And I will not allow your daughter to marry my son, *wherever* she may be hiding!"

The shock of his statement immobilized them all for a moment. Mr. Turner, still huffing, looked at Mam with barely veiled contempt. Neil regarded the man as if he had sprouted a beak.

"She's not *hiding*," Sheena said. "She's down in town right now getting married to Mr. Turner. So you can *haud your weesht.* We don't care—"

"Sheena," Neil said curtly. She stopped speaking but continued glaring, copying her mother so precisely it would have been funny at another time.

"Mr. Turner," Neil began again. "We hold your son in very high esteem. I believe he feels the same for my sister Muirne. Why would you oppose their marriage?"

"You're from an upstart rabble sect, probably in someone's pocket back home into the bargain!" the man shouted. "Even if my son *is* an atheist, I won't have him marrying into a family of Dissenters! Nothing but a lot of rebels, low-lifes—"

"That is quite enough!" Mam raised her voice and cut

him off. "Have you told your son this?"

"He's an atheist?" Neil asked.

Turner answered Neil first. "Yes. Has been for several years. A combination of his schooling, his mother's spoiling him, and the death of a close friend. Of course he didn't tell you; I should have known. And as for you—" He stepped toward Mam; Neil stepped quickly to her side. Turner waved off the implied threat.

"Of course I told him! But just like forsaking his religion, he's determined to thwart me. He only told us of his intentions to marry last week. His mother and I have never met the girl! I undertook this journey post haste to apprise you of his family's feeling since any family of good breeding should not want to upset the normal —"

"Blether," Mam spat. "I'm sorry your horse has had such a long journey for naught, as Muirne's not here. But they'll do what they want. They love each other; it's plain. He's been a good friend to us and I think they'll do fine together." She swished around and strode into the shadowy cabin. Sheena followed suit, shooting a final glare behind her.

From the immediate stillness that followed the door slamming, Neil would bet they were both listening at the window.

"How long have ye been out here, then?" Neil asked.

"My family's been in Colchester County since 1799."

"That so."

Neil kept his voice flat, trying not to sound impressed, but Mam was probably making the same calculations he was. The Turners looked to be richer, better settled, English, *and* Established Church, all of which meant the magistrate would look none so kindly on someone say, breaking the man's arm. Neil let the thought flit briefly through his head before letting it go. They couldn't afford to invite any more trouble into their lives. God knew they'd already seen enough of the uninvited kind.

"I agree with my mother. I think they'll do fine together. But if you're going to make trouble, I'm here to answer you. You'll no' threaten my family and get away with it."

Neil tightened his fists and stood his ground. The man was a hotheaded, arrogant arse. The rational part of him hoped the man would simply storm off rather than risk Neil's fists. He knew if he hit him, the man would go straight to the law and have him fined or imprisoned, and there would go any chance of their starting anew.

"I'll tell my sister and Mr. Turner that you stopped by."

Turner was incredulous; he let loose a high-pitched scoff. "You listen to me, boy. You'll tell your sister the marriage won't happen. She can set her sights elsewhere."

Neil didn't reply. The image of the man's arm swinging useless at his side became another scene: his head being bashed into the large grey rock in the yard. He imagined striking the man with all his force—then saw in his mind's eye the same thing happening to Gillan. He vibrated with the need to stay still. When he remained silent, Turner spoke.

"You leave Edward to me," he began.

"Oh, I'd leave your whole family to rot, if this was how they all behaved," Neil shouted back. "I won't offer you hospitality since you've clearly come to insult us. But

I will bid you good day."

When the man didn't move quickly enough, stuck in his disbelief, Neil fetched the horse by the bridle. He dropped the reins in the dirt, not even deigning to hold them out to the man. *Rebels and lowlifes, he called us. And here I am acting the part. Well.* But he wouldn't strike this pox of a man, this father to his sister's betrothed. After a seething, uncomfortable pause, Turner grabbed the reins and hoisted himself up on the off side, awkwardly spurring his horse away with a furious impotence. Neil hoped he wouldn't simply return with reinforcements.

Neil was straightening his fingers from their clench when Mam came out a few moments later. She placed a hand tentatively on his shoulder blade but he turned away from her to let loose a furious yell. She shook her head.

"It's not fair, is it?" she said. "We're never good enough, not even on our own land. My poor Muirne."

"Aye. I wonder what will she have to say about it."

# Chapter 12

THAT EVENING THEY made use of the last of the neighbors' gifts. Mam mechanically shredded the old potatoes from the Massons' stores, making a slurry before throwing in the last of the animal fat and packing it into the pot over the fire. Sheena carefully tipped the bag of harvested nettles into the pot and placed the birchbark cover on top. The delicious smell of sizzling potatoes in bacon fat enveloped the cabin a few minutes later.

Neil sat on one of the stump seats, his legs wide, his elbows on his thighs. What a nasty piece of work the man was. Could they take his word for truth? Was Edward an atheist? He'd heard the word only once. It was from the Rev. Mr. MacManus on Mull, it must have been almost ten years ago now. He'd been describing the heathens in Asia and the New World and explaining why it was so important to contribute to the subscription for the missionaries to go civilize them.

"Do you want those godless French Boneys to get to them first? Do you want the world to be populated with atheists? People with no moral code, obeying only Bonaparte the Upstart?"

He had been impassioned, his hair askew, his eyes aflame. Lachlan MacManus had certainly felt alive with the fires of the Spirit that day, Neil remembered.

But Edward? The always clean-booted, fast and efficient, going-to-be-a-doctor Edward? How could it be true? And if it were, how would Muirne bear it? She had put such faith in the man. So had they all. He'd been their saving grace when Mam's life had been in danger, for goodness' sake.

"Neil?"

It was Sheena calling. She crouched by the fire, her feet neatly tucked under her, her arms hugging her knees close. He went over an squatted beside her.

"Aye, Sheena."

"What's going to happen to Muirne now?"

Neil looked into the dark wells of her eyes. She'd been brooding. If Muirne had not a chance, what was the likelihood of a prosperous match for Sheena?

"Nothing will happen to her. Dinna fash, now. We'll see what she's done in town. She may have more news to pass on. Perhaps they're married already and that was a madman that visited us."

His mother's strangled cry reproached him.

"Don't, Neil. If that young man disnae believe in God, he's not the man for Muirne."

Neil wished Muirne were there to have her say. He gazed another moment at the hook which held the pot over the fire. Yes, they had made it through a winter here. But would they ever be free of the hunger that drove them to desperation? That had driven Gillan upriver?

"Can we never get a piece of luck?" he burst out.

Sheena flinched and fell over backward, catching a toe in the ashes.

Mam let fly an oath. She came around the table to dust Sheena off ceremoniously and stare Neil down.

"Now you hold yer tongue, young man. When Muirne comes back, we shall see which way the wind blows. Until then, not another word about it. I won't have such a faithless sinner eating at my table. If it is true. Which I canna believe, as yet."

His mother alternated between stern admonishment and confused disbelief. He nodded. "Sorry, Sheena."

His sister shrugged. She rose slowly and fetched the blackboard. Mam sat with a pile of thick woolens to mend now that winter was retreating and they weren't wearing them all the time.

"I'm taking myself out for a bit of air," Neil said. "I'll stay around the clearing."

He went out the front door, away from the women. When he pulled the door shut behind him, he flung himself to the sky, his fist leading the way. He swung his arms down. Pounded his feet into the earth a few times. He stood up slowly, huffing and puffing with his rage. *That felt good.*

He walked carefully down to the clearing—that hopeful exercise—and traced the path around it. He knew Muirne. She would take on such a husband if it meant it would help her family. He prayed that Edward wasn't secretly the horror they imagined. *If Muirne had married him, without knowing!* He prayed harder.

# Chapter 13

"SHEE-NA!"

THE two notes rung out in the cool air of afternoon as Muirne and Alisdair topped the hill. Sheena and Neil looked up from their places down in the furrows. Neil wore the same old linen shirt and faded *feileadh beag* that he always did for work outdoors. He and Sheena looked at each other, hesitant. *Now there's an odd look. I thought for sure Sheena would be excited to hear what happened.*

Muirne waved. "We're home!"

The door to the cabin swung open and banged against the outside wall.

"Mam!"

When she turned to smile at her mother, the late afternoon sun showed the same hesitation in her mother's eyes that had been in Neil's stance. "What is it? What news?"

"You all right? How did the trip go?"

Muirne noticed something edgy in her mother's voice. "We're to be married within two months. Edward talked to the Reverend Balwhidder yesterday. We hope to use his church in Pictou, but there's a particular circumstance, *Mathair*. He doesn't belong to any particular church, exactly..."

When Muirne looked at her mother, she saw the sad knowledge in her eyes, then a hardness.

"How does he propose to marry in the Kirk when he

disnae believe in God? Lie to the Reverend?"

"No. He hopes to have a judge perform the marriage and then have the ceremony in the Kirk for the community." She softened her voice. "But you know of this already. Who has been by? How did you know?"

"His father. Unbelievably rude, that man."

"His father was here? And already gone? He did not want to wait to meet me?" Muirne was disappointed. Her mother's mouth merely quirked at the corners.

"No, he didna want to meet you. And you wouldna want to meet him. He doesna want Ed to marry into a Dissenter family. He was intolerably rude. Poor horse," she muttered.

Muirne's breath caught. She cupped a hand over her mouth. Her other arm curled across her waist as if she'd been punched.

"I thought I'd had the worst of the shock and it was over, but…they don't want me?"

Sheena reached the clearing; Muirne didn't see her so much as felt her lean in and put an arm around her. They walked slowly to the cabin.

Muirne caught another glimpse of Neil before they reached the door. His face. *He knew.* But *what* did he know? She was the one who'd spoken to Edward; they'd only heard from his father. How could the father object to her before he'd even met her? Did Edward know of his disapproval? He must. He hadn't told her of any obstacles with his family. Why wouldn't he tell her? He must be planning to go forward over his father's objection. What kind of family was she marrying into? Her mind clouded over with discord and distressing thoughts.

"He called us rebels and low-lifes, Muirne," said

Sheena.

Muirne felt about to cry. She was nearing the end of her strength. She didn't think she could keep up the brave front any longer. She felt the transition from cool outside air to their warm, smoky cabin. She felt Mam and Sheena sit her on the box bed mattress. The wooden edge dug into the backs of her legs. Mam spoke.

"He looks down on us, *mo fheadhainn ghaolach*."

"He said his family is Church of England," Muirne started to say.

"It's no' that," said Mam. "It's the last generation's spite toward Dissenters. We're nothing but poor, useless troublemakers."

Once again, they were being treated with contempt by those who fared well under the old system. Losing what little they'd gained coming here. What could Muirne do against that great tide, the one that had pushed them out of their island home?

Neil cursed under his breath. His mother patted Muirne on the back and walked after her and Sheena into the house. He looked away, off into the trees. Alisdair had scampered into the forest, no doubt checking a special hiding place. That blasted Turner. Why couldn't he have told them sooner? For his part, Neil was surprised but not hateful toward him for his admission. Mam, though —she would equate disbelief in God with worship of the Devil. But if you didn't believe one, you didn't believe the other, wasn't that so?

He wished Muirne all the hope he still had. Perhaps there was still some way Muirne and Edward could be happy together, but he could not see it. He heard Sheena kicking clods of dirt out of her way as she trounced the path back to her garden.

"Sheena!" Neil called in a warning voice. She immediately stopped. Alisdair came back towards him, watching carefully as he placed his feet along the edge of the last furrow.

"Why don't you go help Sheena with her wee garden?"

Neil followed Alisdair past the turned-over earth. The boy kicked at clods like Sheena had been doing. Neil closed his eyes against his irritation. Sheena had carefully marked off her part of the garden with river stones.

Alisdair seemed untouched by the family's mood. He eagerly asked Sheena what had happened while they were away. Sheena didn't answer him straight away.

She had a thin length of iron and was painstakingly piercing holes in the hard ground. She slipped two seeds from her precious hoard into each tiny hole. She packed each six-inch hole with earth, singing a quiet verse with her eyes closed. Alisdair waited until she finished the first verse, then asked what she was doing.

"I'm singing to the spirit of our ancestors to watch over my little garden," she said. "Know what song?"

Alisdair shook his head. She put a little more breath into her words and Neil could hear them.

*Come from every corner isle,*
*Distant rock and under vale,*
*Come good spirits, do not fail,*
*The MacLean calls.*
*Do the work of God's own breath,*
*Bringing warmth, repelling Death,*

*Nourish us from good green earth,*
*The MacLean calls.*

Alisdair held out his hand for the length of iron. Measuring the row with his eye, he dropped the tip to the ground, got her nod, and pushed the tip into the earth.

# Chapter 14

MUIRNE STAYED IN bed the rest of that day. She didn't rise until supper. When she joined everyone else at table, there was a mark from the blanket that had lain crumpled against her cheek, and her hair was a golden, mussy haze. Neil was tired from the field work, but gave a little smirk when he saw his sister.

They all tucked into the smoky, salty fish stew. Neil was glad when Alisdair finally broke the silence to compliment his mother's cooking.

"Why," said Mam, a smile opening up her face. "I'm glad you like it, dearie. It's too bad the river doesn't wander all the way up to where we are, eh? But that smokiness, we could get that with some of the mushrooms in the forest, y'know. Just put them in the ashes for a bit wrapped in wet leaves."

Sheena, who had become the best forager in the family, asked about something she had seen but not dared harvest.

"Huge, and bright orange like—like a copper kettle!"

"How huge?" Alisdair goaded.

Sheena shifted her hands to indicate a distance almost two feet wide.

"Ye can't've seen one *that* big," Alisdair said.

"Those are called hen-of-the-woods, Alisdair. They grow on the side o' trees. They can get quite as big as that," said Neil.

"So they're safe to eat, Neil?" Sheena asked.

"I believe so. And they're supposed to be good eating."

Muirne looked up from her bowl. "What is?"

"Mushrooms," Neil said, dismissing it as unimportant. "Maybe we'll go on a hunt in the autumn, harvest some that we're sure are safe to eat, smoke 'em up." He grinned at Alisdair.

"Oh, yes," Muirne agreed. "In the autumn."

As her words drifted off, Neil felt his toes curl. He wished so much that he could make things right but he couldn't undo the damage that infuriating fusspot Turner had done. Nor could he knock sense into Edward. Nor could he compel the officials in Pictou to make inquiries into Gillan's murder. All he could do was start growing those oats. He wished he could help but the knots lay in others' hands to unravel: Mr. Turner's, Edward's, the magistrate's. It was bloody frustrating to do naught but wait.

When Muirne stood up from the table after supper, Neil tapped her on the elbow. He cocked his head out-of-doors. She nodded; she would follow. Sheena cleaned bowls and spoons. Mam dried the spoons and tucked them into a clean cloth, then stacked the bowls on the stool to dry. Neil stepped over Alisdair as he aimed his top down the center of the open cabin.

Neil waited for his sister in the dusk. First the ship was taking Turner away to England before he could propose, then they discovered his atheism, and now there was his father's vehement disapproval. Muirne was having an even harder time of it than he was. His love may have forgotten his name but at least no one came to his door to insult his family. He might well be casting his hopes into the abyss, but while he still felt something, he would not throw away his slight chance. Letty's face as the ship pulled away was still clear to him, tugging at his heart. He would wait another year. Write again; see then. In the meantime, there was a farm to get up and going. Plenty to keep him busy.

Muirne finally joined Neil on his log. They looked out toward the sun. It was below the line of hills but sent a cheery haze of orange light skyward. A swallow swooped across the sky, then a bat from the opposite direction. He looked her way as she looked out. The blanket mark had finally faded.

"He must have told his father about me," she finally said. "Seen his reaction. And decided to go through with it, despite the difficulties. No?"

Neil nodded once, thinking it was quite a simplification, but aware that his sister was just warming up.

"And he did the right thing by telling me of his loss of faith beforehand. I would have liked more time to question him about it but I understand Dr. Skinner's decision forced his hand a bit."

Neil didn't bother to respond, just watched her face keenly.

"What confuses me is how he can seem so full of feelings and kindness and goodness. These are gifts from God! Why does he not recognize that? Why would one death make him turn his back on all that he's received? We didn't!"

"No, we didn't," Neil agreed.

"I feel a little foolish saying this, Neil. But I feel that Edward is a gift of God. To us."

The surprise this statement elicited must have shown

clearly on his face.

"Don't you see? He's so helpful and kind, hardworking, skillful at his profession. He will do well as a doctor! And he loves me. I know it."

"How does a person love someone, not believing in the love of God?"

Neil watched as Muirne's face heated.

"I don't know," she said. "I just know it's true. And I don't want to lose it. This gift."

"Do ye not think he'll poison your own mind on the subject? And what of the children ye'll have together?"

"I asked him about that. He said I could raise them in the church. They'd be educated and decide for themselves."

There was a long pause as Neil considered Muirne's words. For the first time he could remember, he couldn't tell how she truly felt about the matter. *Is she sacrificing her spiritual reward to give us a few handfuls of flour?*

"That sounds fair," he pronounced. "But I don't want you to regret it. Regret is a beast of a thing. It gnaws at you."

Muirne tilted her head. Did she suspect the guilt he felt about letting Gillan depart for the wilderness alone and friendless?

Her voice became softer. "I've been thinking about that today. I wasn't sleeping. Just staring at the roof timbers and the cobwebs and the holes patched with moss."

"And?"

"I'll take it."

"You love him then."

She nodded.

"You trust him? Even so?"

She met his gaze straight on. The nod was almost imperceptible. "Even so."

Neil looked down. His mouth worked. He felt full of something he didn't know what to do with. She looked so unearthly calm. She was sure of herself and the step she'd take. Well, if that was the case, he'd trust her decision.

"Aye. Well. As long as he never harms ye, I'll stand by ye both."

Muirne clasped his hand in both of hers. She brought her forehead down to meet their hands. He felt her lips moving. She was so good. Perhaps she was right. After a minute, she squeezed his hand and let go. She sat up with a great sigh.

"Why should his father *hate* us so? Not knowing us?" She turned to him with a resolute expression. "So we are Church of Scotland. We worship in the meeting house. We are deprived of our own ministers here but do without. We blame nobody for the lack. We are able to make do. Why does he have such a store of hatred for someone he doesn't know? Do ye think he knows our family? Something about Gillan? Back on the island?"

"You're grasping at straws, Muirne. Listen, there are plenty of people who canna bear people who don't think like them. Take the fight in Pictou about the Academy. People were doing godly work, looking after the education of the young men around here. They were only asking for the same small monies as the college down in Halifax. But the jealous old Anglican sheepfaces in the Council denied them the funds."

"Is that what that Mr. Fraser was on about when we were visiting? I didn't catch it all but I heard him mention Halifax."

Neil nodded. "Aye. It's a matter of the Church of England folks not wanting the rest of the province to get their own minsters and schools, like ye said. They don't need a reason. They're afeared we'll get on their level if we have the same opportunities. And well we might! But they can't abide losing any of their power. They can think of all sorts of ways to mince around why they won't grant the Academy the title of a College. But it's fear. And selfishness."

"We've just learned better, then, with Mam?"

"Aye, and by our da."

They seldom spoke of their blood father. Muirne was only seven when he disappeared on the Canal; Neil, eight. He'd been gentle, he remembered. Mam had cried for days when he'd been conscripted as a laborer on the Canal. Gillan was rougher. He'd loved them in his own way. But Alec had had a quiet way of asking question after question. *Why do ye feel that way, son? Who told ye that was the truth? Who do ye think wins if ye do that?*

"Tolerance, ye mean." Muirne smiled at him gently. He felt exposed in his memories.

"Aye, and ye know what they do to tolerant people. Start a war and make 'em take sides."

Muirne just shook her head at his flippancy. "Old Mr. Turner may have made it clear he doesn't want me but it is the younger Mr. Turner I am looking to wed. Unless Edward tells me otherwise, I'll hold him to that."

She narrowed her eyes. "But it is intolerable that he should come hear and make threats against you. I wonder what Edward will do when he hears of his father's behavior."

"He may not hear of it," Neil said. 'You can't write

him of it. I doubt he'll return to his parents' house before his ship leaves."

"You're right," Muirne said, taken aback. She scrunched her forehead, trying to think of a way delicately to inform her intended that his father was an arse. The orange glow had long since faded and Muirne's familiar face was nothing but points of reflected moonlight.

"Let it go," Neil said softly. "Ye parted on good terms, aye?"

"Yes," she said.

"Expecting to be married in two months?"

"Yes."

"He'll surely need to talk to ye before then. Take his measure when he visits. Or if it's a letter, see if he apologizes."

"And if I have to tell him?"

"Then you have to tell him."

They both contemplated the ground at their feet for a moment. Neil stretched from his sitting position and pulled his knees up to the log, rubbing his thighs briskly for warmth.

"Aren't we a lucky pair in love?"

Neil shot his sister a look, invisible in the darkness. A helpless giggle escaped her. She reached her hand out to rest on his forearm, grasping their mother's cable-knitting and rolling it between her fingers.

# Chapter 15

MUIRNE SHOVELED CHICKEN manure and ashes over the furrows to nourish the soil, while Neil squatted at the far edge of the clearing, molding river weeds to the ends of the humped rows to the same purpose. Sheena made a racket plunging down the winding path.

"Be careful!" she called out. "It's a nasty fall if you lose your footing!"

"Muirne! There's a letter in yer wee house!" Muirne's skeptical expression changed to alarm.

"Ye didna see Edward, did ye?"

"No. It must've been the postboy. Maybe Mam heard him earlier. We can ask——"

"That's all right." Muirne hesitated, feeling trapped. He'd written! Did he know of his father's visit? Was everything they'd arranged to be turned upside-down again? Oh, what she wouldn't give for a moment alone to read Edward's letter. Finally she said, "All right, let's up and fetch it."

Sheena's excitement was hard to countenance.

"The romance!" Sheena swooned, then stopped short. "Even if Edward's father *is* a pigheaded louse."

They clambered up the hill then back down to the tree. Muirne reached up and snagged the envelope from its perch with moist fingers. She felt Sheena's eyes on her as she scanned the letter's contents. Her hands tightened on the paper as she struggled to decipher the lacey script, leaving little muddy smudges. *That's it, then. He's gone.* Her eyes suddenly bubbled over with tears. She refolded the paper and touched the back of her hand to her runny nose.

"Well?" Sheena prompted. "What is it?"

"He's away to London Monday. A faster ship. He waits until his return in the spring to see us married. He'll consider us engaged until then. Even though—"

Miurne's face crumpled. She sniffed loudly. When next she opened her eyes, Neil was at their side.

"His father is trying to make him change his mind but Edward intends to go on without his blessing. He apologized for him."

She looked to Neil. A small smile curved her lips. "He said he'll keep trying to talk sense to his father but that it might take longer than he's willing to wait to be married."

"So it is good news?" Sheena's voice was doubtful.

"I can't wish to be the source of such trouble but we mun wait it out. Just like Neil," she said. "And hope."

"And pray," said Sheena.


The day came for Edward's boat to sail. At home, Muirne drifted around, a bit of her melancholy seeping into the rest of the family. She'd told them all about Edward's letter. There had been little else to say. They all supported her decision to wait and see, though Mam maintained her tight-lipped reticence on the subject of Edward's atheism.

They got the oat crop underway and quickly moved on to sowing the wheat Bracethwaite had advised them to purchase on their last trip to town. It meant another intense, backbreaking, prickly session of clearing stump, brush, and bramble, but they all pitched in and managed it in under a fortnight. The smaller patch lay south of their oat crop, still within view of the back door of their cabin perched above.

Nights, they rationed out the barley bannocks and potatoes, along with stories of what they would do with the fruits of a full harvest. Mouths watered at the tales each told around the hearth in the evenings. One such night, Muirne was listening as she wound Mam's yarn into a ball by the fire.

"I'd sell all the wheat. We're not so fine that we need fine, floury bread with our soup, are we?" Neil teased. "I'd take the money and buy a pig. There's plenty mast around here in the summer and we'd get it back much improved come winter time. Our own bacon and porridge!"

Muirne's mouth watered at the thought. It seemed like forever ago when they had last tasted bacon: Mrs. Conaghey's last year, in fact. Neil smiled at Mam, whose family had managed pigs and sheep back on Mull. Mam cleared her throat of a sudden obstruction and turned to Sheena.

"And what would you do with a bountiful harvest?"

Sheena looked at Neil. Her eyes wandered up to the ceiling and around their snug cabin. "I'd sell it, too. But save the money. We might need it for something." Her eyes darted toward Muirne then quickly away. Muirne wondered what she could possibly be brewing in that head of hers.

"Are you planting mischief as well as bog myrtle?"

Mam asked. Bog myrtle had been mixed in somehow with the sand and seeds given them by Jenny, and Sheena's little garden patch gave out an unexpected, musky fragrance.

"I don't know how it's able to grow in that soil," Neil said, shaking his head.

"Neither me," said Mam. "But it does smell lovely, for as long as it stays." She poked a finger under Alisdair's chin where he sat by her knee.

"And what about you, my good man. Full harvest. What would be your plan?"

A low mumble was all that came out. He was concentrating on his top, which he'd learned how to spin and flip at high speed on the half-timbered seat, the closest flat surface to where he crouched.

A sigh went round the room. Neil looked pointedly at Muirne. "Well?"

"Oh," she said, waving a hand at him. "I suppose your plan's the one."

"But?"

"Well, if there were enough from the sale of the wheat, it would be nice to have some new clothes. Better tools." She held out her hands, palms up. They showed half-healed cuts, yellowed callouses, and one purple blister.

"And Sheena and Alisdair have both outgrown their shoon. The mountain air's done them a lot o' good, that's all."

There was a silence. Sheena sat up straighter. Mam spoke.

"That's a good idea, Muirne. You are right. I hadn't noticed but Sheena's skirt is showing ankle—she's finally shootin' up!" Mam let loose a chuckle. "And perhaps we could do a barter for some of those hide moccasins. They seem to do very well for hill walking. Did ye not see Mr. Allman, Mrs. Allman, and all the MacGregors was wearin' 'em?"

"Oh, aye," Neil agreed, with a twinkle in his eye. "Must be the latest style from Paris." He ducked as the finished ball of yarn from Muirne's lap sailed in his direction. He laughed as it bounced off his outstretched palm.

The summer passed quickly, with the MacLeans adapting further to the land and weaving themselves more tightly into the fabric of the community. Alisdair got his moosehide slippers for help putting up a fence; Sheena got her new skirt made of local wool in exchange for two handmade brooms. Both were worn and commented on at the next visiting round at the MacGregors'.

They sat around the MacGregors' hearth one night to celebrate the successful wheat harvest in early September. Though small, the yield had yet earned them enough to pay back their debts to Mrs. Conaghey as well as purchase a fine, young ewe. As the MacLeans sat in their neighbors' fine carved chairs, Muirne let herself imagine how she might furnish her own house. *Simple. Colorful. Pillows everywhere.* She almost giggled at the thought.

"Now that's a pretty shade, Miss Sheena," Mrs. Mac-Gregor was saying next to her. She fingered the hem of Sheena's skirt. "Is this chain stitch your handiwork, Mrs. MacLean?"

"Aye, it is," Mam replied. "We've not had much wool

to work with yet but I've got plans to build up a few lambs and have some serious shearing work to do next year." The MacGregors also kept a few sheep for wool, milk, and meat.

"There was enough of the rue root for me to make a nice rose shade for this one. And I believe it does favor Sheena's dark hair." Sheena blushed and glanced surreptitiously at the strange men seated across the circle. Muirne smiled.

When neither of his sons commented, old Mr. MacGregor chimed in unexpectedly.

"Yes, it does, Mrs. MacGregor. Quite puts the apples in her cheeks."

Sheena slumped in her seat, her head sinking into her chest. Muirne came to her rescue.

"What other plants do you find useful for dyes around here, Mrs. MacGregor? I'm sure Mam would love to be able to use some different colors when we have our *serious shearing*." She winked at Sheena.

The conversation wandered on to the local plants, and the MacGregors knew quite a few to recommend. They'd been in the area only a few years longer than the MacLeans, but Mr. MacGregor had had more contact with the Mi'qmaq Indians. A Native family had been living near the river spot where they drew their water. The oldest boy of the family had shown Mr. MacGregor many of the Native foraging techniques and fishing skills.

This topic drew the old man out of his slight doze.

"Perhaps a year ago, it was" Mr. MacGregor said. "They moved to be with others of their tribe north of New Glasgow, on the new reserve."

"I am glad that they passed on such valuable knowledge, so that our family can also benefit from it," said Mam.

"Indeed," said Mrs. MacGregor. "In these parts, a person has to learn local strategies quickly. If a family can't adapt, they end by moving."

Muirne felt a warm little glow at the assumption that they were accepted, part of the group that was adapting and earning their keep, rather than the type Mrs. Mac-Gregor would as soon consign to the pioneer trails west.

Sundays in summer were often passed in this pleasant habit of visiting. The visits helped ease the uneasy silences around Muirne's prospects and Neil's hopes. Neighbors also learned not to mention Gillan in front of Sheila MacLean, as hopes of an apprehension or investigation dwindled.

# Chapter 16

IN THE PREDAWN blue-blackness, Neil was awoken by a kerfuffle outside. Their lamb was bleating to raise the dead. Neil was up first and looked out the front window: nothing to see. He raced to the back door and cracked it open. There his breath hitched in his throat.

A brownish black bear on all fours moseyed in their direction. Its snout wove this way and that, scenting the terrified sheep.

Neil cursed under his breath and shut the door. He scattered the dirty cloths piled atop their scant hunting gear, frantically grabbing for the stock of a rusty rifle. Mrs. Conaghey had given it to them last winter, just for something to frighten off any dangerous men with, but it was not trusted to shoot. Mam kept it to please the old woman, along with a small pouch of bullets. They did fine with homemade snares, Neil had always thought, and those didn't need new ammunition—just the nettle string, which could be made for nothing.

Neil's dashing about had woken his mother. She opened one of the doors to the box bed, blinking at him in the darkness. "Neil?"

"It's a bear, Mam. I mean to scare it away."

"Neil!"

By the time he'd got out the front door and around to the side where the chickens and lamb were held, the lamb's screaming had stopped. It huddled in the corner of its pen, pushing and hopping against the pickets of the fence. The whites of its eyes glowed in the dark as it strove to get away from the bear's scent.

The bear was already approaching the other side of the pen, a mere twenty yards away. Its snout wavered toward the hens' roost to its right, away from Neil. Would it go after them instead? They couldn't stand to be sacrificed, either. Either the lamb's bleating hadn't woken the chickens or they knew enough to stay in the roost. Neil was betting on the latter.

Neil moved away from the house and crouched. He waited for the bear to make a decision. *Damn you*, he thought. *Find your own food. Grubs, or berries, or salmon. Yes! Then we'll have* you *share your fine feast with* us. That almost made him smile. He would have to put more facing up on the sheep pen so that the space wasn't so open and inviting.

The bear turned its head. It seemed to look at him, momentarily distracted from its chicken—or lamb— dinner. Neil wasn't sure of the best course. Yell at it? Make himself look big and intimidating? Or not move, and make the bear lose interest and slouch away? He tried to stay invisible but knew that it was probably up to the shifting wind. *Shift my way*, he thought at the wind. Miraculously, it seemed as if it had: Neil felt no change in the air, but the bear's attention wandered back to its menu choices.

The bear continued waffling. Neil was on the verge of roaring at the creature after twenty minutes when it slipped its head under the bottom spar of the sheep fence. It flexed its neck upward, pushing the stick from where it rested, and taking two or three pickets with it. A section of the fence collapsed.

He would have to try to scare it away with a near shot. He steadied the gun on one knee, the other resting in the dirt. He cocked the hammer, sighted down the barrel, and squeezed the trigger.

An explosion in his hands. The heat seared his fingers and a flash of light blinded his vision. He tasted something metallic and was thrown backwards. Before the pain caught up with his nerve, he had rolled back forward into a defensive crouch.

The thumb and forefinger of his right hand felt like they were on fire. There was a white-hot pain under his chin as well. He tried not to flinch but a terse gasp was wrenched out of him. The bear's nose turned again, away from the cabin. Neil thought about the odds of his survival against a bear armed with nothing but a rifle butt. He would have to make for the cabin and wait it out. Just as he was preparing to rise and make his dash for the door, he heard another explosion.

This one made the bear stagger back. It roared its pain and confusion in one short bark, then rolled onto its side, emitted a whimper, and lay still.

Neil's ears were ringing, either from the rifle exploding in his hands or the second explosion from his right. What was it from? They didn't have any other firearms. When he looked to the right, he saw two men. It was not yet dawn but a little grey light allowed him to see that they both held guns.

Immediately, his body took on a life of its own. He lurched and stumbled over to the door and stood before it, ready to defend the house. One of the men lifted a hand in greeting then pointed behind him. He couldn't hear them but turned to look. His mother emerged from the house wrapped in a plaid. She reached out to touch his shoulder. He couldn't hear her as her mouth moved. Something was wrong with his eye, too.

She raised the plaid to his face. It came away from his chin with blood on the faded blue-green. She looked at him for a frozen moment, her eyes taking in the damage through a silent tunnel. She guided him to one of the stumps by their front door and made motions for him to stay. Neil looked back to where the men stood but the scene had stopped making sense. The world listed; he felt the rough logs of the house against his cheek. He closed his eyes.

# Chapter 17

NEIL BECAME AWARE of the world slowly. The fitful slobbering of a dog slicked at his ear. He felt a little spray of moisture and jerked away, one eye open. He saw the faded muzzle of a chestnut-brown hound not two handspans from his face. It withdrew for a moment to regard him, tail wagging. Then it resumed investigating all his crevices. After his ear, the nose went under his arm where it lay on the bed. The snuffling was not unpleasant but it encouraged him to move, which Neil most certainly wanted to avoid doing. His head ached like the devil. A bandage lay across his right eye and the pressure seemed to make ghostly images float in his vision.

His left eye surveyed the back wall of the cabin. He lay on his bed. All seemed quiet. Where was his mother? Who were those men? He abandoned caution and swung his legs over the edge of the bed, immediately regretting it as a wash of sickness burbled up his throat. A wet cloth fell from his face to his lap. There was some dried blood on its grey surface. He reached up a hand—his right hand—to probe the jaw. Intact, with mushy bits. It was so swollen he couldn't feel to the bone. Probably a good thing.

The dog's nose probed under his right thigh; he obligingly moved: his legs didn't hurt in the least. The dog's tongue licked at something on the coverlet. *Whose dog is this? What happened to the bear?* A low murmur reached him from outside, expanding to a conversation as the back door was pushed open.

Muirne's head appeared briefly, he saw out of his left eye. Upon seeing him sitting up, she grabbed the edge of the door and called backward. "Mam, everyone—he's awake!"

"Whose dog is this?" The words came out garbled, hampered by his injured jaw. Neil gestured back toward the hound, who came to lick his fingers. "Fearsome beast."

"As you see." Muirne smiled. "If you come out, you can meet our visitors. She's their dog. Can you make it all right? Is your head—?"

"Come a moment," he said. She sat beside him and put an arm 'round his waist. He just sat there a moment. Feeling the dry crackle of the spiny straw in the mattress ticking. Holding the wet cloth, feeling its drops fall onto the dirt floor. Something like a hiccup escaped him. He clenched Muirne's shoulder. "I thought that was it," he said. "That I'd wake up with no hearing or—burns across —"

Muirne didn't meet his gaze but looked at the floor as he did. "You do look a sight. I'm sure it'll heal. You've just had a bitty shock, is all. Come, you must meet your rescuers, the Janneys."

She helped hoist him up. The room spun a few times, then subsided. He walked slowly out to the back pens. It was fully light, the fence was still in pieces, the lamb was in the coop with the chickens, and there was a tent pitched just beyond the drainage ditch for the animals.

Two strangers stood as he approached, setting down mugs and bowls on the camp seats where they'd been perched. Sheena and Alisdair took their cue and turned to watch his progress. Mam came over to give him the motherly once-over. She brushed the hair from his face, her eyes flickering over the bandage on his right eye and the abrasions along his jaw.

"Thank goodness that old piece didn't do more damage. It's blown to smithereens. I'm only glad it didn't take you with it. How're you feeling, Neil? We were just visiting with the Janneys while you rested."

Neil executed a nod that was so slow as to be almost a bow, in order not to set his head spinning again.

"Father," Mam indicated the older man, slight of build and grizzled of beard. "And son—Amos and Matthew." Matthew was a blond youth, no beard. His face looked aged by the wild weather and frontier living, but his eyes yet held a glint of innocence.

"Thank ye most kindly, then—Amos, Matthew. I am in your debt. What happened to the bear? Did ye scare it away?"

Alisdair leapt into the fray. "Not on yer life, Neil! They shot him! He's out there in the yard waiting to be cleaned and skinned! They said they'd leave some of the meat to us, Neil!" Neil looked from his brother's excitement to his mother.

"Seeing as how we could use some meat in our bellies and they can shoot plenty more on their journey." Mam nodded her thanks to Amos.

"Aye, that's marvelous kind," Neil remarked. "It's the first time a bear's come up this close. Usually they just avoid our trails. I thought maybe they were a myth!" He worked his jaw which only produced more sharp pain, and decided not to talk as much. His words were still so garbled that they likely couldn't understand him anyway.

"Well, they're not. You'll be wanting a good gun beside you," Amos said, then stopped, evidently thinking better of more advice in case they couldn't afford one.

Neil noticed. Things started to sort themselves out in his head. The dog belonged to this father and son pair. But why had they come so close to their stead so early in the morning? He tried to speak clearly and not grit his teeth.

"What brings you to see us, sirs? Have ye business with the MacLeans to conduct?"

For the first time, the placid expressions of the heroes of the day became troubled. Neil wondered what it was about. His mother's eyes had gone glassy, and he turned back to Amos, fearing he knew not what.

"Yes, Mr. MacLean, we do."

"Neil," Neil flapped a hand at the formality.

"Neil," the man amended. "My son and I, we're traveling labor. We work the forests all the way from Lower Canada to Nova Scotia. Been off a spell, but we had a debt of honor to pay."

"The debt's mine," a quiet, surprisingly melodic voice said. Everyone's attention focused on Matthew. "Yer pa saved my life last year, after I fell into a crick. Pa was attending to the travois some ways away, where we'd stacked the lumber. I was out gathering up the nets of fish to smoke—it was Crown land we was on, see," he said. So they hadn't been stealing anyone's fish. Neil nodded.

Matthew glanced at his father for support. When he got the nod, he continued. "Well, Gillan and that boy Sandy traveled with us for a bit. Eastward, on his way back from Quebec. We went through a town. Bit built-up it was, with a flax mill, sawmill, public house, even plans to connect a railroad through. Yer father saw a man he knew there." His recitation faltered.

Amos picked up the thread of the tale. "It was clear they knew each other. We was waiting on a corner to cross next to him, see. He warn't looking at us stragglers, but Gillan looked at him a second time. Starin', y'know? And this fellow, he got to feel the stare and looked back. Well. Gillan sort of preened. Odd, like. He spread out his hands, looked at 'em, bit a nail or two. The other man, even with his high hat and his shiny shoes—he looked fit to burst in our faces. But neither said nothing. Then we just walked on."

Matthew added, "Gillan looked mighty pleased about something, while the other man just glared at us when we went. Uncanny, it was."

Amos picked up the thread of his narrative again. "When we parted ways with Gillan and Sandy, we made to go north to see about work in the autumn. We worked there for a spell and made some money. When we came back through that same town, we saw that man your father had recognized, Mr. Anstruther Brown, in the tavern. He was boasting of the drubbing he'd laid on an old enemy, working him over but good. Called him 'the new MacLean, the ol' Gillan,' he did, and that's when I knew our friend Gillan had met with trouble."

"We hoped to see him here in spite of everything. We're very sorry that's not the case," Matthew said.

"I'm very sorry, young man. Ma'am." Amos dipped his head to Mam.

The news hung in the air like acrid coal smoke. They

sat in the cabin, feeling it eat at the lining of their lungs. Neil glanced at Alisdair, wondering how he would take the news, remembering how he felt when his own father was reported missing. His brother's face was flushed, he noticed, right before the lad dashed the few feet to hide his face against Mam's shoulder. A poisonous leaden rage made Neil's muscles ache as if he had clenched them in place for hours. He realized his hands were rigid and pried them open, feeling one of the scabs on his thumb split open. Any guilt he felt about choosing differently from Gillan in that crucial moment melted into a blood-thirsty hunger for justice to be visited on this man Brown.

But what was it about? How did such a chance encounter in the street lead to such violence? These two seemed to know nothing more about the event. And neither had Sandy when he recovered from his shock. Despite their revelations, it remained a mystery.

"We thank ye for coming all this way to deliver this news," he said unevenly. "Our father did make it back last autumn, only to die a few days later. We tended him as best we could but his injuries were grave indeed." Neil swallowed painfully past the lump in his throat.

What difference did it make to put a name to an idea that had been beating around his head for almost a year? None. Only instead of ignorance, now he fought power-lessness. He would go to the authorities with the information and they would do nothing. It changed nothing about Gillan's death but everything about how he felt. He had a name now; shouldn't he go after the man?

"We shall find out a solicitor, when the next Sessions meet. Yours may be the testimony we need to hold this man and make him pay for his sins," he said.

The group teetered in silence. Cold air skimmed over Neil's skin, raising the hairs of his arms, even as the bright afternoon sun shone down, warming the puddle of packed dirt where the dog lay curled up, its tail under its muzzle.

# Chapter 18

THAT NIGHT, THEY shared supper with the Janneys. They roasted bear steaks over an open fire, taking care to catch the dripping juices in a pan of potatoes thrust underneath. What could have been a celebratory feast was subdued by the reaction to Neil's face, speckled with clotting blood and bandages soaked in Mam's witch hazel bark decoction. His mute presence, for it still pained him to talk, rendered most of the rest of the company mute also. Alisdair still tore into his portion but instead of crowing over the shooting of the bear, he stuffed his mouth furtively. Neil didn't suppose the boy wanted to hear about Brown's boasting any more than he did.

The Janneys hacked down and stripped a couple dozen stout branches of their bark and drove a circle of them into the ground. After preparing the sinews, they wound them around the tops of the rough poles. Muirne helped Mam wrestle sharply honed wooden stakes through large sections of the bear carcass. The men raised the burdened rods and hung them at angles across the circle. It was a very hastily made smoking shed. More honed sticks were whittled and jabbed into the earth pointing up to deter coyotes and other scavengers. Neil watched, the scent of the herbs around his eye keeping him sharply aware.

They retired early: the MacLeans to their cabin and the Janneys to their tent. Muirne took another look at

Neil's face, inspecting it in the firelight. She didn't look satisfied or at ease, he noticed. She removed the bandage over his eye. She'd put it on when he was still unconscious and couldn't feel it, thank goodness. Now he sat silent but tense.

"It's red and swollen around where your eyelid's cut," she said.

"That doesnae sound good," he said.

"All right. Head back. Eyes closed. I'm going to douse it with spirits like Ed did with Mam." Neil let his head sink backward and squeezed his eyes in preparation. Even that was enough to make him gasp. She poured the liquid over the eye before he could brace himself.

"Agh!" he gasped again, louder. It was the spluttering sound he made whenever he braved the cold waters of the Atlantic. He tried to calm down but couldn't. He stuttered and hissed in agony as she dabbed. He couldn't stop his body shaking; every dab and pull and rub was like fire. Finally, Muirne put her hands on his shoulders.

"Head up now," she said briskly. His neck muscles tightened and he drew his head up slowly. A bead of liquid squeezed out of his right eye. The tremors were slackening but still present.

Muirne looked into his good eye. "It's still brownish-black, coming out. But crying is said to be good for washing wounds. Leastwise, it won't make it worse."

She attempted a smile. *I'm not crying. That's just my eye leaking out.* He didn't suppose that remark would help matters so he kept it to himself. She folded a clean cloth over his right eye and wrapped her kerchief around his head in a thin band, tying it gingerly. It was still unbearable.

"How could it be worse?" Neil said, then added, "Sorry."

It wasn't her fault he couldn't control himself. He felt the odd sensation of his eye rotating and searching without being able to see the light as his good eye followed Muirne's motions. They all knew there was no help to be had in the towns down the hill with Dr. Skinner gone. He'd have to bear the pain and hope that no infection set in. If it did, he'd have to find a ride across the mountains southwest to Truro. Hope there was a doctor there. Lose his eye. *Damned bear.* He would not allow it to spoil his plan to find that bastard Brown.

"I'll not cry, Muirne. And neither shall you. We shall dance on the grave of this Anstruther Brown. And then there will be room for tears. Not before."

Her face was full of pity. He had to resist making another protest, another empty statement.

"Sleep well, then, Neil."

He did not. He had a devil of a time finding a position that wouldn't pull at the kerchief, which pressed against the bandage over the eye. When he finally fell asleep he dreamed of a giant brown bear that pawed at him from its hind legs. He knew it to be that man Brown and let fly his rage, swiping and slashing. A surprisingly high voice emerged from the bear as it tried to defend itself.

"Ow! Neil, stop!" Alisdair was batting at his hand to disrupt his dream.

When Neil realized what he was doing, he froze. "Sorry, Alisdair. All right?"

Alisdair patted himself down. "Yeah."

"Sorry if I flailed about. I was killing that bear in my dream."

Alisdair gave a muffled 'Hmph' and turned back to sleep.

The next morning was slow going.

Everyone was outside by the time Neil stirred. He shuffled outside and was immediately greeted by a rancid smell. Mam stood above the fire from the night before, poking in their iron pot with her biggest ladle. The grey juicy bits popped and bubbled.

Their guests were up and their tent packed. The bear hide was stretched across one of their saddles, causing the horse to sidestep a bit because of the scent. Amos stood near Mam and her pot. Matthew sat on his camp chair while the others squatted on the ground nearby.

"Bear grease is verra useful when traveling on the road," Amos was saying. "Mighty helpful for the leather tack." He gestured to their well-worn saddles.

"And medicine," Matthew added. His father tut-tutted, perhaps disparaging the source of the medicine, the native Mi'qmaq. "Just you wait until you need it, Dad. Then you'll be hollerin' to the Indians for help."

"Has the smell woken you up, Neil?" she asked. "Could certainly keep critters away. You feeling more yourself yet?"

She looked at him a bit anxiously. Muirne rose and came over.

The bandage had been pushed toward his nose in the night. Muirne looked even more alarmed.

"Maybe we'll have to send over to River John for a doctor after all. It's looking streaky and red on the outer edge, Neil."

Muirne's gaze dropped from his eye to a small clay pot in her hand. She whispered, "You scored Alisdair in the face in the night. I've put the garlic paste right over it; he'll be fine after his yowling. Just take care. I'll put it on you now."

Neil stared forward. *How could it be worse, indeed.* After Muirne finished with him, he sat on a stump. His face was on fire and he felt quite useless.

"Thank ye again, missus," Amos said. "We should be getting on our way. Will the young man need a ride west?" Amos asked.

"What do you think, Muirne?" Mam asked. "Will the garlic paste be enough to stop the infection?"

Muirne stared at Neil as if she was making the most important decision of her life. Perhaps it would be the most important decision of *his* life. He didn't want to lose an eye, be less than a whole man. He had faith in their medicine from home, though.

Muirne finally said, "Aye, I'm sure it will. Thank you, Mr. Janney, but I think we'll be able to manage." It was as if she'd read his mind.

The older man nodded and turned to gather the last of his things. Matthew rose and motioned for Neil to follow him. They stood in the last mists of the mountain fog, in the shade of the cabin.

"Ye've got somethin' to say," Neil stated.

Matthew nodded. "If you wanted to go back to that town, I could take you."

Neil looked up.

"It's on the Richibucto River, out by Ford's new Mill. If the law don't work out for you, that is."

Neil wanted to jump at the offer, as soon as he was whole and in full possession of his faculties. But a sneaking note of irrational suspicion crept in. *Why would*

*Matthew go sticking his neck out for us again? He did his duty, came to pay his respects for a man who had saved his life. If in fact he had.* Now he was being downright mistrustful. Could Neil really feel comfortable going on a one-man search for vengeance? Maybe it depended on whether that gave better odds at finding and punishing the culprit. He'd already said he'd pursue justice in the courts, for his mother's sake. He decided to put his legal case forward and hope that got the man hanged. If not, there were other options.

Neil pinned the younger man with a look. "If the law doesnae work the way it should, I may take you up on that." *And how often has the law worked the way it should?* He thought bitterly of home back on Mull. "Until then, I've got my family here to look after."

Matthew blew out a breath. "Don't know where I'll be when that happens but I'll check in on you when we come through in the spring. Best of luck to you until then." Matthew stuck out his hand and Neil shook it.

"Thank you."

The men wished the MacLeans good luck with the law, and the MacLeans thanked them heartily for the hundredweight of smoked bear meat in the insulated hole under their kitchen. The stinging, slogging rains came the same day the Janneys departed.

Neil lay in the cabin, itching to do a hundred things to get the planting going, but obeying his mother and sister. They'd decided the best thing for the eye was coolness, darkness, and a strong-smelling compress made with thyme and other herbs. The smell of it seemed to give him strange dreams. No more bears; instead, he heard the bray of the bagpipes and looked out over many hills toward the sea. Then he felt like his hands were crawling on cobblestones, each individual cobble forcing its shape into his palms as he groped. Then again he stood. Before him floated Letty's face. She looked through him, but with such longing he wished he was the one who produced such feelings. He tried to speak to her but felt painful metal rods wiring his mouth shut.

When he woke next it was passing into late afternoon, to judge from his mother's clangings and rattlings over the fire for supper. He felt less restive but his jaw felt worse.

"Eh, Mam," he croaked. He cleared his throat but she was already coming over to his bed.

"And how is it with ye?" she asked.

"Better." He opened his jaw experimentally. He could open his mouth to a certain point but no more without a twinge erupting under his chin. That could wait. As could the little bits of bone that were no doubt chipped off his jaw. He'd not be chewing anything hard for quite some time.

"There'd better be some of that bear meat left by the time I can chew again," he joked.

Mam smiled. "Sense of humor again. That's a good sign."

"Aye. Do ye want to take a look at it in the light?"

"What light there is," she grumbled. "Sure—up with ye now." She helped heft him up. He walked unaided behind her to the door, feeling the fluid that had gathered in his face shift and drain. He rolled one of the big stumps in their clearing to the doorway where they would be out of the rain and tilted his head for his mother to peer over him.

He talked while she pressed and stretched painfully around his eyelid to keep his mind off it.

"And where's everyone?"

"Oh, well, Sheena's out with the creel gathering river moss. Muirne's been out to look for oak-apples but should be back soon. And Alisdair is—sorry, Neil, that's the worst bit."

"Nae bother. And Alisdair?" He clenched his hands together.

"Alisdair is off setting traps down at the base of the hill."

"Is he hoping to catch another bear?"

She chuckled. "I would say not. But you know, I think you're looking better. The color's changed, and the bruising's started turning, but the eye looks intact. Ill, but whole. I guess there wasn't any metal in there after all. Thank Heaven. Wait here a moment, Neil."

Neil said nothing as she reappeared with a cool cloth, smelling of spirits again. Muirne followed on her heels. She examine the patient, also, and concurred with her mother's opinion.

"Excellent!" Neil said, putting his hands on his thighs to rise dramatically. "Then I'll get a patch on to protect it and head down to town to see the magistrate or his clerk."

The moment of dumb shock on their faces made him smile. As he winced from moving those facial muscles, his mother and sister exploded in a furious cacophony.

"You can't travel like that! Have ye had the sense knocked out of ye?"

"What on earth are you thinking of, I'd like to know!"

He waited them out. "I am going to go slowly, with whatever spirits and medicines you want to douse me with, but I am going. We must act on this news from Amos and Matthew! We have a name and a town. We must alert the magistrate as soon as possible. That's *my* duty."

Mam seemed to realize that he had made some important internal resolution. The bluster went out of her. "Well, take care. I'll go in and start making some bannocks for the road."

Muirne was less sanguine. "We could be wrong, Neil. What if you're all alone and lose your sight? What if your other eye gets infected? What if—"

"Don't go on so, Muirne. It's just a slow, easy trip into town. I may even find that a doctor is visiting and get his opinion."

She pursed her lips, knowing he had little hope of that.

"I must *do* something," he said. "I know it's about time to harvest the oats, and you can start on the south end of the field, take it slowly with the scythe. I'll be back in two or three days, and by then, someone *else* will be doing something—going after this Brown in Ford's Mill. I can't just let it lie, Muirne."

She crossed her arms and stared at him. He saw two of her, one normal and one shadowy and tinted with red.

"Don't be angry, Muirne. Ye've done a fine job. I'll take care to return in one piece."

He left that evening after the rains stopped, his injured eye more comfortable with the long twilight.

# Chapter 19

MUIRNE WAS IN a churn over Neil's departure. She under-stood his desire for action but had a bad feeling about his leaving. The echoes from Gillan's departure were just too close. She was thankful that hoeing the mud took up so much of her physical energies that she didn't have time to uselessly speculate. She did have time, however, to won-der about Edward and whether his ship had arrived safe. She hoped he would write as soon as possible. It wasn't going to change his religion or his parents, but she could at least find solace in his affection.

The mud from the rains was everywhere again. Muirne tried to knock off the caked stuff from her shoes as she came in, but her legs were covered in it as well. Alisdair did the same when he entered, stopping to peer at the dark muck.

"It's not like the mud at home," Alisdair said. "It's redder, and thicker," he said. "Ground up. Ours had the seashells in it, and felt smoother."

It was like Alisdair to go peering into the dirt. Muirne had forgot what mud used to look like, she'd been floun-dering in this stuff for so long. When no one replied to his pronouncement on the mud, Alisdair spoke again.

"What do you think happened to Mr. Janney's wife, Mam?"

Mam's head was bent to her task; she was once again by the fire, using its light to gather and stitch the folds for the sleeves of Muirne's wedding dress. The sight of all that shimmering cloth made Muirne want to run her fingers over and through it endlessly. Good thing Mam had charge of it; it would be worn into nubs if she got hold of it.

"It's not for us to speculate, Alisdair. He didn't tell us and we don't know them well enough to ask. But they've clearly been on their own for a while."

Alisdair digested that. "He's a bit queer, isn't he, Mam?"

"Who, Mr. Janney?" she asked, surprised.

"No, Mr. Matthew."

"Mm. There's a sort of strain about him, you could say. I suppose he was attentive enough. What did you think, Muirne?"

"Attentive? I suppose. Hey, do you hear that? I think it's stopped." Muirne rose to peer out the door. Sure enough, the forest glistened with sunlight on the dripping leaves. It was a picture.

While Muirne set about their dinner preparations, she noticed Mam was sewing with jerky motions, rather than her usual calm, elegant, efficiency.

"What is it, Mam, that's making ye so jumpy? You're not worried about Neil on the road?"

Mam shook her head slightly, but asked, "And if I were, who could blame me, the logging camps set up as they are, and roving bands of single men, clear off their nut, just looking for mischief?"

"Mam, he'll be careful. Neil already knows the places to avoid. He told us them as well."

Mam pursed her lips, as if to say, *And how does Neil know all this?* But she didn't disparage her son's judgment.

She held up the elbow of the sleeve she was working on, feeling the gathers on the underside all the way round with her fingers to make sure it was even, then bunched the sleeve material and her pins back into the muslin sack. She rose and excused herself to the privy. Muirne gazed out at the still-sparkling forest through the doorway, dusting her hands off on the rag at her waist.

Muirne was getting used to the weight of the scythe as she grasped its handles and swung to her left. *Always to the left.* She wished there was some way to switch sides, as her right side was becoming sore. Sheena was working her little garden patch, several rows over. The garden boasted more bog myrtle, whose scent Muirne loved, as well as meadow sage, hyssop, flax, madder, gorse, lesser celandine, coltsfoot, and yarrow. Every third thwack with her hoe, there was a silent pause as Sheena glanced at the road. Muirne took a break to stretch to her right and watched her sister, amused at her optimism.

She, too, was keeping an eye out for the postman, just not being so terribly obvious about it. When Sheena looked up and started, Muirne followed her gaze to the silhouette of the postman with his bag. An unknown visitor trailed behind him, taking the hill at a slower pace. Muirne could tell nothing but that it was a woman; her shape and that of her bonnet made that clear.

The postman, a middle-aged man with black hair in a fringe 'round his head, was called Tommy, or more properly, Tom McClelland. He was naturally quiet, as might be expected of someone who spent days at a time crossing empty forests to reach far-flung settlements. When the pair reached the cabin, Muirne squinted and saw a slight, trim, older woman dressed in black lace.

"Mr. Tommy!" Sheena squealed.

He looked down the hill and acknowledged the address with a wave, then knocked on the cabin door. The woman took in the landscape. When she turned, Muirne gaped.

Unless she was quite mistaken, this woman had to be a relative of Edward's! Muirne could see her striking eyes, her wide forehead, even from this distance.

Alisdair, usually ready to leap toward Tommy for the post, halted in the doorway at the sight of the new visitor. Mam swept forward to issue a welcome. Muirne and Sheena waited in the field. *Is it Edward's mother? Why would she come?* Muirne hoped it was not to be a repeat of the father's visit.

"Afternoon, Mr. McClelland. You look well. Have you brought us a special visitor?"

"Afternoon, Mrs. MacLean. Yes, this is Mrs. Turner, who I've helped to your property from the post road, some two miles west." He executed a perfunctory bow and bid them a good day before walking briskly off. No doubt he had been severely delayed by his feat of chivalry.

Muirne heard his words clearly fifty feet below. She left the field slowly, scythe in hand. As she came to the edge of the field, Mam called to invite the girls up to the house. They watched her usher Mrs. Turner in first, then turned to each other, aghast.

Sheena's eyes were so round the whites looked like saucers. She grasped Muirne's hand.

"Is that her? Why would she come?" Sheena asked.

Muirne only shook her head mutely.

It was the hottest part of the day, almost four o'clock. It would be nice to finish early. Sheena scurried up the hill. Muirne, much more thoughtfully, brought up the rear.

# Chapter 20

THE WOMEN SAT around the table in an uneven distribution. Muirne and Sheena squished close together to give Mrs. Turner a bit of space at the other end of the rough bench. Their mother took the tree stump seat facing their guest. Alisdair went out back to procure the large hawthorne creel pressed into service on such occasions.

Since Mam had already introduced herself, she did the honors for her family, treating Mrs. Turner as an esteemed guest.

"This is Mrs. Turner, everyone: the mother of our good friend, Mr. Edward Turner."

Muirne twitched, torn between fetching the oat bannocks with their gooseberry preserves and staying at table to hear Mrs. Turner's first words. After an agonized glance at her mother, she rose to get the tea things from the cupboard along the back wall.

She assembled the knit bag of nearly-powdered leaves and filled the pot with water from their barrel outside, setting it over the ever-burning fire, which she stoked up for good measure. She listened as she broke the bannocks into pieces and placed them on a large wooden trencher, along with the pot of preserves and a pewter spoon. They were still speaking about the settlements and the town's growth by the time she laid the trencher on the table. She went back for their supply of four cups, whittled by Neil over the winter.

When she returned to her seat, Mam had introduced the topic of Ed back into the conversation.

"It was a miracle that Muirne was able to find him so quickly, and that he had his wits about him. That brandy and the poultice were what kept my throat from closing. Poor Neil said it was quite a scare."

"Yes, his father and I are very proud of Edward." The woman looked over at Muirne. Her expression was one almost of bemusement. "And he is our only surviving child, which may be partly to blame for some of the tension between father and son."

"Yes, of course. When there is only one chance of continuing the family, everything must seem important, every decision a wrench," Mam murmured.

"Exactly." Mrs. Turner seemed comforted by her mother's reply. Her mild expression turned somewhat more brooding. "But that doesn't excuse his father's behavior." She locked gazes with Muirne.

"I understand Mr. Turner—George, I mean—came here some weeks ago and made a rather bad impression. I undertook this visit today to beg your forgiveness; Edward has been so worried for you. He is unflagging in his efforts to champion you at home in his letters. I was quite convinced before meeting you that I would approve, based simply on Edward's obvious esteem. He does have such good judgment.

"My husband is a good man, it is just that Edward's decision makes no sense to him. He is still adjusting to his son's independent way of living, you see. It is only because George is away at sea that I am here now. He feels deeply affronted and can not quite give up fighting for Edward to come back into the fold—his fold."

Mam nodded. Muirne realized she'd been gaping—not breathing—and made an effort to close her mouth and inhale calmly. She dropped her gaze to her lap. Was his mother really here to make amends? To try to undo the offense of her husband? Or was she merely here to inspect the goods, to see if Muirne was deserving of her son? The bitterness washed up Muirne's throat. A lady like Mrs. Turner would not take an expensive eight-hour carriage ride across the countryside merely to look down her nose at a future daughter-in-law, would she? Muirne fought to keep her thoughts from veering wildly from hope to resentment and back again. The lady seemed kindly disposed toward them.

She was jolted out of her reverie when she heard the pot boiling. Everyone remained quiet as she moved to pour the tea. Muirne fought to keep her hands from shaking. Muirne and Sheena didn't need to share a cup, as Alisdair was more interested in the bannocks and preserves than tea. The lull in conversation felt like a roaring wind in her ears. Muirne took hold of her courage and dove in.

"You were saying something about Mr. Edward's judgment, Mrs. Turner, and his letters?"

"Yes. Well, after hearing from him how deserving you were, and hearing from my husband how badly he'd behaved—he does regret it, believe me, he just can't reconcile himself—I determined to visit you myself. I took the post gig as far as the spot where Mr. McClelland found me. It was quite a bumpy ride but an adventure nonetheless, and it gave me time to think away from the house."

Her eyes were lively as she exclaimed about the bene-

fits of comfortable travel. Muirne put on her most understanding expression, endeavoring to appear *deserving*.
Mrs. Turner turned abruptly to Mam.

"I am afraid I will need to presume on your hospitality somewhat, as it is two days before the next return gig
will be passing. I asked Mr. McClelland when I alighted."
She smiled; Mam was already nodding. So that explained
her large brown case sitting outside the door in the yard.

"We live up west from Pictou along the coast. Has
Edward told you about the place?"

"No, I don't believe he has," said Muirne. She didn't
want to offend the lady by saying he'd been reluctant to
talk about his parents at all. She wondered why he would
be, as his mother seemed pleasant enough.

"Well, we shall have to have a visit." The woman's soft
pink and white cheeks wrinkled in a broad smile. "I
couldn't think of a thing that would please me more.
After the harvest is in, of course. I don't want to take you
away when you're needed."

Mrs. Turner spoke this in Mam's direction, expecting
her to give her permission for the venture. Mam turned
to Muirne. Muirne blanched, fumbling for a polite reply.

"That is most kind, Mrs. Turner. Perhaps I can come
with Sheena or Alisdair? We don't take the post gig but it
is easy enough to travel in pairs."

"Of course. A companion would be wise, coming
across the wild country that is our forested hill. Although
I would be happy to pay for your journey. Two fares that
distance wouldn't be more than—what? Four shillings
and sixpence?" She smiled again. "Consider it George's
penance, and then your sister or brother may come with
you. Miss Sheena seems eager for a journey."

"Oh, we couldn't——" Muirne began.

"Oh, but you can," Mrs. Turner countered. "And if you can come with me when I leave, it should be much more convenient. We can have a few days together without George sulking in the background."

Muirne was hesitant. "Then you are certain Edward intends to proceed without his father's blessing?"

Mrs. Turner sighed. "Yes. I am. We will have to continue working on George. Now, do say yes."

It was harvesting time. Neil was gone. She could get the oats started the next day, then leave the day after that in the gig. Neil would be back that day, he'd said, and could continue with the rest. *As long as his eye gives him no trouble.* It seemed an awful gamble.

The silence was marked. Mam must have been making the same calculations. She said, "Go on, Muirne. We'll have the one day and then Neil will be back. Take Alisdair with you for a companion."

"But the fares, I'm not sure——"

The lady proceeded as if the matter was settled. "Blether. It's nothing. It's our pleasure." She smiled. "And now we may talk at leisure—or is there still work to be done in the field today?" Muirne felt too strangled to reply. Four shillings and sixpence was *nothing*.

"Just need to set up those stooks to dry before nightfall. Right, Muirne?" her mother asked.

"And some of the tools need seeing to," Muirne added. She rose and turned to Mrs. Turner.

"We are so honored to have you here, Mrs. Turner. We're all so grateful to your son for his care of our mother last year." She was so nervous her palms were slippery with sweat. What if the woman wished to speak to her alone? What if she made a mistake? What if the lady saw she wasn't deserving? She could mess it all up.

Muirne escaped to gather the oats into stooks and clean the tools.

The first task was easily dispatched in a quarter-hour. Muirne carried the scythe and *cas-chrom* back up to the cabin. Heat suffused her face as she sat on the bench at the back of the house, rubbing the cloth over the wood and metal joints. She flapped the cloth impatiently at the handle, out of temper. Sheena struggled out with the straw mattress from the box bed.

"Here, Sheena. Let me help," Muirne said.

She reached to catch the end that was almost dragging in the dirt. Belatedly, Alisdair appeared with the wicker carpet beater. Muirne held the heavier end as the two younger children set about hitting and slapping the lumpy cover to upset the dust and unsettle the bugs. Their hearty whacks echoed in the quiet of the hilltop at dusk. It only took a few moments, then brother and sister staggered back inside with the awkward load. She heard the noises, the general settling in of bodies, the general good nights, and finally Mam, smooring the fire.

Muirne straightened her shoulders. She placed the clean *cas-chrom* in a cloth and lay it on top of the chicken roost. Neil was out fighting one of their battles for them. She could certainly fight her own here. She sincerely hoped she could pass whatever tests lay ahead.

# Chapter 21

MUIRNE WOKE THE next morning with goosebumps. She slept next to her mother and Sheena on the mattress usually occupied by Neil and Alisdair. It was stuffed with whins: spiky, spiny branches of the ground cover that grew on the hillsides in the autumn. For the time being, Alisdair was curled up by the hearth.

Mrs. Turner was in the box bed, which had enclosed panels around a mattress stuffed with the last of the old wool and more whins. *I didn't know what I had until I lost it*, Muirne thought testily. She pulled the blanket, pooled under Sheena's side, enough to cover her chilled arms. She thought about the night before and tried to resign herself to another whole day of that awkwardness. She dreaded the necessity of being so careful in her speech with Edward's mother. Yes, she seemed sympathetic, but so foreign. She hoped only that she would not make an ignorant misstep. She would have plenty of time in the field in the morning to think up pleasant things to say.

When she and Sheena took their break from cutting the oats for breakfast mid-morning, they had made a noticeable dent in the field. From up top, they looked down, proud of their work, for there they could see better that they were more than halfway done. They crossed the threshold into the dark cabin, where Mam greeted them with a smile. Alisdair was tasked with crushing the oak-apples and apparently he had been hard at his work too: the brown powder clung to his hands. Muirne closed her eyes briefly, happy and thankful. She opened them and Mam was motioning for her to join Mrs. Turner at the table. She washed quickly and went in.

"Mrs. Turner was telling me last night of her husband's growing up near Tatamagouche. He had a private tutor as well, just like we wish for our Alisdair."

Mam was pressing bannocks on the hot girdle for their breakfast. Sheena sat across from Mrs. Turner this time. Alisdair hurried in and sat cross-legged on the floor, still rubbing his hands against his pants. Muirne hoped the quick splash of water before entering was enough to take off the sheen of her exertions. Her mother seemed oblivious to these concerns about the impression she made. She wore her same stained work apron, her same summer muslin skirt.

"Yes, that is what we wish for Alisdair. He's very quick to learn." Muirne's words sounded stilted to her ears. She couldn't make a comment about the father. Better to turn the conversation to the mother's family.

"And yourself, Mrs. Turner? Were you raised in Nova Scotia also?"

"Oh Heavens, no!" Her lips curved into a small, secret smile. "No, the lack of women in the colony thirty-five years ago led George to write to his family. He still had relatives in Dumfries, whom he asked to find him a bride."

Muirne stared. The woman was a frontier bride. She tried to recover her aplomb. "I see. Then you are from Dumfries?"

"Yes, down near Wigtown. It's a lovely area. Full of Bells; that's my maiden name. Haven't visited since, much to my sadness." The smile turned wistful, then rounded back on Muirne with an amused tilt. "But I have had enough to occupy me here. The place was much wilder then."

"Does Mr. Edward have any brothers or sisters or cousins back in Scotland?" Alisdair interrupted.

"Alisdair." A stern note from Mam.

Another smile from Mrs. Turner, who indulged the curiosity of the young boy. "Yes, George had one sister and she one son: therefore Edward has the one cousin. He is very close to George's family in Wigtown. He is to fill a living in the church there."

The irony! Two cousins only, and one a vicar while the other was an atheist. She felt her eyebrows flickering and threatening to break her careful composure.

"We also had a daughter—Clara—but she died of yellow fever just after her second year," Mrs. Turner said quietly.

The pause that followed was respectful, rather than awkward. It purged Muirne of her urge to laugh.

"I'm sorry, ma'am," said Muirne. "Perhaps that was an early reason for Mr. Turner to think of medicine."

She dipped her head graciously. "Perhaps."

"Was there a different line of work Mr. Turner intended for his son here? Following him into the merchant marine?"

"A perceptive question, my dear. But Mr. Turner is not in the merchant marine. He invests in ships and their cargo."

"A profitable venture, when Britain rules the seas," Mam said.

Muirne wished she had something to contribute that

would not reveal her ignorance of commerce. She also thought how peculiar it was that Edward would turn his back on his father's profession. His passions must be great for medicine, for denying the Church—and for her.

"Maybe Edward will be able to make use of his father's business connections once his practice is established."

Mrs. Turner observed her with coolness. "No," she eventually replied. "I don't think George's contacts would be useful in Ewdard's line of medicine."

"And what does your own family do, Mrs. Turner?" Mam interjected, saving Muirne from another fraught interval.

"Most of the Bells of Wigtown are minor gentry. There are a few restless Members of Parliament, a handful of gentleman farmers. But no doctors."

Muirne bit her lip. What was she to say to that? This recitation sounded like the lady was wistful for her family's rank. How she must have come down, to suffer the indignity of a Church-of-Scotland-peasant for a daughter-in-law. Och, this was bad. Two days of this here, *and* a return visit?

Muirne shook herself mentally. She reminded herself how much her family could gain if she married into this family. If four shillings and sixpence was nothing they could have a flock of sheep in no time, enough for milk and cheese and meat all year long, not to mention buying more than one type of seed to try each growing season. She strained to think of more to say that would show how *deserving* she was, even as her skin crawled with unease at this idea of marrying for money and safety.

"Speaking of education," Mrs. Turner continued.

"What has been your upbringing? Edward informed me you received his letters."

"Yes. I can read, thanks to my brother Neil. And write. He taught me when they would no longer take a girl at the village school. My writing is still very bad but I do read when I have the chance," she said.

"And where is this Neil now? Will I be able to meet him before I go?"

"I'm afraid not," Mam replied. We're expecting him back from New Glasgow tomorrow afternoon."

"And the gig leaves in the morning. Ah, well," Mrs. Turner said.

Muirne had her fill of bannocks and tea. She left Mrs. Turner to her mother and returned with Alisdair to the field. It was Sheena's turn to stay behind, to render some of their wild game fat into tallow for soap. It was a reeky task and Muirne was glad she wouldn't end up smelling so with Mrs. Turner there.

When they returned for dinner, Muirne tried to smooth her hair back into its rough knot and wipe her face with a cool cloth, but she entered feeling overheated, sunburnt, and sticky. The conversation pattered on as before, her mother guiding and her siblings interrupting. When the onion soup with stew meat was declared delicious by their guest, Alisdair piped up about their visitation by the bear. He relished being the storyteller, casting Neil as quite the hero until the gun exploded in his face.

"Goodness! That is quite a story—and I've heard quite a few stories of bears in these mountains," said Mrs. Turner. "And you say he's gone to town to get it looked at

—well, it's good that he can travel."

"No, it's so he can talk to a judge or someone. The men that shot the bear came here to tell us who—" Alisdair faltered.

"Who may have been responsible for an attack on my husband last autumn," Mam finished quietly. "Neil went to start inquiries into his arrest at once."

"Edward did tell us something of the circumstances last year. I am so sorry. Such a terrible misfortune. I'm glad your son has been able to take up the slack so easily, Mrs. MacLean. Others might not have been up to the task."

"Thank you," Mam murmured. A grey chill swept the room. Muirne took the trencher with the remaining bannocks and cut them into wedges for later.

"Mrs. Turner, we don't usually have supper until six o'clock. Are you quite satisfied?"

"Yes. Perhaps you'll give me your receipt for the blackberry preserves we had this morning. Mine comes out quite a bit sharper."

"I'd be glad to," Mam replied.

When they had finished, Mam swept the crumbs into the pan and gave them to the chickens out back, all the while reciting her process for boiling down the blackberries and her secret ingredient: bay leaf. Meanwhile, Muirne removed the ashes of the fire and put them in a new bucket with clean water. Sheena would strain them tomorrow to make potash to go with the tallow.

The children moved purposefully about, each to their own task. When Muirne had retrieved the eggs from the chicken run for supper and put them in the bowl for Mam to cook with, back she went for her third shift of laboring in the fields. Tomorrow it would be Neil's turn again. She mulled over the conversation thus far; it seemed to be getting easier to be in Mrs. Turner's presence. But would that continue in the post gig? In her house? Without the calming presence of her mother?

Muirne had been surprised when Mrs. Turner seemed at ease using her hands to break apart the bannocks. They had also shared a pewter knife for the preserves and she didn't hesitate. Surely gentry in Dumfries didn't eat so? Muirne was sure they all had silver service and clean linens at each meal. Perhaps this was an indication of the lady's great adaptability. Or was her background not what she had told them? No, she wouldn't start thinking Edward's mother a liar, not when she behaved so kindly to them.

# Chapter 22

MAM PREPARED THE breakfast early, for Muirne and Alisdair would be leaving to catch the nine o'clock post gig with Mrs. Turner. There was a thrilling atmosphere of excitement in the cabin. Peals of laughter escaped from Muirne and Sheena. Muirne had taken her sister aside to make sure she wouldn't dream away the week but help Neil to thresh and winnow the oats.

"And then the wheat harvest is almost ready as well, and it needs to be cut at just the right moment. You heard Neil."

"Of course," Sheena promised. "Only Muirne, do promise you'll tell me all about the visit—every detail?"

Muirne laughed. "Aye, I will, and I'm sure Alisdair will fill in any details I miss!" Muirne finished folding her clothes and packed the necessities for the week. Alisdair did the same, even more excited than Sheena because he was going along.

They said special prayers for the harvest, Mam a bit more solemn than usual. Mrs. Turner observed them respectfully then turned to Mam.

"What a very orderly household. Quite successful management of every detail. You must be very proud of them, Mrs. MacLean." Mam, who had folded their utensils away, acknowledged this with a smile and a blush. Muirne was struck by it because she couldn't ever remember seeing her mother blush.

Muirne and Alisdair marched out after many embraces, with requests still being hurled at their backs. Muirne let Mrs. Turner take the lead, allowing precedence to overtake practicality for the first time in her life. She hoped that this secret visit would go well, that there might be more visits, that Mr. Turner might come to regard her as an acceptable daughter-in-law—so many things. It was with her heart on her sleeve that she traipsed out.

Sheila and Sheena stopped calling after them when the little group dropped out of sight behind the spine of their hill.

"Well," said Sheila. "Let us hope Muirne does the right thing." She was softening in her thoughts about Edward, having met his mother.

"And that Alisdair does not blurt out anything improper," Sheena added. Sheila smiled.

"Yes, well. He's growing up, is Alisdair. You're both studying your letters, isn't that so?" They turned to go back into the cabin to put the sleeping arrangements back to rights.

"I would help him learn if he would concentrate," Sheena said crossly. "He's always off to the river or the woods. Sometimes it's useful—when he's checking our snares—but most of the time he gets away with doing nothing."

"Don't take on so. A few years ago, you were the same."

"I wasn't! I was always out gathering kelp, is what I was."

"Oh, aye." For the first time in over a year, the image of the underground kiln where they had burned the kelp for potash to sell came to Sheila. She picked up the cups, needlessly swiping the inside of each one for moisture and dust, even though she'd done so less than half an hour ago. The interior of the cups peered back at her, looking like the underground kiln where first she, then her children had tended the kelp day in and day out. Until one day it was all worth nothing.

The conversation fell away. Sheena put on a kerchief for the bright sun that now shone. "I'm away to finish Muirne's work on the oats. Don't be surprised if I get it all done in an hour. I feel in such good spirits!"

Sheila shook herself from her memories of the island. "I'm glad, Sheena. Be careful with the scythe now. Muirne's just sharpened it for ye."

Sheila picked up the silk that Muirne had brought back weeks ago. She would continue work on the wedding trousseau in the faith that Muirne would win over Mrs. Turner, and that Mrs. Turner could turn her husband's heart. After dinner, perhaps she would give Sheena a hand with the threshing when the girl's energy would be flagging.

After setting pins for the neckline, Sheila attached the sleeves, basting first to see that the fit would be loose enough for Muirne. She dipped the broad loops under and out, cinching each one just enough so it wouldn't be likely to catch and tear. She brought out the box that Jenny had given them at their leaving. The battered thing still smelled of the sea air from the ship, she fancied. She lifted the latch, opened the top, and pulled out the tray full of sewing notions.

Bobbins of thread Jenny had dyed and wound herself, the colors of their MacLean tartan. Sheila's eyes misted as she pulled them forth: blood red, moss green, the light blue of the summer sky, the yellow of the thorny gorse, white, black. Should she choose all one color to use for an embroidery design for Muirne's dress? *Nay. In this one thing, I shall not conserve and pray for another day. I shall spin it all into one dress and have faith that more thread will be given.*

After using the yellow and blue, she threaded the dark red into her needle. That gaping hole in the ground, the unused kiln, came back to her then, as well as the memory of her misplaced faith in their laird. But she wasn't trusting anybody but her family now. Couldn't afford it. Neil would come back, they would get the harvest in, put it all up in time for the snows. And if Sheila had her druthers, Muirne would be married to Ed —who would find God again—Letty would write back to Neil, and that bastard Anstruther Brown would be strung up from the nearest tree.

She remembered his wild jealousy when he had tried to court her nine years ago. His boasts to other men. Hearing his lies had made her ashamed. Afraid that people would believe him and no one would want her. She had been so happy to put herself and the three children under Gillan's protection. She'd had no idea that the two men knew each other back in Torloisk. Gillan would have kept it from her, not to worry her.

Neil had asked her whether she believed the Janneys, but the tale they told of the encounter in the street was too like the blackguard she remembered to bother denying it. Obsessed with competition, never a graceful competitor. Oh, Gillan. She didn't tell Neil the details, merely that it sounded very like him. And now Neil was off to combat the malevolence that was Anstruther. She fervently hoped the man didn't hear of the suit before being apprehended or he might just make his way here and terrorize——but what if he did?

Sheila stilled. She blinked hard. Neil had only left three days ago; it was impossible.

"Tcha!" she chided herself in the empty cabin. She yanked the red through and jabbed her thumb with the needle. She hissed more in annoyance than pain and sucked at the pinprick.

*She and Sheena were alone on their land. Sheena was alone in the field. What if he sent men to do the same*——no, it was ridiculous. Neil would come back today or tonight and they'd figure out some way to guard against such a threat. It wasn't time yet to worry.

Sheila didn't trust her hands with the thread again. She got up, stuffing the work back into its bag. It fell from the seat and slumped onto the floor. Sheila didn't notice. She strode to the hearth and picked up the fire iron. She jabbed at the coals until they glowed red.

*There's no reason. It's not possible. He can't be actually here. He's miles away.*

Before she knew what she was about, Sheila bolted toward the doorway and almost fell over the wadded fabric at her feet. She grasped at the logs of the wall to stop herself then stumbled her way out into the sun.

*See, there's the sun, sunny day, perfectly fine. I'll just go check on Sheena, see if she's finished the oat field yet.*

She reached the edge of the cabin clearing and peered down through the thorny brambles to the small arrow of land they'd started to cultivate. The afternoon sun was behind her and the fields were in shade. She didn't see her daughter in the field. The scythe lay visible where the oats had been cut.

"Sheena!" she screamed. She scrambled directly down the hill instead of taking the trail along its side. She slid on her bottom through dusty soil as dry branches snapped and her hands caught on blackberry thorns. *Where have they taken her? Where is my daughter? I will kill him if he harms her.*

She plunged downward in a panic until her shoe ran straight into a large rock. Her foot stayed put and she went flying. Expanse of blue sky. The weightlessness. A flash of red—*Sheena's kerchief—*

Ten feet below, her back connected with the solid, tamped-down dirt next to the oat field. She lost her breath then convulsed, gasping for air. The red kerchief bobbed into her field of vision. She realized there was nothing wrong with Sheena; here she came. Her daughter was fine. But she'd done herself an injury, panicking like that. At least a broken toe. As she breathed out, she felt her limbs go numb. *Oh no.What is this? It feels like drowning.*

Sheena came close. Her "Mam?" was so tentative, so fearful, that Sheila tried to sit up. No. Tried to speak. No. But the Adam's apple bobbed in her throat. She tried to twitch her fingers. Was that a response? Her daughter knelt at her side and moved her hands over her body, searching.

"Mam?" Her voice was high and querulous now. "Where are you hurt? I can't tell where anything's wrong without ye moving. Oh God! What happened up there? Why did ye fly like a demon down that hill? Oh God."

Sheila wanted to reassure her, calm her, but all she could feel was the pull downward toward unconsciousness.

# Chapter 23

SHEENA HAD THOUGHT it was another bear, the way the breaking thorns and branches had snapped and stolen her attention. When she saw it was her mother careening down the slope calling her name, she scrambled up from her sprawl in the shade and snatched up the scythe.

She waited, her eyes on the top of the ridge, to see if danger followed her mother. She saw nothing but the bright sunlight, burning her vision. Then the branches had stopped cracking. Mam flew over the last ten feet of scrub to land at the bottom of the hill. Nothing moved above. Sheena darted forward.

"Mam?" she tried to whisper. It came out faintly.

"Mam?" she tried again, getting a harsh squeak for her trouble. She swallowed and threw down the scythe. Her mother was hurt. She knelt in the flattened grass where she lay; a foot looked askew and she wasn't moving.

"Mam!"

Sheena panted, wanting to scream for help. Help from someone else. But there was no one. No Neil. No Muirne. Not even Alisdair to send for help. Should she go?

She talked to her mother, a stream of worry and unconscious terror that fell from her lips that she didn't even realize she spoke aloud. All the while, she touched tentatively the forehead, the cheeks, the neck, the hands —a finger twitched.

"Mam? Can ye move? Should I move you? Tell me what to do!"

The eyelids fluttered, then closed.

"No!"

The strength in Sheena's voice echoed across the small cleared field. The echo reminded her that they were a target, alone and unarmed. She had to get her mother up the hill and in bed, then go for help. Sheena scoured the ground for something to help her carry someone heavier than herself. The sled that Neil had fashioned for ferrying goods was stored behind the cabin; she could drag her on that.

Sheena ran up the hill, her heart skipping beats in her ears. She dragged the awkward bundle down from the rafters hanging over the byre, flinching when it banged down in front of her and sent the chickens into a tizzy. Her hair frizzed and stuck to her cheeks as she pulled the stiff leather bottom, reinforced with wood, and the attached wooden runners down as carefully as she could.

Twenty minutes after she'd left, she was back at her mother's side. Mam's face had gone pale and her lips were blueish. Sheena managed to keep her frustrated scream in her throat as she unfolded the leather flaps with shaking hands and drew it even with her mother's body. Her mouth was clamped shut and her heavy breathing was making her nose run. She swiped a sleeve at her face, wiping away the sweat, slime, and tears. She took a breath in through her mouth and dove in.

First, the head and shoulders. She positioned herself at Mam's head and squatted down to grab hold of her linen shift at the shoulders. She pulled and yanked as gently as she could. She fell down twice. Finally, she had

Mam fully on the sled. She crawled over to her mother's face, putting the back of a hand to one cheek. It was pale but warm. *That's good.*

Sheena pulled at the sled with all her body, digging her heels into the dry soil and heaving them up the hill with all her strength. She slipped and landed on her bottom more often than not. Each time she rose, she loomed over her mother's face, checking for a change. And each time when there was not, she gritted her teeth and pulled again. Her vision was blurred with tears; her face became smeared with the dirt from her hands when she wiped them impatiently away.

About three-quarters of the way up the hill, Sheena fell and lay there. She stared at the blue sky. She heard the chickens, calm and amiable once more. She thought of the lamb, her mother's idea to keep them in a bit of milk for cheese and wool for spinning. Such a little hope. But it had worked.

Sheena sucked in the next breath. She rose slowly. She didn't check the sled. Instead, she picked up the two tow ropes she'd been tugging and pulled them over her shoulders. She bent and dug into the ground, walking forward now. *A little hope,* she thought. *That's all we need now.*

She went more slowly, less frantically, walking forwards, and she didn't fall. Her whole body was one rigid bone, from the stiffened back of her neck to the straining core of her down to the lead she felt in her legs. She made it to the house and stood there, spittle blowing in and out of her mouth as she panted. *Bed, water, blankets. Then to the MacGregors'.*

The sled glided over the smooth dirt of the cabin

interior without a struggle. Sheena bent and tried to pick up her mother in front of her box bed. She got her arms under her back and knees, but pitched forward when she tried to hoist her upward. Her right hand shot out to break her fall, and she landed with a thunk on her right knee. The shock was breathtaking. There'd be a big egg on that knee in no time.

She tried laying across the mattress and dipped her arms down. She used the heavy pallet as leverage and pulled her mother up into bed. Now her arms ached. But it was done. She put a hand over her mother's brow. It was warm. *A little hope.*

It was enough to get Sheena limping over to the wash basin for a cloth. She dipped it in the cool water and brought it back to lay on Sheila's forehead. She knew she should go for help but her body cried out for a rest. *Very well. A rest. Then I'll leave at nightfall for the MacGregors' cabin.*

When Sheena woke hours later, she heard snoring noises. She turned in bed and felt an exquisite pain in her knee. It all came back. She jolted upright, smiling incredulously at the snores from her mother. She peered closer. A bruise, a few welts. How could she tell how she was if she didn't wake up? She must go. But when she moved her right leg to stand, she gasped. It wasn't merely an egg: any sideways movement drew fire along the joint of her knee. She couldn't walk like this. She might not even be able to hop.

Sheena took the cold cloth from Mam's forehead and went to wet it afresh with cool water. She struggled across the floor of the cabin, a defiant, high-pitched mewling escaping her with every step. She dunked the cloth jerkily and sat on the floor near the basin. She hoped it would help ease the swelling of her knee.

Wasn't Neil supposed to be back this night? Would her mother hold out til then? Would *she*? It would be a week before Muirne and Alisdair were back. *Maybe the knee will get better in a few hours*, she reasoned.

*And maybe I'm a chimpanzee.*

# Chapter 24

As Neil walked toward town in the morning, he remembered at the crossroads that one of the Allman women had worked at the Halifax soldiers' hospital. He took the turning for their property, which was fairly close to New Glasgow. *Miss Allman must have seen a lot of gore. She may know better than Mam or Muirne if my eye needs to be operated on.*

It was only an hour's walk from the crossroads and it was in the comfortable shade of heavy spruce and fir. The Allmans hadn't harvested much timber; they'd come here with the grant a generation ago, with help from the government. Neil was careful to keep his right hand stretched out to the side in case he ran into something he couldn't see.

The Allmans were at work in the fields. Neil felt a twinge of guilt for leaving Muirne with the worst of the oat heading, but let it pass. He hallooed Angus, the eldest son. The pain of moving his jaw was getting lesser with more usage, at least.

"Is your sister at home?"

"Delilah? Aye—is it doctorin' you need, Neil? What's happened to your eye?"

"I used a bad gun. It turned on me, blew up in my face while I was shooting at a bear."

"A bear, is it? We've had one or two here this year but not nearly as many as when we had the livestock. Oy, it looks like your jaw got a bit mashed as well. Come away in."

The burly man led the way to the snug cabin. His dark hair, which was not pulled back but chopped short to his chin, gleamed in the sun. His red face and sweat-soaked limbs, as well as the wide swath of rows and full buckets, showed that he and his brother Patrick had been at it since first light. They passed the brother, still laboring. Neil felt another twinge of guilt about Muirne, but really, their field was much smaller.

He was told to sit on the wood bench in the yard. Delilah came out and nodded at meeting him again. He remembered her being very quiet when they'd visited. He hoped she would give him good news. Her touch was cool as she apologized for laying her hands directly on his skin.

"More like I should apologize for having skin so dirty for your hands," he quipped. The elbow of the girl, at his eye level, cringed closer to her body. She seemed a little older, perhaps twenty. She must be sensitive when it came to young men making comments. Well. Others might like her church mouse quietness but Neil wanted the impish grin of his girl across the sea. As Delilah prodded, Neil flung his thoughts away from the present. It was an easy habit with him.

He felt at a loss when it came to Letty. How many times could he bear to write to her with such little hope? Every year, those hopes diminished. She was probably married now. Of course she was. Her father would have married her off as soon as he got an offer. He thought of Letty's old man, how cold he'd been that last New Year's Eve in Scotland. Even in baking sunlight, Neil shivered at the thought of the lonely alley to their pub, where his family had been denied the hospitality of a First Footing, and he'd been disappointed in his own hopes. *Not good enough.*

He wondered if anyone here would ever catch his eye the way Letty had. If he would settle down with someone else, like his mother had done after his father died. With Gillan. At the thought of his last view of his stepfather, bitter frustration flared up, his errand into town remembered.

"There, then, you're back," Delilah said. "I think your eye's healing fine. Mind how the lid heals, though. Don't want it sticking together." She gave a hesitant smile. "Your mind does seem to wander."

"Ah, I am sorry. I was wandering it a-purpose, in case there was a jab or a poke that I didna like." He smiled back.

On his way again after a hearty shared meal, he thanked the Allmans and bid them a good day. He was in New Glasgow before five o'clock, and thought he just might catch someone at the tiny courthouse chambers where visitors came for legal matters.

He entered the yard of the building, which usually housed all manner of officials and their errand boys. He asked one of the latter, the only one left hanging around the hitching post, where he might find the officers of the court.

"The Law, ya mean?" said the impudent youngster. "Turning yerself in, are ya?"

"No," Neil said, more patiently than he thought he could manage. "I'm looking to get someone *else* arrested. You volunteering?"

The imp gave a grimace of respect for his wit. "Awright. No need to get salty. Only one left is me master, Mr. Wemyss, who handles King's Counsel. I'm waiting on a last commission from him. Welcome to wait."

He gestured at the top rung of the fence. Neil leaned against it, crossed his arms, and stared at the doorway. He hoped this wee scrapper wasn't playing a joke on him. His face was starting to itch.

Not more than ten minutes later, a man came out wearing ancient robes and a white powdered wig as if from the last century. He stopped briefly to hand the boy a rolled up paper and a folded-up paper. Both had seals.

"Take these. They're for Carey in Foxhill, both of them. Stay to get his answer. I need it by Monday week so hurry on back."

The boy said nothing, merely put the papers carefully in his leather shoulder bag. When the top flap was secured, he pointed at Neil.

"This gentleman wanted to talk to an officer of the law, sir," he said. As soon as Wemyss turned his eyes to Neil, the boy hotfooted it in the other direction.

"You wish to prosecute?" the man asked, leaning toward Neil to peer into his face. He got an impression of minute spectacles perched on a red, bulbous nose. "Good god, what happened to your face?"

"A gun exploded in my hands when I tried to fire it."

"Well," the man said. He was clearly disconcerted but motioned for Neil to explain his purpose.

"I've recently received new information about the circumstances of my stepfather's murder."

"Murder?" The man's tone changed to distaste. He stepped back, for which Neil was glad; his breath smelt of sourness, old fish and sharp mustard.

"Yes. His name is Gillan MacLean and he made it back to our family in Pictou but died two days later of wounds from an attack on the road."

"Oh, yes," Wemyss drew out the syllables. "Now I remember." Neil's nerves were on edge. He was so ready to give responsibility for this to someone else, someone whose job it was. Someone who knew what he was about.

"Well, what is the new information? I remember hearing the news last August. What has since come to light?"

"Two men who met him along the road. They were witness to an interaction between my father and a man named Brown near Ford's Mill. There was obvious dislike. Then," Neil raised his voice, as Wemyss was about to protest. "They observed this man weeks later boasting of having put down his old enemy, using Gillan's name."

This gave the lawyer pause. "Well. The testimony of these two men may help your cause, but you'll need to engage a solicitor and have him file motions and open an actual case. I don't believe you have an open case for this murder yet?"

"Well, no. We'd no idea what had happened before."

"Find a solicitor. He may hire an inquiry agent, or not, but they'll need to act quickly. It is the end of the summer," he said emphatically. Neil had no idea what significance this fact held. His face must have shown his ignorance.

"The end of the court! They won't convene again until March! Now if you'll excuse me, I'm late to an appointment."

He doffed his wig as a salute and shoved it under his arm as he walked away, back straight and head high. Neil called after him.

"Can't you help me? Aren't you a solicitor, sir?"

He turned briefly. "Technically, yes, but you'll need someone else. You can't afford my fee. Best of luck."

Neil gaped. Where else was he to look for a solicitor? How did he know how much he could afford, anyway? In point of fact, he couldn't afford anything. He'd been rather hoping that it was the state's duty to round up dangerous criminals. He was doubly astonished: first at the additional difficulty he would have to surmount, and second by the careless way the man had sized him up. Neil looked down.

Homespun wool trousers. Brown, loose. Homespun linen sark. No longer white, torn near the right wrist from the gun's explosion. Native-made leather moccasins. Thick woolen socks. Even in summer. He wiped his forehead of sweat with a forearm. *I guess he sized me up right.*

Wemyss was almost out of sight. The boy to whom he'd handed the papers was long gone. Neil leaned back against the rail again to think of his next course of action.

It was frustrating, sure, but nothing he couldn't handle. He'd make camp back in the woods and come back tomorrow morning. He'd engage a solicitor. How would they pay him? How long would it take? He quizzed the splinters of grayed wood as he thought. *Better hope for a more malleable fellow in the morn.*

Finally, he took himself off to find somewhere to sleep. As he did so, he caught a glimpse of a young woman watching him from the middle of the street. She had honey brown hair which sparkled with gold in the sunlight. She was alone in the street holding a big wooden tub on her hip.

Her mouth was quirked as if she was contemplating laughing at him but Neil wasn't offended. Rather, he was intrigued at her boldness. Sooner than he wished, the moment was over. She broke eye contact and continued on her way past him, wearing a completely sober expression. Neil was puzzled. He shrugged it off and repaired to a clearing a half-mile from the town. A spare dinner of bannock crumbs and oat mash answered his stomach's groaning and he nestled into his plaid.

The next morning, he returned to the same squat building with its maze of offices. The corridors were wide and he wandered past several closed doors with bronze name-plates before finding one that was open. He saw a round head, with scant black hair combed across it, bent over a large ledger. When he knocked on the door, the head did not move. Neil wondered if the man were deaf. He was about to knock again when the man spoke.

"Yes, I heard you. A moment."

*Quaint manners in this high and mighty place.*

He finished the line he was tracking with his finger, then the next, and the next. Neil's eyes wandered down the corridor seeking other open doors but this was the only one in sight. Somehow he knew he would have an even worse reception from a closed door.

Finally, the man made a little sound of satisfaction. He wrote down a number on a nearby page filled with notes, then closed the ledger carefully and looked up at Neil for the first time. His eyes narrowed when he saw the healing cuts to his face and the swollen, bruised eye, but he refrained from commenting.

"Are you looking for someone in the building, young man?"

"Not someone in particular, just a solicitor who'll hear my case," he replied.

"And what is the case?"

"My stepfather, Gillan MacLean, was beaten savagely last autumn on the road and died of his injuries soon after he made it back home to Pictou." It was getting easier to say with repetition. Not to mention his jaw felt almost normal again, except for the little specks of scab that were healing from the burns. God, he must still look a sight. *No wonder that young woman yesterday laughed at me: a cripple-face lost in thought by the courts of justice. Poetic.*

"Yes, I heard the news and remember some of the particulars. Do remind me," he said. He indicated the one chair facing him in the office. Neil sat. He didn't pour out his troubles but marshaled all the facts he knew: Gillan departing to look for work with Sandy Wilson, his late return in dire shape, his inability to speak, Sandy's incomprehension of the attack on the road by two men, and the Janneys' recent account of the man in Ford's Mill, before and after Gillan's death.

Neil waited to hear the man's opinion. He eyed the black suit, the messy cravat, the pale hands stained with ink. He didn't look as well-off as that man Wemyss. He hoped he wasn't as high-handed, either.

"I may be the best man for the job you will find here," he said. "I have an office midway between here and the area around Ford's Mill. It's where I usually work. This is just a secondary office for those who travel for the court session."

"That's why there's no name on the door?" Neil asked.

"Yes," he said. The man didn't seem concerned with the lack of status. Maybe he would be a decent sort. "By the by, I haven't introduced myself. My name is Caleb Drexel. I am a solicitor from Amherst."

"Amherst?"

"It's about four days' walk west of here."

"I see. My name is Neil MacLean. Pleased to meet you, sir. If I could ask about fees—"

"There's no question of fees in a high crime case like this. It is the state which pays my fee. Indeed, someone should have been notified to start an investigation last autumn, more's the pity, but I don't suppose you knew to ask."

Neil felt the condescension and parlayed it into a virtue. "No, sir. My family was not well acquainted with the law, never having much contact. We're regular dependable folk, sir."

"I'm sure. Now, just write down these names and addresses—you do write, yes? Good. Write their addresses so I can visit them and we'll see what it comes to. I'll send you word in a few weeks when I've made some progress. If and when we need to take testimony in the form of an affidavit, I may ask you to come to Amherst. Is that satisfactory?"

The words blurred past Neil. He nodded. Without standing up, Drexel opened the ledger back up and started scanning his next lines. Neil rose from the chair, uncertain how to respond to such a dismissal.

"Thank you, sir," he said quickly. He bumped the chair and heard it squeak in protest as he hurried to leave the office. He winced, didn't look back, and was back out in the hallway, feeling gauche and clueless and annoyed at himself.

The gauche and clueless feelings had left him by the time he reached the outskirts of the town, retracing his steps from before. But annoyance only increased as he made his way home. A small twinge in his jaw served to remind him that he was clenching it, all that day and into the evening.

# PART TWO

# Chapter 25

To ANYONE FROM Glasgow or London, the Turners' house might have seemed paltry, but it was the grandest home Muirne and Alisdair had ever been in. They had been in the countryside most of their lives and on the knife-edge of urgency most of those years, and so it was grand indeed.

The rains had followed them westward and they presented quite a swaddled and steaming picture when they arrived. Mrs. Turner tut-tutted about water seepage in boots and the taking on of chills. She signaled the driver with a tap to the roof with her walking stick, and maneuvered out easily for a woman of middle age.

Muirne, already soaked from rain at the window, peered out into the fog. The house sat at the top of a hill, a small remove from the town of Tatamagouche. It commanded a decent view of the forest on one side and the tops of houses in town on the other. Beyond the houses stood a sluggish river. It was to this view that Mrs. Turner drew Muirne's attention.

"Well, Miss Muirne, Master Alisdair: welcome to our home," she said as they alighted from the mail coach. Muirne stopped Alisdair from running ahead of their hostess and they followed her as she picked her way carefully across the muddy ground. A thin woman stood with the door open, an umbrella extended half out of it for her mistress.

"You must change out of those drenched articles at once,' Mrs. Turner said. She bid the maid see to their guests' outer garments. Muirne took off her sopping wet woolen cloak at the door to avoid spoiling the rugs and wood floors she glimpsed within. Alisdair followed suit with his woolen pullover. They stood shivering in the hall, awaiting direction.

"Now, go on up to your room. It's the first door on the left from the top of the stairs. Dry yourselves as best you can. I'll be right up."

They clomped up the stairs, leaving a soggy trail. Alisdair's shoes were soft and soaked, where Muirne's had wooden soles and sloshed. The appointed room had its door ajar and a merry fire was visible in a hearth surrounded by white tile. Two small beds stood side by side, each with a dark wood headboard and a white coverlet. A soft blue braided rope rug covered most of the floor. Muirne ran her eyes over everything, remembering her promise to disclose every detail to Sheena.

Alisdair ran to the fire and put his hands out. "Lord Almighty, this room is almost as big as our cabin!"

"Alisdair, don't swear." But Muirne wasn't really scolding. She kept her shift on and put on her change of skirt and bodice. The wet one she hung by the fire, careful not to set it too close. Alisdair took off his breeches and put on his plaid, copying Muirne's example.

Mrs. Turner was on their heels five minutes later. She indicated with a hand that they should follow her back down to the sitting room. They sat on a settee with a shiny, bristly brown surface. It was strange; it bounced beneath them somehow when they sat. Mrs. Turner had already changed into a fancy burgundy dress with a patterned skirt and elongated bodice. The skirt's panels were in shades of lavender and plum, which Muirne knew meant it cost a pretty penny. No plants around here produced that royal hue.

The heat of the fire soon did its work, and even Muirne's' hair started to dry. She felt a fine flush spread across her cheeks. Alisdair was in such a good mood after twenty minutes that he was tapping the toes of his new leather shoes.

"Do excuse us, Mrs. Turner," Muirne said, tugging Alisdair's elbow. He stopped his tapping guiltily and sat up straighter. "Your home is so comfortable, quite—"

"Oh, don't trouble yourselves. I'm sure it's been a very exciting, and tiring, journey. You will have plenty of time to recover. I don't believe Mr. Turner, my husband, will put in an appearance until next week, so do make yourselves at home. I hope you will."

She smiled particularly at Muirne. After some restorative tea, the lady showed them the house where Edward had grown up.

There were three main rooms for visitors: a parlor, a dining room, and a library for the men. There were two sleeping chambers and a large kitchen on the ground level, as well as a three more upstairs, and garret rooms for the two servants, a female cook and a man-of-all-work. They returned to the parlor. Muirne noted how warm and dry it felt. No chinks in the logs. No stumps for seats.

As the serving woman brought in warm cakes and more tea, Muirne's thoughts wandered from Mrs. Turner's local gossip to home. A note of their safe arrival would be sent with the next morning's post carrier. She hoped Neil had returned home before the rains started again, for it would be miserable on foot. And his eye! Did he find a solicitor? When was the next Session to meet? How were they to pay a solicitor's fees? Then Muirne thought of her Mr. Turner, growing up in this style of life. How would she ever manage to please him? And when would she meet the imperious Mr. Turner the Elder? She felt as if she was doing something vaguely wrong by visiting in his absence.

"Of course, we were here before most of the trades-people," Mrs. Turner was saying as she bustled around, checking doilies and straightening afghan blankets on the backs of furniture. The trim figure in a burgundy dress was completely at ease holding court in the parlor. Muirne had not yet learned her given name, but she knew it started with an M, as the chatelaine the lady wore bore the initials M and T. At least that was what she thought the letters said, though there were a lot of curlicues in the chased bronze. As Mrs. Turner continues to talk, Muirne learned a number of things, besides the last year's fashions in England.

"We got to see them move in, one by one, and it was the most marvelous luxury to be able to walk to the shops, rather than send Mr. Hammond a day's ride away. We don't keep animals here, you see, and so—"

"Not even for butter and beef? Why, if we had all—" Alisdair's outburst was cut off by Muirne's sharp shake of the head.

"Well, we do have a dairy cow, and the horses, of course, but I meant *herds*, my dear. *Flocks*. George didn't want to bother with animal husbandry, occupied as he was with the ships and tides and timetables and whatnot."

Alisdair relaxed; he was intrigued. "What kind of ships does Mr. Turner work on, then?"

"Oh, well. He has invested in all sorts of ships and cargo. But more recently, my husband has specialized in being a prison ship escort."

Shock and awkwardness met this announcement. Muirne blinked and cleared her throat. Alisdair's face puckered.

Mrs. Turner affected not to notice. "And he loves it so much, he does not wish ever to retire, which I think to be a very fine sentiment. George loves law and order, he does."

After a second's pause, Muirne recovered and moved the conversation along. "Was he always happy with Edw —your son's choice of career?"

"Certainly not. It was quite an argument when he realized Edward was serious, I'll tell you. But eventually Edward brought him 'round. We both saw the respect accorded to the new Physicians' College. I think it's a fine profession, being a physician. Now, surgery..." She gave a delicate shudder to indicate her opinion.

In more conversations over the next few days, Muirne learned that Edward's favorite food was oysters, said to be because he was carried across the seas while still in the womb. His studies with a tutor did not seem promising until they moved west into Tatamagouche. Then, he studied with Mr. Wilburforce, a highly sought-after master from down Halifax way, who was enticed to stay with them for a year. After this, Edward's focus seemed to be razor-sharp. However many angry parents remained in Halifax to resent his absence was not thought on by Mrs. Turner, Muirne noted.

Muirne also learned that there had been no other potential-wife shadows before her, which was comforting. It surprised her, for he was in a promising profession, and of a marrying age. She wondered if there had been any others to whom Edward had revealed his godlessness; if he had, perhaps that was why none had accepted. *She* would not be so narrow-minded.

Several days passed in quiet seclusion. Muirne marveled at the lack of activity: nothing more active than walks about the perimeter of the yard, nothing more disagreeable than sitting up straight and being attentive. She felt a little glee at leaving the scything and winnowing work to her brother and sister. Mrs. Turner became easier to talk to, less of a foreign species, and more of an older, wiser woman. By the fourth day, Mrs. Turner had become Matilda, and Alisdair was telling the poor woman all about the best way to find winkles on Mull's shores. Muirne looked on with pride and a little hope.

The day before the visit was to end, Muirne entered the dining room for breakfast and saw not Mrs. Turner as she expected but a squarely-built man, in a finely spun navy coat with silver knots down the front. He rose from the breakfast table to bow a greeting. Was she supposed to introduce herself? Mrs. Turner hadn't mention a visitor. *Oh!* Muirne thought. *Is this Mr. Turner? Does he know who I am?*

"Good morning," Muirne said, and came in slowly with Alisdair just behind. They seated themselves at the opposite end of the table from him.

It was an impossible moment. Muirne didn't know whether she should pretend everything was all right, or whether she should stand firm and confront him about his opposition to her marriage. She started with polite flattery.

"Mr. Turner! I am so glad to see you. I had hoped to speak with you a little before we must leave. Has your business kept you in Pictou Harbor this whole week?"

His eyes glanced up at her from under beetling brows as he sat back down. He harrumphed and looked at his porridge and kippers. Was he avoiding her? Was he ignoring her?

"Good morning, Miss MacLean. Master——?"

"Alisdair," Muirne supplied, as her brother just stared, goggle-eyed.

"Master Alisdair. Pleased to meet you."

Muirne let pass the fact that he had already met the rest of her family in much less courteous circumstances.

Muirne strained to keep a pleasant smile on her face while inwardly she was shouting at this repugnant man. *How dare he threaten her family in their home? How dare he judge them, after making his living shipping off poor folk for no other reason than their poverty?* Could she live with such a man for a father-in-law? Could she just ignore his existence altogether?

Alisdair lifted his plate and cocked an eye at Muirne. She nodded and he went to the sideboard to fill it with food. The boy was for once remaining silent when his oblivious chatter might have helped fill in the awkward silence. Muirne wondered whether Matilda had known he would be there this morning. Whether she had a hand in this awkward introduction.

The master of the house tried to pose a few enquiries about their stay but the atmosphere was much too strained. She didn't know how to return the same level of affected civility. Alisdair attacked his plate with gusto. He seemed as much at a loss as she was.

Muirne managed a 'yes, sir' and a 'no, sir' before Mr. Turner stopped asking questions and pulled at his lip. He kept his eyes down, as if a very interesting speck on the tablecloth held his attention. She prepared to sail to her family's defense if he let loose with any of his vile statements again.

"My wife Matilda informs me that you are to be Edward's wife."

Muirne felt unbalanced. *No attack? Not yet.*

"She asked you here. She intends to support Edward's choice."

But *he*—what would he do to stop it? Disown Edward? She couldn't bear being the cause of such a rift but she knew Edward would not be put off by his father's disapproval. He hadn't been so far. How could he bear it? Maybe it had to do with his lack of religion.

"I have nothing against your person, but your family are penniless Dissenters. You can not expect me to rejoice at such a match for my only son."

He looked steadily at her then. Muirne kept her gaze on her plate, the white porcelain, the silver fork and spoon and knife. What Edward must have grown up with. Her heart shrank. How would she be able to give him what he was used to? She felt Mr. Turner's eyes, dark under those black-and-white eyebrows, inspecting and dismissing her, and her defiant nature rose up to support her.

"I have often been afraid of fortune-seekers in this colony, Miss MacLean, and sought to save my son the misfortune of being caught by one. But I believe my wife when she says you are not such a one, after hosting you for a week."

*It is only five days we have been here, and we hosted her first, without any notice at all!* Muirne wanted to scream at him. Something in his voice told her that he merely humored his wife; he would always be guarding his family against her. *If only I could lay into him about his own faults.* She glared back but did not say anything. The clang of metal fork against china plate signaled Alisdair's abrupt abandonment of his meal.

Muirne rose and took her plate to the sideboard. She spoke with her back to him. "I'm glad Mrs. Turner has faith in my good character."

She scooped a wobbly poached egg and some black sausage onto her plate. Her mouth was watering at the prospect of it. She wished she could simply stuff her face full of food like Alisdair and not have to talk to this odious man. He was not ranting in his own house but Muirne could tell he still bristled with the indignity of hosting them.

"It remains to be seen whether Matilda is correct." Abruptly he switched from barbed insults to conciliatory nothings. "I was thinking we might have a walk into town later, now that the mud has dried. You could meet some of the residents and tradespeople. So they will know you when you return."

Mrs. Turner entered the room, all smiles, adding her entreaty for a walk that day.

"Of course, sir."

He expected her to return. He was bowing to his wife's pressure. No one would stand between her and Edward when he returned in the spring. She glanced at

Alisdair. He was staring at Mr. Turner, probably imagining torture.

"Thank you, sir," she said, a little louder. Alisdair squirmed in his chair but said nothing. He did not know that their fate had just been diverted onto a new course. They had just been ushered in through the golden gates.

# Chapter 26

MRS. TURNER STOOPED by her husband's seat and leaned close. He gave her an absent-minded peck on the cheek and she swept around him to sit next to Muirne.

"It was quite a surprise to see you early this morning, dear. I had not expected you back for another two days."

Muirne kept her head down. Did the woman think she was fooling anyone? If he had come in this morning, they would have already talked. Why was she bothering with this blether?

"I do recall our guests were planning on departing today. We do not want to leave it too late. When is the gig passing through town, Mr. Hammond?"

The man had come in to take one of the serving dishes away. He bowed to his mistress.

"Half one, Mrs. Turner. But there's another one tomorrow at half ten."

"That would do us better. What do you say, Muirne? Can you and Alisdair be spared another day?" Her eyes twinkled.

Muirne glanced sideways at Alisdair. He was making big eyes at her, plainly begging to be gone. But this was to be her new family. She thought she'd won over Mrs. Turner, only to be backed into a corner with Mr. Turner by her design. Tricky woman. That bit of pique decided her.

"I don't think that would be a problem," she said.

Mrs. Turner dimpled.

"Well, then. That is settled."

Mrs. Turner carried on with more small talk, which Muirne struggled to respond to in the same trusting spirit as before. *A den of vipers*, she thought. *I will have to ask Edward pointedly about this sort of thing. How did he turn out so differently?*

When they had finished this miserable breakfast, the four of them walked down into town. Muirne's stomach was in knots and she kept taking deep breaths to calm herself. She marveled at the attentions Mr. and Mrs. Turner were paid and quailed a little at the thought of taking on a family that had such influence—whether she had not better keep to her own humble kind.

The town of Tatamagouche was less self-consciously important than Pictou, but no less a center for commerce and news in the region. Muirne could sense the eyes registering her presence on the arm of Mrs. Turner. They stopped in at the greengrocer's, the new haberdashery, and the side office of the blacksmith's, who was also a town official of some import. Mr. Turner asked him about some new rule governing shipworkers' wages while Muirne and Alisdair watched his apprentice at work. They had never been this close to an anvil and tongs before and emitted small screams when the sparks flew.

Mr. Turner introduced her each time as a friend of his son's, visiting from down East River way. The tradesmen acknowledged her graciously and engaged in small conversation, as if they had no urgent business on hand. When this happened for the fourth time, she wondered how Mrs. Turner took this sidestepping of their real relationship.

When she met Mrs. Turner's blue eyes, she saw kindness in the wrinkles and contentment in the lined mouth that spoke of her approval of her son's choice. *Edward's choice*, she thought. *He did choose me. Forget his family's squabbles.*

Mrs. Turner squeezed Muirne's arm a little tighter against herself as she spoke in a murmur. "It is hard for us both, letting Edward go, Miss MacLean. But George and I must remember he has already left."

"Yes," she murmured back.

And she saw that his attending school in Halifax, his traveling to England and Scotland for his profession, even going back to his disagreements about his faith—these had already created a gulf between Edward and his parents. His mother sought to ignore that and have him close at whatever cost, but his father had trouble bowing to that level, wishing to exert control over him still. Muirne could understand Mrs. Turner's feelings, which were like her mother's feelings about Gillan.

"Miss MacLean, would you walk a few paces with me?"

The muscles in her neck seemed to clamp down. She swallowed past the feeling. This manipulative woman. If she could not win over Edward's parents, at least she would show them how wrong they were to doubt her. They ambled toward the riverbank.

"I'll be right back," she said to Alisdair, who lagged behind the party, looking through all the side alleys at the hills behind. The two women proceeded along the boards of the jetty, keeping Mr. Turner in sight as he continued talking with the blacksmith.

"You have no way of knowing how important religion

is for George," Mrs. Turner began. "But he quite depends on it. That is one reason why Edward's decision four years ago has been so hard for him to bear.

"Another reason is the hopes we cherished for Edward. He is so bright that quite naturally we thought he could gain a place in the Council with George's connections, but no one with Dissenting views would be tolerated there."

Muirne kept silent as she spoke. The spool of history pushing Edward to where he was today—it was being unraveled before her. Perhaps this information could help her understand him better. Perhaps there was something in his family history that would explain the paradoxes surrounding her fiancé.

"He seems determined to throw away everything we have tried to give him. Any opportunity to improve the stature of our family, any political connection—he runs from it!"

The lady sounded distressed but when Muirne turned to look at her as they walked side-by-side, she appeared more exasperated than sad.

"I can tell your family means a great deal to you, Mis MacLean. As does mine to me. That is why I trust you to do what we cannot. You must work on Edward, bring him back to the Church. The Church of England. I cannot abide the thought of his soul being damned forever, never seeing him after we die. Tell me you will attempt it!"

*Convert Edward?* The thought hadn't even occurred to her, but Muirne suddenly wondered why not. *Because he is firm in his purpose and not the type to be swayed by such arguments as I have*, she thought. But should she try? Was it right to marry someone and try to change one of their firmest beliefs? It felt wrong.

She looked at Mrs. Turner and saw desperation. *But of what kind? Is she desperate for her son's soul? Or desperate to control him?* She didn't know. She wouldn't until Edward returned and she could talk to him.

"That thought gives me no pleasure either; I assure you, ma'am. I will do anything I can to help Edward live a moral life, in line with his principles. It is the only way I think he could be happy."

Mrs. Turner leveled her gaze at her. She knew she was evading her question.

"Very well. We will see what results your efforts yield."

*Question my duty to family, will she?* Muirne steamed quietly. She longed for a time when it would be just Edward and her and they could talk. She wanted his assurance that she was good enough for him.

They wandered a little bit more, looking in silently at window displays of tobacco and cloth, before rejoining Alisdair and Mr. Turner. Muirne felt like she had given something away when she had resolutely not promised anything but attending to her husband's happiness. She passed an uneasy evening, despite the sumptuous supper offered: roast lamb with potatoes and mint sauce, smoked whitefish for starters, and frumenty, cool and sweet, for afters. Muirne had warned Alisdair not to eat quickly or he might appear rude, but his bulging eyes told her he was regretting his promise not to do so. Muirne almost regretted extracting it when she remembered what they had been through but consoled herself with the thought that the first winter was over, and this one coming was bound to be better.

Talk at table touched on the winter forecasts, as well as hopes for development of the colony. Muirne struggled to resurrect scraps of news from Neil to appear informed.

"Indeed, Hammon says the timber is failing, and we fear shipbuilding will remain in its slump until there is another war. I have heard of the canal improvements the Americans are making. And Stephenson with his marvelous new steam locomotive. Still won't get us through the Harbor in the winter, though," Mr. Turner said.

"No, indeed. I think we will always need our sleds for that," Muirne agreed.

"Oh, do you have a sled, then?" Mrs. Turner asked.

"Well, not a sled for a horse, but a sled to pull our goods over the rivers when they're frozen," she admitted.

"We pull it ourselves," Alisdair said with an edge of pride to his voice, pride in his small role. "Horse-drawn sled wouldn't do much good when we've no road anyway," he added.

"Well, there is the post road that comes rather close," Mrs. Turner prompted.

"There'll be roads out there before you know it," Mr. Turner said. "But not for doctors in the near term." He cleared his throat, switching tacks. "Have you had any indication from Edward where he'll want to settle his practice, Matilda?"

Mrs. Turner sighed and shook her head. "I think there are still too many details to be decided," she said. "Or perhaps he has spoken of it to you, Miss MacLean?"

Startled by the intimacy of such a suggestion, Muirne recovered and shook her head. She had assumed he would be in New Glasgow. But if he hadn't told his parents, she didn't want to break the news either.

"No, ma'am. He had not yet decided the last time we talked of the matter."

"Oh?" said Mr. Turner. He glanced at his wife. "So you've spoken of it. What did he say?"

Muirne grasped at the most polite commonplace she could think of. "He was looking to Dr. Skinner for guidance, I believe. We only had the one visit before he left. We were all feeling a bit rushed by the necessity of his trip."

Mr Turner answered with a noncommittal grunt. The lady of the house twitched her gaze to the ceiling then sallied forth.

"Perhaps he does not yet know if Dr. Skinner will cede some of his territory. The last I had from him, there was a question of when and how the old doctor would choose to retire. I am *sure* Edward would not have wanted to burden Miss MacLean with such a question."

Her husband grunted, allowing the small check to his gruff line of questioning. While Mr. Turner had gone on, Alisdair helped himself to the last of the pudding. As the adults sipped their tea, Muirne almost moaned from the depth and richness of the concoction. Her spirits rose further as she watched the boy wolf down the gloppy, stewed fruit, trying to keep his chin dry. He wasn't embarrassed. No, her family was doing the best they could. If she could be sure of Matilda being on her side, she could make this marriage flourish. Even without her, her own family would buoy her up.

"I hope you don't think it presumptuous of me, dear, but in Edward's absence, and in the surety of his regard for you, I wondered if I might help you to arrange the wedding upon his return in the spring."

Muirne turned to look at those kind blue eyes in shock, suddenly afraid she was being outmaneuvered. "Why, that's very kind, but I'm sure there's no need to —"

"But it would be wonderful fun! It could be private that way. No banns for the whole church to hear and gossip about, and only inviting those who would wish you well. And you could have it here, where we have room for guests..."

*Ah, that's her tack.* "Mrs. Turner, you are too kind. It sounds a wonderful idea, but until I am able to ask Mr. Turner his plans and whether—"

"Oh, tosh, I've had his letters; they speak of nothing but you and the grisly details of the surgeries in London." She made a face. "I'm sure it would be his wish that we forge ahead."

Muirne looked to the father to second her attempt at prudence but he was staring deep into his tea. He seemed to wait for her assent also. Muirne smiled nervously. *Why does she want to have the wedding here? And why does Mr. Turner seem amenable to this?* Wary of making any decisions without full knowledge of the situation, she answered carefully.

"Let us proceed like this. I will talk to some of the merchants in New Glasgow when I travel to town next. And I will write to your son," she smiled awkwardly again. "To ask about his prospective employment." She gulped, which made an odd squirrelly noise. This was impossible. She tried to hold on to her pretend authority.

Mrs. Turner's brow puckered. Mr. Turner sat up with a cackle.

"She's got you there, Matilda!" he said through the laughter.

Mrs. Turner leveled a quelling gaze on her husband but took a deep breath and nodded slightly to Muirne.

"That sounds very good, dear. You write and we'll hear about his wishes for setting up practice before we decide on the wedding," said Mrs. Turner.

Mr. Turner seemed to be in a better humor as he retreated to the library for his cigar. He found no need to talk to Muirne, but then she had no desire that he do so. If he left them alone to marry, she and Edward would do just fine.

Mrs. Turner eased off her pressing insistence to move forward with plans. They retired to rest for the next day's journey home.

The next morning Muirne and Alisdair were seen off with their sacks and a providentially-sized hamper of cold meats and jars of pickled vegetables and jam. They waved goodbye to Mrs. Turner, who waved her handkerchief until she was no longer visible. Mr. Turner failed to show himself again before their departure.

# Chapter 27

NEIL RETURNED A day later than he had originally planned. By the time he left the post road for the trail to their cabin, it was almost a week since the bear attack. He rubbed at his eye whenever he wasn't thinking about it. It itched because it was healing, he knew. That was a good sign. There was still a mealy feeling to the bone of his jaw and angry red scabs still puckered the side of his face and forearm, but on the whole he was glad to be in one piece.

He took this inventory of his pains every hour to keep his mind off how cavalier and uncourteous the lawyers had been. *Wear a wig and count yourself above the ways of men,* he grumbled. *I could bring them down a peg. But I need them for the present. Damn!* He stopped and pressed the heel of his hand against the top of his cheekbone. It would not stop buzzing like a beehive.

He was a little lightheaded with the heat and the sun. He was also at the end of his rations. He looked forward to coming upon the house and hearing his mother banging together the pots or seeing Sheena tending the chickens. When he crested the hill, though, he saw and heard neither. He passed the cabin in the sun of midday to peer down to the field: empty. No—there was the scythe reflecting the sun from where it lay in the oat field. Neil's senses were sluggish for a moment.

*Where did they go? It's not laundry time for the potash is waiting for the lye to be mixed*—and then his pulse quickened. His first instinct was to call out for them all but he curbed it instantly. Someone else could be nearby. He walked back to the cabin's back entrance, edging away from the chickens and the lamb in their pens, lest they give him away. *But no one's made off with the animals. Then is it sickness?*

He stood close to the back door and pushed it open slowly. It made a slow scree and Neil was about to step inside when a bucket careened around from behind the door and banged into the wooden frame. The clang set all the livestock squawking and bleating. Neil grabbed a hold of the door frame, jumped inside, and slammed the door. He blinked to adjust to the dark but before he saw her, he heard her.

"Neil! Thank God!" It was Sheena. She was holding out her arms to him. He grabbed them without thinking, looking this way and that for everyone else.

"Where is—" His eyes fell on their mother. She was propped up in the box bed, its doors open, with a hunting knife in one hand and a large ladle in the other. Both weapons fell into her lap, lax. "*Mathair,*" he whispered. "What's happened?"

Mam merely smiled. She sighed deeply and crumpled forward, then flopped sideways. Neil saw the scratches across one side of her face and the bruising around her neck. He had barely opened his mouth to ask about it when Sheena spoke.

"Mam fell down the hillside. She's still a bit dazed. She's slept a lot since it happened yesterday. I hurt myself getting her into the bed. My knee." Neil finally saw that his wee sister favored one leg, and that the sled was indeed propped up against the wall instead of outside where he'd left it.

"But what happened? Where are Muirne and Alisdair? Why did she fall? It's not as if it's a cliff—"

"I haven't exactly figured that out. She hasn't said a word all day," Sheena said in a low tone. Neil looked to see if Mam had heard the comment. It didn't appear so. In fact, she appeared to have dropped off to sleep.

"But she was running like the devil was after her. I watched her coming down. I watched her trip and flip and land on her back." Sheena's voice was choked. "I even waited to see if whatever was chasing her would show itself, but there was nothing."

Neil had nothing to say. He'd gone to chase down justice and been away for something important here at home. He stood a moment, trying to fit back together his life of ten minutes ago and the one he had now.

"Muirne and Alisdair went away day before yesterday with Mrs. Turner. They're fine, as far as I know."

"They went where?" It was too much. He sat down on one of the stumps and unslung his pack roughly to the floor. There was no fire. He stretched his legs and took a deep breath, swept a hand over his eye again. "Tell me again. From the beginning."

Sheena related the surprise visit from Edward's mother, the invitation to Muirne to return with her, and the horrifyingly breakneck fall that seemed to have knocked Mam senseless. Sheena eased back into one of the chairs and propped her leg up onto a stump.

"She needs to see a doctor, Neil, but I couldn't even make it outside the house with my knee like this. Can you go find someone? I know they're gone from New Glasgow but surely over in Pictou or—"

"Wait a moment." Neil thought through the difficulties. Would he do better to stay with the injured, or go find medical help? Internal or external enemies: to which were they more vulnerable? The potential for an attack had been in the back of his mind when he knew Drexel would be sending an agent into Brown's town of business but now he had to gauge how credible that threat was, faced with his mother's affliction. Mam was out cold for the moment. Was that good? Bad? He had no way of knowing. Could he go back for Delilah Allman?

"When are Muirne and Alisdair expected back?"

"They meant to stay a week and only left the day before yesterday." Sheena looked so forlorn. He went over to kneel by her seat.

"What have you done for Mam or your knee since yesterday?"

"Just cool cloths for Mam. I didn't touch the smelling salts. I figured she needed to rest after the fall. But I tried to make one o' Mam's concoctions for my knee—just to dull the pain."

*Screaming agony is more like*, Neil thought as he saw the large protuberance on top of Sheena's kneecap. He covered it gently with his palm, barely touching. Sheena opened her mouth in a grimace and squeezed her eyes shut.

"Well," he said brusquely, taking away his hand from the area, which felt warm. "I'm going to go down and find some leeches. That should help the knee. Then we'll think about who to seek out for Mam."

Sheena looked bleakly at their mother, whose head was folded awkwardly against her chest.

"I'm sure she'll be all right, Sheena." She looked at

him with fresh tears.

"You can't say that. Go. Fetch the leeches, then find someone."

Neil raised an eyebrow at her abrupt tone of command. The catastrophe had apparently shaken her into taking charge. He didn't try to con her out of her gloom. Better to go straight to the river and see what could be done.

# Chapter 28

SEVEN DAYS LATER, Muirne and Alisdair returned home laden with the gifts from Mrs. Turner: salted whitefish, hardened cheese, precious wheat flour. Muirne felt ill at ease with Edward's mother's intentions, but looked forward to the satisfied look on her mother's face when she announced that the father was reconciled to the marriage. *More like 'resigned,' but I won't say it.*

As Alisdair ran ahead up the trail, she wondered if their first wheat harvest was in and the winnowing done. She would definitely needle her brother about having got him to do all the work.

When she entered the cabin, she was surprised to see Neil at the hearth, poking at the pot with a ladle. Sheena stood by him, as if supervising. Muirne smiled. "Is it Neil's turn to be cooking, then?"

It was then she noticed Alisdair kneeling by Mam's bed. Neil unbent himself and faced her with a grimace.

"We have suffered an accident, so yes, you'll have to hazard my burned neeps and tatties tonight." He spoke in a murmur. Muirne felt her heart seize.

"Mam?" Neil pointed to the box bed where she lay propped up against one of the walls, eyes closed.

"Is she asleep?"

"Sort of. I brought the Allmans' daughter here to check on her after I got back. She fell down the hill. Seemed spooked by something. Sheena didn't see anything, though, and she hasn't spoken since to tell us what. As near as Delilah could tell, she's had an attack of nerves, as well as a broken ankle. Delilah's made some boneset and comfrey and left us some black tonic that she's to take after supper."

He wrinkled his nose in distaste. If it didn't smell good, it was probably laudanum. Muirne frowned.

"And I fell trying to get her into bed and bumped my knee. It's stiffened a bit."

Muirne faced Sheena. She favored her right knee, which remained slightly bent.

"Should we not have gone?" Alisdair cried. He was petting Mam's hair and tracing the line of her jaw as she slept. His face screwed up in remorse, as if his reaching out to enjoy the journey and visit and food had brought down this misfortune upon his family.

"No, of course not. One had nothing to do with the other."

Neil remained silent at that, merely turning back to the pot suspended over the fire. Muirne showed them all the food gifts before placing them on the shelves by the back door. She changed her clothes, donning the more ancient chemise and the battered skirt, as the mud was still evident in their hill-shadowed glen.

After supper, which didn't turn out half-bad despite Neil having made it, Muirne found Sheena outside the chicken run squatting with a stick in her hand. Before the summer light faded, Muirne found a stick of her own and traced out the layout of the Turners' rooms and the beautiful patterns in the china she had seen. Sheena showed a bittersweet wonder and awe.

"Their roof was very high! And they had silver settings!"

Alisdair was finally joyfully revealing details from the visit to the Turners' house. Mam remained weak and did not try to move from her bed the morning after they were all back together. Sheena's knee had not yet decreased to its normal size but she minced around, adapting quickly.

"Yes, it was rather impressive," Muirne admitted. She was a little wistful about the nice things they'd seen, and needed to remind herself that with all the nice things came that atmosphere of trickery and challenge that she'd never had to negotiate at home.

"They took us to Tatamagouche, as well. They must be quite important to the town."

Neil let that sink in a moment. "They didn't tell ye such a thing?"

"No. They walked me down to the shops and introduced me, so I'd be known to the owners, the residents. For the next visit, I suppose."

"I hope she doesn't think ye'll be moving in with them?"

This comment came from Mam. They all turned to see her smile, then close her eyes again.

"Mam?" Sheena grabbed a cup and filled it with water from the bucket. She approached the box bed and cradled her mother's head. "Mam," she prodded again. Eyelids lifted slowly. Sheena poured a little water into her mouth. Muirne was touched to see her so carefully tending to Mam. She hoped the bed rest and nourishing food —for Sheena's garden was now producing all sorts of

turnips and cabbage and onions as well as fragrant weeds
— would work its magic and bring her back to her normal self.

When the excitement had subsided and Mam seemed
not likely to speak again soon, Neil repeated Mam's
question. "Well, do they expect ye to go live there?"

The thought hadn't even occurred to Muirne, and she
felt a cold flood of fear. In addition to trying to convert
Edward to something that was not even her faith, was this
what Mrs. Turner's maneuverings about the wedding
location were leading up to? It made no sense, but then,
she was looking at it from the viewpoint of Edward's
professional ties and community need, which he had
discussed with her. Had he not indicated it to his parents
as well? Or were they too blind to see further than their
own interests? That she could well believe.

"Oh, I don't think so. Mr. Turner asked where Edward might start his practice, so he must just be curious.
I thought he'd be down in New Glasgow myself but he
didn't positively say it. I didn't want to presume and give
them the idea—"

"Course not. That was right. You didna get the sense
they were related to any of the shopkeepers, then?" Neil
asked.

That idea hadn't occurred to Muirne either, but this
one she was surer of discounting. "No, I dinna think so.
His family are so..."

*Overbearing? Controlling? At odds with his own nature?*
*How to describe it?*

"His father invests in prison ships," Alisdair pronounced.

Neil raised his eyebrows. Sheena dropped her jaw.

Muirne suddenly felt defensive. "Well, someone has to."

Neil swallowed. "Even so. It's detestable what the Crown is doing, shipping people off across the world for crimes of no import. If he's got a hand in, you can tell he doesnae care for the poor who steal to survive."

Muirne felt torn. What Neil said was true. She'd felt revulsion at the discovery of the practice as well. And Mr. Turner's treatment of her family was rude, discourteous, and petty. But now that they had allowed her into their family—or as good as—she felt duty-bound to defend them.

Neil forestalled her weak riposte by turning to Alisdair. "Well, my able-bodied lad, are you ready to help us get two harvests in?"


Over the next several days, Muirne and Neil continued the work of the harvest. Neil threshed, swinging the length of rope to crush the grains in the tall bucket. When he was done with a batch, he passed it to Muirne, who winnowed each load carefully, using the large flat woven-reed basket that had come from home. Sheena had made another in their new home last winter, but the holes in its bottom were a little too big. She used it for collecting her vegetables.

As they worked, Neil told her about his visit to town, the strange ways of town lawyers, and his discouraging acquaintance with Mr. Wemyss and Mr. Drexel. Muirne marveled at this new world Neil was navigating. It seemed not that long ago that Mam was going to plead with the Laird MacLean about their rent, and here was Neil, going to make his own plaint with the local authorities.

Muirne observed her brother as dinner was shared out that evening. Everyone was a little more light-hearted from being together and having the harvest go well. The steam of the cabbage mash and mushroom soup warmed Neil's ruddy face, the red making his hair appear blonder by contrast. He didn't smile as much as before. There'd been more laughter on the ship coming to Canada, when they'd all been pulling together for each other. *All that weight*, she thought. *He must be feeling responsible for all of us. What can I do?*

She looked to her younger brother and sister. Alisdair seemed to have forgot his guilt at not being here when the calamity happened; so much the better. Sheena was listening raptly to his account of how many of each dish —even those he couldn't identify—he had consumed on the trip. Before long, their talk had descended into taunts.

"Stuffed your face, I'm sure!"

"Just because you're a skinny besom doesn't mean I never get a treat!"

And indeed, Sheena was slender. Sheena, at thirteen years old, had arms that could still be circled by Neil's thumb and forefinger. Alisdair had grown taller where she hadn't.

"I'm still better with the spade than you, though," she said.

"But can't set a stake without cutting yourself," Alisdair retorted, referring to several weeks before when Sheena had sliced her palm while trying to set a snare.

She sniffed at him, not deigning to continue the argument.

*Sheena is still not thriving with the regular meals, but at least her mind is healthy. She no longer pines so for the home croft, at least. That is something. She has had to grow up because Mam needs her.* Muirne glanced at the box bed; yes, she was dozing again. She knew Sheena's knee was healing but saw no evidence of her mother's distraction dissipating, or her left side returning to normal. Mam's left leg hung like a dead weight and her left arm clutched and contorted but would not obey her.

Neil distracted Sheena, educating her and Alisdair almost without their knowing. He had a knack for it, carrying on about the silliness of English grammar. Neil had the book from the Reverend Balwhidder and got the younger ones to read from it before the waning autumn light failed. While they were all thus occupied, Muirne sat with her mother. She had fits of wakefulness more often after the first week, but still wasn't able to concentrate on a task. But Muirne had an idea.

Mam had shown Muirne her plan for the wedding dress: the white-on-white embroidery and the small flourishes of color by the bust and sleeves. Muirne gathered the bunched material and placed it in her mother's lap. She still slept propped up against the wall in what could not have been a comfortable position. Her eyes opened slowly. She looked directly at Muirne as her hands spread forward over the dress. Her gaze was drawn downward; Muirne followed where she looked.

One thumb was circling the smooth facing she'd placed over the bottom of one sleeve. Muirne plucked the needle from where it was tucked into a fold. She put it in Mam's hand and held her breath.

The thumb and forefinger held the needle limply. She

loosened her hold and it fell into the folds of fabric. Mam rolled to the side, and Muirne dove for the pile of cloth, snatching it out of her way so her mother wouldn't lay on the needle. She spread it back out in her lap, carefully searching. There it was. *Well. If she can't do it, I can try.*

Muirne looped her stitches as she had seen Mam do, knowing hers were not as neat or consistent. But preparing the linens for her wedding did make her feel closer to Edward. Instead of being heartbroken over her mother's condition, or worrying about the uncertainties of her married life, she could sit on one of the logs outside their front door and draw solace from the confidence and solidity of her intended. *Escape.*

# Chapter 29

ANOTHER WEEK TURNED the leaves a brilliant array of colors, a brilliant celebration of what had been a good weather year, but a trying emotional one for the MacLeans. They expected another furious winter lay behind it, with long, dark hours in close quarters. Yellow light flickered from the hearth in the afternoon, as the fire did double-duty warming the pot on the hook suspended from the roof timbers.

Sheena now did most of Mam's chores. Her knee healed enough to be able to walk on, and the terror of that night and day she'd been alone with Mam started to recede. Neil was back, Muirne was back, and Mam was alive. Sheena had heard Delilah Allman tell Neil when she was making her potions that it was paralysis. Apoplexy. Something people tended not to recover from. It broke Sheena's heart to see her mother alternate between the hazy fog of tired stillness and the frustrated attempts to make her body work as it used to. Sheena was staring down weeks, months, years of watching her mother like this. She couldn't bear it.

What about all her plans? Sheena had intended to earn some money with her baskets again that Christmas, enough to buy a loom so that Mam could weave again, and teach her how. What use would it be now? The sight of Mam's limp left hand on the blanket every night as she slept made her heart ache. There was nothing she could do.

She remembered having nothing to worry over but the romantic entanglements of her siblings, mere weeks ago. Pining after a Michaelmas cake would have been a top concern, which almost made her laugh. She tried to bury her sadness in her new duties; Muirne went to the fields with Neil while she stayed in the cabin to cook and clean and mend and watch over Mam. Alisdair took over her snares, so she didn't go outside much that autumn.

Everyone was occupied that October, preparing for the winter when so many things would be unavailable. Alisdair scoured the pots with river sand. Muirne used the stored bear grease to waterproof the plaids Neil and Alisdair would wear while felling trees. Neil and Alisdair worked to get some of Sheena's onion and kale seeds buried under the cover of the byre so they'd be accessible over the winter.

Under the first gentle patter of snow, the post carrier was not afraid to make his rounds. One Wednesday in mid-October he brought them two letters. Neil banged into the cabin with them, eliciting an excited clamor. He opened the one addressed to himself first. It was a single piece of note-paper from the solicitor in New Glasgow.

"Says he'll send to the bailiff in the town closest to Ford's Mills to find out the public opinion of Mr. Brown. If there's something to go on, he'll order a discreet investigation and keep us informed. We may be called as witnesses, as Sandy certainly will, for any inquest." Neil read over the same short lines again, before folding the paper back up and setting it inside the cover of the family Bible for safekeeping.

"Pretty much as we expected. But I am hopeful; he

didn't immediately move to delay it until the spring. Maybe I've impressed him that this should be considered a serious crime."

"Lord knows that would never ha' happened in Scotland."

The abrupt comment came from Mam. Sheena was more used to it because she spent the most time with her, but the rest of the family was still adjusting to her drifting in and out of the conversation.

"No, Mam, it wouldn't," Neil replied.

She didn't expect an answer; Mam usually only stayed coherent for one idea at a time. Sheena turned back to see what the second letter was about. Neil handed it to Muirne.

"Your turn, Muirne."

"Oh, pffft," she chided, snapping the letter out of his hand. It was a proper envelope. She gingerly pulled out the heavy note-paper within. She looked back at the envelope: wavy slashes of ink crossed the franking of the king's figure. "It must be from—no, let me check."

Several pages unfolded in her hand and she skipped to the last page to glance at the bottom. "It is from Edward."

Muirne scanned the first lines. Everyone held their breath. Alisdair's eyes flicked among the adults' faces. Sheena shushed Alisdair's fidgets with a sharp tap on his shoulder. Muirne paused, then looked up to ask, "If I could read it first in private, please?"

Neil backed up a step. "Of course," he said.

Muirne pulled one of the stump seats closer to the fire to read. Sheena sat at the foot of the box bed, where her mother lay sleeping. She watched her for a bit. Mam looked too much like an angel. Sheena noticed how much of the lines of care and suffering had been removed from her mother's face in the past few weeks.

Alisdair rocked back and forth over his drawn-up knees by Sheena's feet. Sheena tapped the back of his head at each pass, happy to see him break into that innocent grin she loved. Neil stayed by the table, his head down, as he beat out an intricate rhythm with the toe of his shoe, his thoughts no doubt returning to the solicitor's letter. When Muirne turned from the fire, three heads twisted to see her.

She started off calmly reciting the common sentiments, then consulted the paper as she continued.

"Mr. Turner is very well. He sends his compliments. We are the best family in the world for putting up with his inconveniences. He hopes to be reunited with us a week after April 3rd, when the very first passenger sail of the year arrives in Halifax. It is a journey he would not wish on anybody—either the winter sea crossing or the overland mail."

A sneaking smile crept over her features. "That's well, isn't it?"

Sheena contributed an encouraging smile.

"He does not speak of having the wedding at his parents' but down in New Glasgow," Muirne continued. "I shall have to disappoint Mrs. Turner's hopes."

A grimace at that task distorted her face for a moment. "He also speaks of setting up his practice there and asks me to speak to someone about letting a house."

"I wondered how he would assert his independence," Neil said. "Well done, I think. The town is well-known to us and established enough to keep more than one doctor busy."

"True," Muirne said. "I was supposed to write to Edward about this exact detail, but in the commotion of coming home and Mam's accident, I forgot. Well, now, how shall I go about it?"

"I can help you make enquiries and establish credit for a new household over winter, so that by the time Turner comes, you can have the house all ready. If there are any difficulties, I'm sure the good old doctor's name would set them to rights. He did send a letter of introduction from him, didn't he?" Neil gestured to the letter.

At Muirne's nod and withdrawal of a second page, he brightened. "That would be proper, wouldn't it?"

"I admit I've felt like I'm dancing on the edge of propriety, what with visiting Edward's parents and having them push me to make all these decisions," Muirne said. "This letter helps somewhat."

But Sheena thought they were on the wrong side of convention. Her fear made her speak sharply. "And how proper is it for the groom to ask the bride to conduct his business before they're married?" Sheena asked. "What next? Is Muirne to have her own account at the bank?"

Muirne was shocked into silence.

Neil said, "Sheena, there's no call to be unkind."

Sheena felt bad but didn't want her sister to become disreputable before she was even installed as Edward's wife in town. Hadn't Mam told them that their reputation and integrity were all they had?

Muirne said, "It's true, though. Things are being done in a rather unusual order." Some of her inner turmoil showed as agitation on her face. "But I think expectations are different here," Muirne said slowly. She looked at Neil. "And they're changing. We must change with them.

I trust Edward, and that's his bidding. Let's make sure we do it right."

Sheena gritted her teeth. She would not be so showy and pig-headed when it came to her marriage. She sighed. No, she was just being bitter. She must remember to be grateful for all the good things in their life, or it was going to be a very long winter, indeed.

# Chapter 30

WINTER QUICKLY CHASED down the sweet last hours of chilly autumn. Neil made their last trip to town for a while and returned with a young heifer. The animal's black hide was covered with burlap sacks for warmth, and on top of the burlap lay other supplies. Their credit was still rated worthy by Mr. Bracethwaite and Neil had made free use of it, carting home new wool, salt, flour, and beans, plus a few dozen turnips.

He wore several layers of leather and had snowshoes strapped to his feet. It was mighty cold for the exposed parts of his face, but the leather and the exercise made him sweat. As he came up the road home in the dark twilight, he sang.

*"O lassie, art thou sleeping yet,*
*Or are you waking, I wou'd wit?*
*For love has bound me hand and foot,*
*And I wou'd fain be in, jo."*

He forgot the next verse and went cannily on with the one he did remember.

*"The night it is bath caulk and weet,*
*The morn it will be snaw and sleet,*
*My shoen are frozen to my feet*
*Wi' standing on the plain, jo."*

Neil battled for breath, climbing up encumbered with the cow's lead and his bulky shoes, trying to throw all his breath into the song. He was feeling good.

*"I am the laird of windy-wa's,*

*I come na here without a cause——"*

Finally light spilled out into the night. From the dark silhouette of the cabin about fifty feet away, he saw two candles lit and dancing toward him. He didn't finish his verse before two girlish voices soared above his:

*"O gae your way this ae night, this ae, ae, ae night,*

*O gae your way this ae night, for I dare nae let you in, jo!"*

Raucous giggles followed, and he saw Muirne and Sheena smiling, wrapped in their shawls, beckoning him in.

"Laird, indeed," Muirne scoffed with delight. "Hadn't you better get that bonny cow into the byre out back?"

"Oh, she's a beauty, Neil. And the rest are all safe in," said Sheena.

"Are they now? Isn't that fine. Aye, I'll just lead her in and take the load off her back. I'm sure she'll be grateful."

Neil took off the snowshoes and handed them to Sheena, who clapped the snow off them and took them inside. Muirne waited while he took off his own pack. She held the candle with one hand while he slung it across her shoulder. She leaned to one side to accommodate its weight and galumphed inside after Sheena. Neil was still smiling as he stretched backwards. The cow pulled at the lead, perhaps knowing food would be found once it was under a roof.

They would have a couple weeks to mark out favorable trees. He would bring Alisdair with him to do it and not venture too far. Mam was not so sleepy lately but still fragile in mind. He dared not leave her alone for too long without Muirne on hand. And Muirne would be leaving them in a few months. Neil wondered at her strength of will. *Through hell and high water, indeed*, he mused. *High frozen water.*

He let go of the cow's lead and scattered a spare amount of hay from the bulging bale she'd been carrying. Enough for three months, Bracethwaite said, if used carefully. *Then we'll have to make a deal with the Massons for some of their hay.*

Thoughts spinning through his head about their economy for the winter were sent packing as soon as he entered the cabin. Four candles and the hearth glowed. His family arrayed themselves around the table and its tall chair. Even Mam was out of bed, sitting to the right of the place for the man of the house.

"I hadn't thought of that song in ages, Neil. I'm glad to hear you sing it." Muirne beamed at him.

"What's it about, Neil? Will you finish it for us?" Alisdair's face lit up.

"I don't think that's the thing for tonight, Alisdair," he replied. "Maybe when you're older." Sheena hid a grin. Neil raised an eyebrow.

"Same for you, lassie. I don't believe you should know that story yet, neither."

Muirne laughed. "Oh, let up, Neil. Course she does. It's one Uncle Charlie sang whenever he was trying to make Aunt Jenny forget something he'd done."

Sheena nodded, clearly pleased with this allowance from Muirne.

Once they were seated and trading steaming dishes of potato and cabbage, Neil related to them the report from Mr. Drexel.

"All action is to be suspended until the spring."

A sigh from Sheena. Muirne shook her head and spoke. "I suppose there's little investigating to be done when you can't travel."

"True enough. Speaking of travel, are ye ready, Alisdair? To pick out our trees?"

Alisdair blinked. "I am to go?"

"Aye, for this part, at least. Dinna fash, Sheena will take care of the snares for ye both." He raised his brow at Sheena and she nodded enthusiastically. Poor thing probably wanted to get out for a bit.

"We'll leave on the morrow." Alisdair puffed up, proud of his new role. "And we should only be a couple days, Muirne. I'll be careful."

In his mind was something they'd heard first from the Janneys, then again from the MacGregors: it was the practice for men to go to big logging camps to work for a large landowner over the winter, making sterling cash to the tune of eight guineas a month. As often as not half the fee was paid in rum, and the other half in credit to a company store where a man would be beholden to the owner in no time at all. Neil was warned to stay away from such roaming gangs of desperate men and he fully intended to make the cabin like a fortress so they wouldn't have to go far afield scavenging like they had last winter.

They had enough food to last them and the animals, they had neighbors a few hours away that would help them if necessary, and he'd brought back enough wool fleeces for Mam or Muirne—or Sheena, even—to spin and card. He noticed she seemed less animated than usual, but as she'd always been a brooding type of girl, he decided to let it go its own way. Lord knew they were all stewing a bit, anxiously eyeing Mam and waiting for what spring would bring them: for Muirne, a wedding; for Neil, perhaps a letter. And some conclusion to the investigation for them all, so they could lay Gillan to rest in peace.

They held a Christmas fast, staying up the night in vigil to pray.

When New Year's Eve came with a howling storm, they were content to stay inside, reminiscing about past celebrations and dreaming about the future. Muirne was particularly tight-lipped about her wedding arrangements, saying it was bad luck to make plans aloud. But he knew why she did it. You had hope for something but you didn't tempt fate by speaking of it overmuch. The devil would come take it from you if he knew what you desired. At least that's what they used to say back home.

Once January was underway in earnest, Neil watched the sky for breaks in the snow storms. Whenever there was a long break, he and Alisdair went to work on a marked tree. They bundled themselves up in their warmest clothing, only to shed half of it when they started swinging the axe. Alisdair was starting to fill out and get some muscle on his frame with the steady milk and cheese and eggs in their diet. He was turning into an able companion in their quiet treks around the property.

Neil did feel some loneliness, though. Working with Alisdair minded him of his own boyhood and dashed hopes. He missed his beloved nooks in the hillocks and the squishy peat moss of the old country, all lost with his family's land. For a moment, he'd thought that Letty was the replacement for his lost home, a joy taken and a joy given. But then she'd turned away from him... Until his going away! *Why* had she done it? He could have long buried her memory if she hadn't come just as their ship was sailing off.

Whenever he caught himself being too maudlin in his thoughts, he had only to start Alisdair off on a subject of debate or a catechism. The boy would be occupied for half an hour at a time, without seeming to stop for breath. The boy would have done very well at school, if only he'd had the chance to go. A born debater, that one.

In early February, the snow lay stacked feet high but the sun had miraculously decided to return for a day. Neil took the opportunity to tramp with Alisdair about a half-mile from the cabin to bring down their farthest tree. It had been a thinner one, the job was quick, and Neil hammered at the larger branches for firewood as Alisdair talked. Neil had asked him a catechism about the trials of Job.

Twenty minutes later, he was winding up.

"And so, when Abraham decided in his heart that he would give up his son, the Lord knew, and would not allow this misfortune to happen, but having tested his child, allowed the blade to be stopped at the right moment. So, it is a story about trusting in the Lord's Purpose, even when we cannot see it, nor the benefit of it." The boy finally fell silent. Neil put by the mallet he was using to slough off tree bark. He was about to propose a logic problem when Alisdair's face turned thoughtful.

*Oh, brother, here it comes*, Neil thought.

"Neil?"

"Aye, Alisdair," he replied. He picked up the axe.

"Can you see the Lord's Purpose in Da's death yet?"

The axe stopped mid-swing. The question was unexpected only because Neil's mind had been amused by Alisdair's style of debate. He'd known it would come to this; it had been over a year. He wished Mam could be the one to answer this for Alisdair. She would know just the right mix of empathy and faith and logic that would make sense to the boy. Neil himself had not a clue.

"I canna say, Alisdair."

"But you still think it was part of the Lord's plan?"

"Well, it must be."

"But what if there's no plan? What if Mr. Turner is right and there's no God ordering everything, just people being good and people being bad?"

Also unexpected, but it should not have been. Neil should have known the talk about Edward's faith, even in hushed voices after the fire was banked, would seep into Alisdair's curious brain. Neil paused to feel for his own certainty in the answer. For he knew what he should say. But they were alone here in the wilderness; trusting to anything, even to God's plan, might well work harm on a person's will, his self-reliance. He felt a trembling inside his chest as he had that traitorous thought, but ploughed on.

"There are two parts to that question, Alisdair, and only one that I can answer. Ye'll have to appeal to a minister about the Kirk's view of free will. For me, I believe there are people being good and people being bad. I do what I can to act as the Lord would to both of them. Be good to all, but steer clear of those who would do ill. They'll land themselves in their own just deserts, you'll find, often enough. And that can be called God's plan, if ye like."

Alisdair kicked some of the bark off the tree, digest-

ing this. Neil wondered if Alisdair might have heard anything in town during his visit with Muirne. *Surely not.
Edward's business is not widely known there yet, I wouldna
think.*

When they returned for a late supper, Alisdair gave
no indication of further deep thoughts. He was his
greedy, hungry, growing, impish self again. But Neil
watched him more closely. Was this a new threat, one
whose effect was impossible to ascertain? Should he talk
to Edward about this atheism nonsense, or stay away from
it altogether? He knew Muirne would be talking to Edward about it before they married. He'd leave it to her.

Muirne, whose evening ritual was darning stockings
and reworking old garments into new, pieced together
squares for a colorful blanket. When the younger children
went to sleep, she took out the wedding linens with a
hunched sort of reverence. She was working with the silk
by the fire in her customary spot when he introduced the
subject of Alisdair's questions.

Her brow furrowed.

"Perhaps if we had a regular preacher who did the
circuit, he'd feel the strength of the Bible and the Gospels
sure enough, but—the broken services we've had for the
past two years—and the troubles—but don't they say
that the true believer questions before coming further
into the fold? Oh, Neil, I don't know how my own home
will succeed if I can't even keep my own brother on the
right track!" She scrubbed her forehead with the back of
her hand, agitated.

"I'm sure ye will, Muirne. Ye'll figure how. Turner's a
good man' and ye trust him, aye?"

Muirne nodded.

"If ever ye start not to trust him, you know where to come."

Muirne met his gaze. She covered his hand with her own.

"But I'm sure he'll let you work the way you see fit, Muirne. He's...modern like that."

"Well, I hope so, since there'll be little enough time to talk when he gets back before we—before we're—married."

The word was reluctant to alight on her tongue, and she spoke it hesitantly. She rolled up the silk and put it in its protective muslin sack. She rose from the fireside chair and tucked the bundle into one of the cubbyholes on the back wall.

"How's the dress coming along?" Neil asked.

She sighed loudly, leaning back for a moment against the wall with her eyes closed. When she opened them again, she was more composed, and smiled at Neil.

"I'm getting the fit right but Mam will finish the embroidery. We've still got two months."

Neil was surprised. He hissed at her as she pushed the ashes over the fire. "Whhshht. Suppose she can't?"

"She'll recover," Muirne whispered fervently. "Sheena will see to it."

Neil couldn't deny that Sheena was growing into the role of chief caretaker, becoming less of a child each day. But that wasn't what worried him. "I'm not worried about Sheena. I'm asking you. Are you truly ready?"

"A house in New Glasgow will make it easy for you all to visit. And the post will come more frequently," she said, with a slight tease in her voice.

She was trying to put the focus back on him and his

hopes for Letty. Neil stood stiffly, and Muirne sighed. In the darkness, she passed him and clasped his forearm.

"And with spring will come more chances," she whispered. She patted his hand. He stared into the fire, as unwilling to relinquish hope as he was to be hopeful.

# Chapter 31

THEY DID NOT have a chest, but there was a large hope *pile*. By the end of February the pile contained bedsheets, coverlet, nightrail, extra chemise, cloths for drying and covers for pillows. The wedding dress remained almost finished, the colored embroidery thread lacking a resolution to its wavy curl. Muirne shook open the folds of silk and turned it in the firelight to make it shimmer. Her mother's golden yellow and sky blue spirals chased each other down the bodice while the dark red only covered a quarter of their length. She couldn't look at it without pain, thinking of her mother's careful, loving stitches giving way halfway down to her pinched or loopy ones.

Mam was able to focus on her children's faces for longer but still unable to help with the physical chores. She spoke rarely, and her speech was a little slurred, but they could understand her, and it did not seem to be getting any worse. Muirne anxiously hoped their mother's energy and lively spirit would return. If they did not, the family would be back to where they were last year, not enough people to do the considerable amount of work it took to survive. She could not in good conscience leave them.

No transatlantic news had reached the MacLeans since December, but one letter from the Turners came through in February. Mrs. Turner had found a property to let from the tanner in New Glasgow, a Mr. Newmand.

She had also gone and engaged their Tatamagouche minister to perform the ceremony, a Mr. Tunnithan.

"Tunnithan? What kind of name is that?" Sheena said shrilly when Muirne read it out to the family.

"I don't care what kind of name it is," Muirne said. "As long as it is our wish. Which it isn't. And they know that. I wanted to ask Revered Balwhidder in Pictou."

"But you hadn't yet?" Neil asked.

"No. I thought Edward…"

"It's not important to him, Muirne. You should do it. Or the Turners will win!"

She wrote to Mr. Balwhidder the next day, explaining her husband's lack of wishes and her very strong convictions. Since they had no Church of Scotland minister, she would appreciate his presence at such an occasion. She waited a week before Tommy came by to collect the post.

The reply came quickly: he was unable to legally preside over a wedding where both people were not of his sect, and therefore suggested she give the honor to one of the Anabaptist ministers that were to be found in the eastern townships. This response received its own round of scathing commentary from Sheena when Muirne read it out in March.

"Anabaptists? Anabaptists? Does he think we are heathens? You'd as soon be married by a Catholic priest!"

Muirne held back a grin. "It is disappointing. But also rather funny." She let the smile bloom on her face. "To think I am the one who should disqualify us from a religious service!"

"You?" said Neil.

"Me," Muirne confirmed. "I did not tell him about Edward's views, merely his lack of particular wishes for the ceremony."

"Well, there you are," Alisdair said from his stool. "You should have told the truth. Now ye've a penance to do."

Muirne rolled her eyes. "Of course, Master Alisdair, as soon as you do yours for spilling the ink that I labored over for hours!"

Later that night, Muirne and Neil discussed the wedding plans more soberly.

"I don't want his mother to be constantly exerting her will over our house," she said to Neil. "Could you imagine our Mam telling us when and where and whom to choose?"

"No," Neil admitted. "But she's a rare case, our Mam." They both looked over in silence to where their mother lay sleeping.

"I do so wish she would recover her strength. I wish there was something we could give her," Muirne said.

"Well, if Balwhidder willna do it, why not take the man the Turners found? I'm sure he'll be fine. Besides, the day's for you and him; no one'll notice the man reading the lines."

"But it's not just that! I feel like she's running roughshod over me, even from afar, even before I'm her daughter-in-law! She's looked into a house to let, put down first month's rent—and we've never even seen it! I'd like to think she is acting under Edward's bidding, but why should he not write to me as well? I don't understand. He's become a blank to me all of a sudden." She put her head in her hands.

"Dinna worry so much, Muirne. Honestly, you act as if it's all your responsibility. It's not. I'll go and see this house. Where is it?"

"It's a small house in the high street in New Glasgow owned by Mr. Newmand the tanner."

"Well, at least it's in New Glasgow; isn't that what you wanted?"

"Yes, but not like this."

Neil tsked. "Wait and see. Ye might actually like it."

Muirne smiled at his chiding tone. "Very well. I'll stop worrying." She snapped her fingers. "There," she said.

Muirne lay awake on the edge of the mattress with Mam and Sheena. She was picturing a house, try as she might not to. She imagined dinners like the one at the old doctor's, when the men had talked of surgery practices, professional opinions, and new contraptions that physicians were using. She wondered if she would be equal to the role he saw for her.

There was little time left to wonder: a few scant weeks left before the ship was due into Halifax. *Am I right to commit myself to such a man? One who does not believe in God?* Muirne daily revolved the question in her mind, wishing for the chance to talk to him about it in person. She would even have settled for talking to her mother about it but that did not look like a promising prospect, either.

*I will be sure of him before I truly say yes,* she promised herself.

A few days later, in the brief dark interval for leisure between dinner and sleep, Mam beckoned to her daughters. Muirne and Sheena knelt as she withdrew from under her pillow the threadbare and dusty sacking. It had done its job through the winter: she unfolded the top and took out the layers of silk Muirne could no longer bring herself to work on. Mam spread the dress across her lap, the neckline visible with its careful embroidered crescents and descending spirals. But the yellow and blue were now joined by chevron lines of green and red! Muirne caught her breath and looked up at Mam. She pulled the folds apart and saw a green thread winding down the front with the yellow: a spiral that suggested a vine pattern. Muirne traced it with her finger.

"It's beautiful, Mam. Thank you. How ever did you manage?" Her words were barely audible but her mother seemed to understand. Muirne left off looking at the dress to throw her arms around her mother. "Thank you," she said again.

Muirne couldn't believe it: her mother was going to be all right! Her eyes went first glassy, then weepy, and then she laughed, hugging her mother and rocking back and forth with her.

Sheena stood and hovered until Muirne moved to wipe her face, and she joined the embrace. By that time, Alisdair and Neil had noticed the commotion and came over to see Mam's work. They marveled first that she was looking so self-possessed, and then they erupted into a clamor about her ability to be so duplicitous. While Neil was holding Mam's hands and rubbing them for warmth, Muirne sat back on her heels to enjoy this homecoming of sorts.

"You'll need a new shift as well. Ye canna wear yer old one under this now," Mam said.

"Yes, Mam. I can manage that on my own."

Muirne glanced at Neil. She'd have to go to town to purchase it, though. Perhaps Neil would go for her.

"Will you teach me how you made that pattern down the front?" Sheena asked, her eyes soft.

"Yes, Sheena, when you're sure of your writing."

"Yes, Mam."

"It's proud I am of everyone in my house being able to read and write." She looked hard at both her daughters in turn. "I hope it helps you keep what is yours, and … help your families to survive." Her voice petered off.

Muirne squeezed her mother's shoulder before moving off. She felt the regret coming off her mother in waves. She doubted it would have helped Mam plead their case with the laird in Scotland had she known to write. But if ever someone came to threaten her children, or her Edward, *she* would at least know how to read the law. Now, *finding* the law was another point altogether…

When Muirne looked up again from her thoughts, Alisdair was watching Neil carve a piece of wood in his lap with the rasp. The tallow candle that stood on the table was dangerously low, which meant activity was almost at an end for the night. Still, Muirne enjoyed watching the turning, the scraping, the methodical back and forth of Neil's movements. Her quivering thoughts stilled. When he stopped, she looked up, her eyes unfocused.

"What is it?" she asked.

"I think it'll be another spoon," he replied.

"That's not—" A lightning glance from Neil; a subtle shake of his head. "Oh. That's nice." She took Neil's hint and changed the subject. She nodded in Alisdair's direction. "And when'll you be trying your own hand, wee man?"

"Maybe after the moose-hunt," he said, sleepiness slurring his reply.

"The what?" She turned to Neil.

"The Frasers were by yesterday with an invitation to a moose-hunt. Seems the best time is the tail-end of winter. I've agreed to go but Alisdair shouldn't come to the field with the men. Maybe next year," he said. Alisdair's face screwed up in sleepy protest, and he sighed and fell back against his skins just as the first candle guttered out. No doubt there would be protests in the morning.

Neil and Muirne swept up the scattered wood shavings with their hands and dropped them into the wood basket by the fire. Neil sat on his own pile of plaids, the sound of him settling against the four or five layers of wool making only a slight *scritch*. Sheena blew her candle out after carefully folding her handiwork into cloth sacking away from the fire. She was practicing the same design on Muirne's bodice but on a spare scrap of muslin. Muirne thought it was quite ambitious but that Sheena would have no trouble—*that girl is so stubborn it does her good*. Muirne heard Sheena get into the box bed, Mam's voice speaking soothingly.

Muirne sighed, waiting to ask Neil what she'd wanted to ask, but not in front of Alisdair. The boy was sound asleep but still they moved toward the near side of the hearth to prevent overhearing. Muirne felt his hand at her back and appreciated his presence as a guide, though there was no spare furniture over which to stumble.

"What is it, Neil?" she asked when they sat close together on the near side of the log bench.

"I'll miss ye, when ye settle in town, you know."

"Of course you will, so will I miss you, but there will be visits, don't forget." She latched onto his forearm, wanting to pull the truth out bodily if need be. "But that's not what's troubling you." She turned beseeching eyes on him, willing him to feel her plea, even in the dark.

"Well, when you go," he asked, clearing his throat as silently as possible. "It occurs to me it'll be rather a sad house up here. Mother regretting Gillan, me regretting Letty, Sheena regretting home. Mark how well she tends that garden row. She needs something to look forward to here to occupy her thoughts."

Muirne wanted to protest, but didn't. She thought Sheena'd been coming along well this winter, strengthening in body with the hard work, if not blooming quite yet. Still, she was only thirteen years old. They had hope of steady food now. But where was Neil going with this? He knew Edward couldn't live on the ridge.

"What do you want to do?"

"I'd like to look for a tutor in New Glasgow. For Alisdair. My lessons may be good enough for Sheena, but... I'd like to give him at least that."

Muirne drew a deep breath.

"This is about your own missed chance back on Mull. Oh, Neil." Her heart cringed for him. He stood before her having lost his first love, his stepfather, his right to family land, and his hopes of higher education, yet he wanted to pass something of those dreams on to Alisdair.

"That's past. I want something better for Alisdair. For Sheena. Have them come stay with you where there will be more opportunity, in the town."

"I'll ask Edward about it as soon as I can. Alisdair

could live with us for the first year and we could see how he gets on. Is that what you want, Neil?"

"Aye." After a pause, "And Sheena after that."

"All right. I'll ask."

Muirne didn't know that they would have the means to educate her siblings in town, but they would try. If all went well…and when was the last time things went well?

"Are we ever to rid ourselves of this tightrope feeling, Neil?"

"Oh, I still hope so, Muirne." She felt his other hand close over hers. "Give us a few seasons, yet." She heard the smile in his voice and relaxed a degree or two, now that his seriousness had passed. She gave his hand a squeeze, then climbed into bed with her mother and Sheena, who was already curled tight into a ball, asleep.

# Chapter 32

THE MOOSE HUNT proved an exciting diversion as well as an available source of good meat in the lean times before anything could be sown under the snow. Neil enjoyed watching the other men, seeing how they interacted with each other. He didn't take a shot, but learned a lot about timing, observing signs, and selecting the right stand.

When the men returned to the MacGregors' house and divvied up the spoils, he heard Muirne being besieged with every type of advice imaginable for how to preserve the moose meat. She must have listened to at least six different instructions from their women neighbors before salting down their share of the two moose downed in the hunt. Back home afterwards, she and Alisdair flayed the raw meat, while Neil had some time with Sheena.

"What do you think of being as talented as yer ma when it comes to the dyeing and weaving? Have ye a talent for it, then?"

"I would like to be as good as Mam but we've not got the tools, have we?" She looked forlornly down, kicking one of the border rocks of her garden gingerly back into place. It marked the line in the snow where her precious plants ended, and the rows of oats started.

"Well, we may be getting close to being able to buy a new loom. It's that or another sheep, but that can be got in spring with the price of a tupping. We'd have to go without the milk and cheese for a while, but it's only a matter of weeks before weaning. Anyway—household economy," he said with a smile. "Back to the loom. Does it interest ye?" He looked her in the eye, even as she seemed to curl up into herself, squatting close to the ground.

"Maybe. I would like to make the plaids like Mam did at home. Some of them are so beautiful. Muirne learned, didn't she?"

"Aye, she did but I don't think she loves it as Mam does. She'll probably buy her cloth in town, once she's married. But is there anything else? Anything that your— that is—" *How was he to say this?*

"In a few years you'll be thinking of marrying and starting your own home, Sheena, little as you may heed it now. Since things have been somewhat topsy-turvy for you, I wanted to ask if you felt something was missing, in terms of learning. I'd give it to ye, if I could."

Sheena looked up at Neil towering over her, blocking out the setting sun. "Father's missing," she said in Gaelic. *Tha Athair a dhìth oirnn.* But nothing can bring him back. Don't worry about me, Neil. I'll be fine."

Neil let out his breath as they marched back up the snowy, shady hill. Perhaps once Sheena mastered the writing, and the weaving, his wounds from Gillan's death would have healed.


Neil next ventured into New Glasgow in March. He headed straight for Drexel's old office, but another man sat at the desk, the door open wide. Before the man could be distracted by Neil's presence, he dashed to the door nearby that showed Wemyss' name. Placing his rucksack and snowshoes outside the door, he knocked. When there was no response, he opened the door. Mr. Wemyss was there with another man. They stood across from each other across the desk. When Neil opened the door, the man on his side of the desk hustled out of the room, his head down.

"Ah, MacLean. What can I do for you?"

"Good day, sir. What is the address for Mr. Drexel's office? Or is he coming here for sessions soon? I need to see him."

"Drexel...let me see." The man's spectacles seemed fogged up, preventing him from seeing the papers on his desk. He peered over the half-moons, stretching his squat nose. "Here is his card. You should think to get one next time you see him."

Wemyss held it while Neil read the address, committing it to memory.

"And how do I get to Amherst, sir?"

Wemyss turned the card around to look at it. "Amherst. Don't have much occasion to go that direction, myself. Ask Carson at the door. He's a fine man for finding his way through woods."

Neil found Carson hanging around the door of the courthouse building. He had longish straggly brown hair, none of it on the top of his head. He wore a thick cloak with fur at the top, and well-worn, travel-stained leather clothing. When Neil asked his help, he spoke as little as possible but gave fairly clear directions out of town.

"Follow the Northumberland strait shoreline northwest until Pugwash, then you're off westward over the hills." His voice had a sour quality to it, as if he already bore Neil a grudge. Neil assumed it was his general demeanor, thanked him, and stopped by Bracethwaite's to send a quick word via the informal post office there. He would be continuing on to meet with the solicitor in Amherst and be back on the ridge in eight or nine days' time.

The route was well marked, at least for Neil, who was used to depending on the slight markings on trees called blazes to guide him in the snow. He slept once in the open on the mainland, after striking out from Pugwash. A queer feeling, that. To realize he was on an island, technically. *It sure doesn't feel like the island of home, where you could look in any direction and see water. No: here, everywhere you look are trees.*

He came down from the hill the fourth morning and saw the tamped-down road and heard the clanging of a smithy in operation. A cooper was wheeling his product onto a wagon for transport. Neil stopped the cooper to ask him if this was Amherst. It was. And where might Drexel be found? The cooper pointed him down the street to the right. Again, it was easy to find. The heavy iron sign outside showed a big 'D' and silhouetted scales and a crown.

Neil was welcomed by the magistrate's clerk, a Mr. Brown. The name didn't give him a jolt until he was sitting with Mr. Drexel in his inner office. He gave his head a shake to clear it of uneasiness at the closeness of the coincidence.

"Thank you for coming to pay me this visit, MacLean. To business. You'll need to have those Janney men return and give their statement in front of an impartial witness. Amos and Matthew, that's right. They've said they'll do that? That's good. But that's your only evidence so far, and that's none so good. Have you had that young fellow who was with your stepfather write down his statement? No? Well, maybe you can find him on your trip home and get it done without delay."

"He's in Pictou, sir. It's on my way home. I shall find Sandy and do as you ask."

"Good. Now let me tell you something of the delicate nature of my handling of the prosecution here: my clerk is related to this Mr. Brown of Moncton."

At Neil's look of confusion, he explained. "Most of his holdings are in Moncton, but he resides currently in Ford's Mills, because of the works currently underway there."

"Anyway, he's a cousin to my clerk, who noticed the name on my correspondence. So far, I've kept the nature of your inquiries private from him, but it is not a point in your favor—or rather, it is not a point in Brown's disfavor, since my clerk comes from a very respectable family. It is hard to believe someone of their standing could be involved in such a crime."

"Perhaps people who know Anstruther Brown's character in the town where he lives would give statements, sir?"

"That is possible. Or if he had an associate."

Neil's logic rejected the idea. An associate? With what motive? Young Sandy had only ever mentioned the two hired men, and the Janneys had made it clear that Anstruther Brown had been the one bragging of doing the beating. An associate—a hunt for another culpable party—was a distraction, a complication, and Neil feared it would just make things go off-course.

"No, I don't believe it. I think it's as simple as it looks. It may be harder to find the two hired men, but if Brown hired them——"

"You can't prove a crime without a weapon, boy. You can't prove the crime without the men that did the beating. It would be just one man's word against another's."

Neil resisted the urge to splutter. *Drexel, you can go hang! If we have to find the two bloody thugs who attacked Gillan, there's no hope! We can't drag poor Sandy around every trash heap and logging camp looking for those good-for-nothings!*

Neil sat tight-lipped through the rest of the solicitor's explanation of the process then left, saying as little as possible. He worried his lower lip as he walked out of the solid wood door of the office, wanting to slam it and set everyone else's teeth on edge, too. He managed not to, but collected his travel gear from the porter by the door. He didn't thank him.

He stood in front for a moment, watching someone else's horse at the post roll his eyes at him warily. He took a breath, let it out. Took another. When he was calm enough that the horse dropped his head and lipped at the grass sprouting by the rain barrel, Neil started out on his return journey with nothing to show for his effort.

More waiting. More writing. More impossible tasks. Matthew's offer was starting to look very tempting. Neil actually paused by the sign to Fort Lawrence, looking north toward Ford's Mills. Brown lay in that direction. Matthew had offered to show him his house. But Matthew was probably still away in New Brunswick cutting and hauling trees with his father. Which reminded Neil of his responsibilities. He had to get back home and help pull those trees down to New Glasgow soon. But first, Sandy in Pictou.

Sandy was at home with the other Wilsons. Neil carefully recorded his words on clean paper and had him make his mark to authorize the testimony. He crossed the harbor once again, this time on the tiny ferry, passing through New Glasgow. As he was walking down the main street he remembered his promise to Muirne to check on the house that the Turners had engaged for April. He was bone-tired after the lonely time spent traveling and the frustration with Drexel. He stopped at the well to heave up the bucket and quench his thirst. While he was sitting on the edge of the squat wall, a voice from behind surprised him.

"Are you always this thirsty, young man?" There was some amusement in the voice. A young woman in cream linen and flaxen bonnet smiled at his jumpiness. She looked familiar but it wasn't the dark blonde curls visible or the small shapely mouth. It was the mocking laughter in her expression. The girl with the washing bucket who had laughed at him outside the courts! She gestured to the bucket. He refilled his canteen and lowered the rope down for her.

"And always this mute, as well? Thank you for the help." She spoke wryly, with a world-weariness that disconcerted Neil.

"I'm sorry. You surprised me."

"Ah."

"You live in the town?"

"Yes. My uncle is the grocer."

"Mr. Bracethwaite?"

"Yes," she replied, a moue of distaste quirking her lips

for a moment. "I care for my mother and do the laundry for the store and a few others. I'm Jemima." She bobbed a perfunctory curtsey and he noticed the freckles across her collarbone. The skin of her forearms was roughened and red, that of her face less so. *A laundress' skin but not yet in ill-health.* She went on staring at him and he realized he should introduce himself.

"Neil MacLean, from back of McLellan Mountain," he said.

She pursed her mouth and gave him another knowing look that he couldn't interpret. It made him tingle and he felt self-conscious.

"I've come to town on some business. My sister will be moving here with her husband soon." He glanced at the position of the sun in the sky. He'd better find this Mr. Newmand and be on his way. Whatever it was that intrigued him about this new acquaintance also made him want to flee.

"Pleased to meet you, Miss Jemima. I'd better be getting on. I'll be sure to say hello when next I'm in Mr. Bracethwaite's."

"I should be very pleased if you did, Mr. MacLean." He passed the full bucket carefully to her. She placed both hands on the rim as he rose, bowed, and walked away. He heard a loud splash and turned back to see her with the bucket upturned, smirking at his reaction. He smiled uncertainly, nodded again, and found his way to Mr. Newmand's atelier.

Mr. Newmand was a leatherworker. While his tannery was located outside town by a waterway, he had been in business long enough to have someone else supervise the management of that enterprise while he took on the cleaner work of cutting, stamping, and tooling according to customers' needs. As Neil entered, he was working on a saddle, only identifiable to Neil because of the other saddles further along in the process arrayed along the wall.

Mr. Newmand looked up, noticed his visitor, and gave the saddle tree in his lap another calculating look before swinging his leg over the bench and rising to shake hands.

"Hello and welcome. Do you come with custom for me, sir?"

"Not at present, Mr. Newmand. I'm Muirne MacLean's brother, Neil MacLean. I was visiting to see about the premises you were——"

"Ah, I see. From Mrs. Turner. One moment." The little man pulled down a shade on his front door, turned his sign around to read *Closed* to the outside, and locked the door. "Let us use the back. I'll take you there directly."

Neil followed in silence. It was merely a formality, of course, since he was sure the Turners would know what they were about. Still, he'd not softened to Mrs. Turner as Muirne seemed to have done. The sight of that hateful man and his poor horse——he would not soon forget the vile things Mr. Turner had said to them. But he did want to have some good news to bring home, not just his disappointment and frustration with the solicitor.

They walked past a few structures on their right, and Neil saw the raw, unfinished ends of these residences: crumbling back porches more like his own than he would have expected from the street view, refuse, scavenged roof materials, and a spindly wooden post strung with whitened laundry snapping in the cold breeze. While there was little snow down here by the river, things were still frozen, and the woman whose yard this was had snagged an opportune moment when the sun was shining to dry her linens.

Mr. Newmand withdrew an impressive set of keys from his work apron and entered the next building from the back.

"Here we are, then." The man's bald spot was visible in the sunlight before he ducked inside. Neil followed and was pleasantly surprised by what he saw. Wooden floors with the cracks filled in with—he looked closer—gypsum. A hearth in the middle of the wall that stood next to their neighbors with the laundry, and two deep-set windows across from it. A small enclosed room in front, and one in back, with the kitchen space supposedly behind that. Neil poked a head into that space, and noted the lack of kitchen fixtures: a hole for smoke, a tub for water, a shelf for plateware. He turned back to the man, who stood by one of the central windows, poking at the glazing.

"Still good, that. Aye, a bargain."

"Mr. Newmand, did your last tenants have the use of a kitchen? I don't see—"

"Ah—yes. They hired the girl next door. There's a woman and her daughter there with not much money. Your sister and her husband might want to do the same." Glancing at Neil, he took another tack. "Or you could have an oven built, have some more shelves put in the back there. As you like. If you improve the property, I'm sure we can see a way to pay you for the trouble."

Neil nodded. "Obliged, I'm sure." He looked around again. "Well, I'm well pleased for Muirne, Mr.

Newmand. Will you be glad to have a doctor here?"

"Oh, sure. Long as they can pay regular-like. I'm none too particular." The man's sharp eye and business standing gave the lie to this statement, but Neil let it pass. He figured he should stop taking up the man's time.

They went out the back way and parted company affably. Neil used the alley on the side with the windows to enter the street. He paused for a moment to look at the face the house presented to the world: a sturdy brown door, one window, a fairly new coat of whitewash.

*This will be her place; I can see it. Alisdair will go to school —yes, I suppose I should see about that next.* He had just turned to step lively up the main street to the rectory where he could ask about local tutors when a voice raised the hairs on his neck once again.

"Neighbors, are we?"

Neil turned to see the girl from the well. She leaned against the doorframe of the house next door.

"Miss Jemima. You live in the next house?"

"Yes, with my mother. You'll be wanting our cooking before long with that drafty hearth."

Her knowledge of the interior disconcerted him and he stuttered through his reply. "It is my sister and her husband who will be living here, as I told you."

"But you'll be visiting."

Something about her tone discomfited him further. He nodded, excusing himself to retreat up the street. There was much business to attend to, and he didn't have time to examine his feelings about the smiling looks this woman gave him, or to discern her character. The unwelcome tingles that Jemima stirred in his body he physically shook off. He had enough to do preparing for Muirne's marriage, Alisdair's schooling, and the murder inquiry.

*Murder inquiry*, he thought with a chill. That would probably wipe that smile off her face.

# Chapter 33

MUIRNE WAS RELIEVED to hear from her brother that the house the Turners had scouted out looked eminently suitable. She agreed with Neil that it would be better to build their own oven and chimney in the back. But she dared not make such a costly decision without consulting Edward. There were so many things she needed to talk to him about. The date of his ship's return in Halifax came and went, and Muirne was irritable and short-tempered by the sixth of April. He could arrive any moment, and there were so many things still up in the air.

"If I had any more worries, I'd need to make a bleeding list!" she swore aloud.

She was alone at the creekside, having filled one bucket with clean snow for the next morning's washing, and another with the juicy leaves of purslane and cow parsley that came with the first wakening of spring. She squatted by the creek, watching the slow movement of water beneath the top coating of ice. It was only by staring at, but not watching, the blackness that one could sense any sort of movement.

She tired of it eventually, and picked up her buckets. Her heart quickened with the tramp uphill. She trudged upward, passing the rows where their first crops had been harvested. Pride swelled in her breast. The ground was clear, but not soft enough yet to start turning over. Neil was talking about breaking it up with a hoe if it didn't warm in the next week. 'Time to be getting on,' he'd said.

*Indeed.*

Edward might be here tomorrow. He'll ride up—

*No, he'll be obliged to wait for the sled, together with all the people coming to the north side of the island.*

He'll walk from the sled, then.

*With all his gear from the trip on his back?*

No, he'll have to go directly to town first. Then he'll ride up to us.

Muirne abandoned arguing with herself. *He'll come when he comes.* She called to Sheena, who was still inside the cabin.

"Sheena! Your gloves! Your turn for the nettles!"

The wooden latch made a sound as it was knocked back. Sheena rushed out to her, grinning madly. The late afternoon sun hung low in the sky behind the cabin and Muirne couldn't see into the shadows of the doorway. Sheena grabbed the bucket of snow and spirited it to the back of the cabin without saying a word. Muirne's forehead wrinkled. She was about to call after her, when a familiar form stepped out of the house.

"Edward!" He was dressed in layers of wool and furs when he caught her up. The smell of animal musk mixed with his own dank sweat. His face was paler than she remembered. But his dark eyes were warm and bright. He hesitated for a half second then kissed Muirne's cheek. If it was possible, he looked anxious. Muirne enjoyed the shivery feeling his kiss provoked.

"Edward! You've just arrived?"

"Yes. I couldn't rest until we had a sled immediately set out from Halifax over the inland route. I left the rest of the party at the road and practically ran here." He drew back from her to rake her form with his eyes, then sought her hands with his. He gently took the bucket of greens from her and placed it on the ground. "You are looking well."

"Did you see Mam?" Muirne didn't know where to begin with all that had happened in his absence.

"Yes. Just now." Edward's features closed a little. "Sheena tells me she is much better than she was in December."

"Yes. She will recover fully, though, won't she?"

Edward merely sighed. He hugged her to him again. His warm breath stirred the hairs at the nape of her neck and his hand cradled the back of her head.

"I'm sorry, my love."

Muirne scrunched her eyes closed and pressed her forehead hard into his chest. *He doesn't think Mam will recover. Oh Mam!* Could she still leave in a few short weeks? Leave her family? She trusted Neil not to let them starve, but with the investigation hanging over their heads...She breathed in deeply. Here was her choice, then. I can't do it, she thought. But when they separated, Edward's face looked so compassionate, so understanding, she was sorely tempted. *Very well, I shall ask my questions and see where that puts us.*

Edward spoke softly, breaking into her inner turmoil.

"My things will be sent round by coach to New Glasgow. My mother informed me they've secured a house there?"

"Yes——"

"They haven't been too much of a burden, have they? My parents?"

She cocked her head at him. "Why didn't you tell me?"

He just shook his head. "They'll come around. It is your opinion which matters most to me. You like the house they chose?"

"Neil says it will do very well. I have yet to see it myself."

"Then I shall settle in straight away, and wait most impatiently until we are married and you can join me."

His hand, previously light on her forearm, snaked around her waist. He smiled wider and kissed her mouth. His lips hummed against hers. She closed her eyes, holding back the many thoughts that wished to intrude at this very moment. He drew back, breathing in measured doses, and she realized he had closed his eyes as well. *Well, I suppose that is how it is done.* She watched them open slowly. *Oh, how beautiful is his face!* The sound of Sheena noisily sweeping muddy slush from the back door made them step apart.

"We need to speak privately. Soon," she said.

He nodded slightly. His eyes scanned her face, and she was torn between wanting to soothe his anxiety and needing the answers to her own questions. *That list,* she thought.

Mam came to the door, looking slightly rumpled from sleep. She was supported on one side by Alisdair, who looked ready to burst out laughing at the guilty-looking pair in the front yard.

"Welcome home, Mr. Turner," Mam said. She let a bemused smile show. "I'm so glad you found our Muirne. Won't you come in for supper?"

"Indeed, I will. Thank you, Mrs. MacLean. I'm sure

everyone has all sorts of news to relate since I was here last. Right, Alisdair?"

The little boy started talking a mile a minute of all that had happened: the visits, the bear, Neil's accident.

They proceeded into the dark house. Muirne was drawn in after them, pulled by the nearness of her fiancé. The man of the hour sketched in broad lines what he had seen and done back in England, then gave more entertaining details about several of his adventures: how he had come by a dozen sweet buns for nothing in Chatham, and how he had lost his best pair of surgical scissors in Wapping. The children were largely entertained, and the nettles and the hoeing were forgotten for the evening. Shortly before true sundown, Neil came in from mapping out his new field. He was shaking after sweating in the cold and looked worn when he grasped Edward's hand. Muirne wished he wouldn't work himself into the ground so. He changed his shirt and sat by the fire and was soon set to rights.

The fire crackled while the wind rattled the trees outside. There wasn't a better place to be, or better company to be found, anywhere else. Supper was a merry affair. Muirne enjoyed the banter, all the while holding back the jitters in her stomach. Her questions and worries would only be held back for so long, she knew.

At last, Sheena and Alisdair both began yawning. Mam and Sheena retired to the box bed, the doors mostly closed. Neil dragged his bedding farther from the fire and settled Alisdair under its blankets. He made up another bed of their extra plaids and animal hides, placing it near where Edward and Muirne sat by the fire.

"Good night, Muirne. Edward."

She and Edward looked up briefly to bid Neil good night, then fell back into their own world. The light from the fire stretched shadows one way, while the light from the candle Neil left on the table cast a faint shadow toward the fire. Muirne watched the fluttering wisps play in the firelight. She composed her thoughts.

"What was it you wanted to ask me about, Muirne?"

"So many things, really." She felt nervous now that he was here and she had to bare her fears to him. "For one, would you like to have a kitchen in the back of our place, or have the girl next door do our cooking?"

Edward looked taken aback at such a practical first sally.

"Well, I suppose I'd just as soon have our own kitchen to use, if it can be got without too much expense. What do you think? Mother says—"

"I agree. It would be better to have our own kitchen." Had she jumped in too quickly? She didn't want to hear what Mrs. Turner had said before she made her own opinion clear.

"For another, there's Alisdair." She cleared her throat but kept her voice low. "If there's any chance of him getting any more schooling, it's in New Glasgow. I thought we might host him, once we've settled in, and inquire about a tutor. It was Neil's idea."

Ed matched her confidential tone. "Splendid idea. Alisdair's a quick lad. Does he intend to go into a trade in town? What does Neil think? Does the boy show any inclination?"

"I'm not sure. I believe Neil thinks only of providing us the opportunities he didn't have. He's done a braw job of teaching us all to read and write, but I think he's done all he can for us in that respect. "

"Of course. Neil seems to have fit into the role of man of the house well enough. Alisdair should be able to make progress easily." Edward smiled lopsidedly at her. "Anything else?"

His face once again wore that somehow tentative look. She didn't know why he would be feeling uncertain. Her nerves were from not feeling worthy of this marriage; he could have no such worries.

"How did it go, really, on your voyage? Are you still sure you can move into town and start practicing without going into debt? I have all the faith in the world in you—that is, only, I wish you to succeed, and I'll need to know how I should run the household."

"Dearest. Here, listen to me." He took one of her hands in his. "It will be a little uncertain, it's true, but I don't foresee any difficulties. Those that have heard of my name have no cause to deride it. There is no ill will against my family in the area, and I can depend on Dr. Skinner to give a very fair recommendation of me to his patients on the West River side that will become mine. We will be very conservative to start with until we have a regular income, if you like, and then go on as we can when things become more dependable."

He brought her hand up to his mouth and grazed her knuckles with his lips. "And it touches my heart that you have faith in me, Muirne. I, who ask for so much, and give up so little..."

He met her eyes; the tingling that had started with the touch of his hand, and crept up her arm with his kiss against her fingers, changed to a strange numbness, and she couldn't feel the rest of her body for a moment. Then feeling returned, and the blood rushed to her cheeks. Muirne wanted to turn her face but held his gaze until the breath held in her chest made her gasp.

Edward smiled, glancing to the box bed doors. There was a little rustle from where Neil and Alisdair lay.

"I'd better turn in, unless there are any other questions," Edward whispered.

"You're sure that you—love me?"

In answer, he squeezed her hand, and leaned over to kiss her for a very long moment. When at last he drew back, she kept her eyes closed, but did not miss his "Yes," next to her ear.

Muirne was jolted out of a pleasant dream the next morning when Sheena jerked awake and jostled the mattress. Mam was already awake and smiling sleepily at her daughters. Sheena stared at Muirne, her dark eyes wide and excited. She was worrying the corner of the quilt with her fingers.

"So it's really going to happen? He's back, he's here, and the wedding's in how many days?"

"Wheeshhht!" she hissed at Sheena before realizing how foolish it was to try to conceal anything from the man who was no doubt awake, mere yards away. Muirne broke into a smile. Sheena's answering smile sent sunbeams into Muirne's heart. It *would* happen. They *would* be married. Muirne let it soak into her bones. Her family could survive without her. She wasn't so necessary after all.

"All right, come on. Let's get breakfast going. Run and fetch the eggs," Muirne said softly.

The girls clambered out of bed, smoothed the blankets and quilts over their mother, and dressed quickly using the doors as screens. Even though their bare feet were visible, there was at least that level of propriety. Muirne wanted her best gown, the one she had worn to Mrs. Turner's, but it was folded in the basket where they kept the clothes in the main part of the cabin. Sheena went out first in her working dress and apron. Muirne heard Edward's greeting to her. Her heart leapt and she swallowed wrong, sparking a coughing fit.

"You all right, Muirne?" Sheena called. She poked her head back around the door, grinning. Muirne swatted at the girl, annoyed that she was making fun. But then Sheena presented her good dress, folded, in one hand. Muirne grabbed it. She used the sleeve of her shift to dab at the tears streaming down her cheeks and smiled her thanks. Her breathing slowly returned to normal and she hurriedly pulled on the dress, brushing her long hair back from her face. She was still beet red but at least the gasping for breath had stopped.

She took a moment to compose herself, pressing her hands to her face to no avail, then stepped around the box bed door.

Edward was standing by the hearth. He met her gaze with a smile. His Adam's apple bobbed down and up.

"Good morning, Miss MacLean."

"Good morning, Mr. Turner. Excuse me a moment." Muirne ducked out the back. She plunged her hands into the ice-cold bucket of water sitting on the work bench and patted her face and neck. When she opened her eyes, Neil stood nearby, holding out a cup for her. Her throat still felt rough from the coughing, so she dipped it into the water and sipped gratefully, carefully.

"The milk for the porridge is already skimmed and waiting. Sheena's bringing the eggs. Why don't you serve?"

The sparkle in his eye told her he was having a good tease. But to Muirne it also meant something more: a passing of the torch. Muirne was serving in Mam's house. She felt a bit shy of that sensation: presiding over the table. She was going to leave, and then it would be Sheena's turn. She banished her woolgathering when she saw Neil's eager face. She nodded and went back in.

The porridge was hearty, the milk sweet, and eggs were positively squandered that day. Courteous remarks were passed about the day's plans, the weather, the new premises in New Glasgow. Muirne sat between Sheena and Alisdair, across from Mam and Edward. Neil sat at the head of the table.

While ancient bone forks scraped newly cured wooden bowls, Edward thanked everyone for their hospitality. He raised his eyebrow and looked in Muirne's direction. She pursed her lips and looked down.

"I'll be right back to help you," Muirne whispered to Sheena, squeezing her arm and rising from their bench. Muirne strode out the front door. She stood facing south, feeling the strengthening sun rays fall on her eyelids.

In a moment, steps followed, and she heard the door roughly fall to. Should she turn? A hand passed over her forearm, barely touching, and the hairs on her arm stood to attention. She shivered.

"Cold?" Edward's deep, cultured voice asked from near her ear.

Muirne colored, wanting to tell him how heated he

made her blood when he was near. Did he not know? She longed to feel comfortable enough to say the words, to describe her bewildering reactions to him. A new thought came to her: perhaps her reaction was not at all shocking to a doctor?

"Nay—a bit jumpy, though."

His hand tugged at one of hers, liberating it from its tightly-clasped comrade. "Worried?"

"Not about *you*. But your parents, and the folks in the town, and the reverend, and the investigation—"

"One at a time," he interrupted gently. "My parents."

"Your father does not like me." She forestalled his protest. "I met him last month and it was very clear he holds a grudge. I thought about it. It's not necessary that he like me."

Edward stepped around to face her and she saw that he looked at her with pride. She felt bolstered.

"At least he is convinced I'm not after you for your money. But your mother, she is very kind, but—" How could she question the credibility of the woman who had raised him? No, she couldn't do it.

"Possessive?" he supplied. "I would agree with that. But she is only trying to help us."

"Help you." Muirne thought of the request to convert her son back to the Church.

"Yes," Edward murmured. "But we will be in New Glasgow, far enough away." He rubbed the inside of her wrist with his thumb.

Muirne felt a giddy wave of excitement. Her breath came in short, rushed gasps.

"Now what is it about the folks in town?"

"Well, they—and the reverend—will no doubt find

out about the——" She cleared her throat. "Your atheism. And I do wish us to fit in. We had—my family had an unpleasant experience of feeling unwelcome when we were in Glasgow."

The shadow that crossed her features at the memory of that lonely New Year's Eve was reflected by the concern and sadness in Edward's eyes.

"Well, I don't know, but I predict that once it has made the rounds of the town and is no longer news, those ruffled feathers will settle back down for someone who can do his job ably, and tend to those in need. And Tunnithan already knows."

He attempted a smile for her sake. She complied, but it faltered not long after. Here was the piece that Edward had not known about when he proposed to her.

"Then there is the murder investigation," she said quietly. Edward shook her wrists for emphasis. His voice was low but insistent.

"Which I will be there to help you through. I will stand by your family through it. I never was able to speak to the man but I collect that Gillan did his best by your family, that you loved him well, and that his violent death is a gruesome stain in all your memories of him."

Muirne's lower lip buckled at this speech.

"Muirne, tell me. Trust me. Your husband."

And as she stood there awkwardly hugging her arms to herself, Edward listened, lightly resting his hands on her upper arms to provide tangible support. It all came tumbling out: Neil and Gillan's bad blood at their last parting; the disappearance of her own father, their mother's first husband; Neil's disappointments in school; the loss of their home; the foreignness of this pile of rock, so different from their own pile of rock.

"So Mam and Neil both feel guilty, and it's none of their own fault! It's that man Brown, if the Janneys are right, and he should be made to make restitution!"

She hiccoughed and worked hard to catch her breath. She was so angry. There was no self-consciousness as she stood there in Edward's arms, though. As she realized this, the anger lightened perceptibly. Like a burden had been lifted.

Edward stood very still. When she finally looked up at him, his eyes were patient pools of understanding. He gave her a sad smile and raised a hand to caress her temple, pushing away flyaway strands of hair.

"Let us hope that the investigation brings the right man to justice, and that clearing up the mystery of his death releases you all from this sad cage you are all in."

Muirne blinked. A cage. That's what the last year had felt like. A bird cage being swung around wildly by an unseen hand with malicious glee. Maybe she was angry with God. Maybe she was closer to Edward's point of view than she thought. She pulled him closer and pushed her face into his shirt.

# Chapter 34

WHEN THE DAY for the wedding came several weeks later, all the MacLeans could be found sleeping in Muirne and Edward's new house in New Glasgow. The cabin on the ridge stood empty and locked.

Neil woke late after a night spent comfortably on the thick horsehair mattress. He thought about the first meeting they'd had with Edward, when he'd ridden up like a knight in shining armor to rescue Mam from a swarm of wasps. He'd no doubt made a firm impression on Muirne then. And since. He was exactly the kind of well-balanced and sensible man that would suit Muirne. He even answered her romantic notions, it would seem, as Neil remembered Muirne turning girlish and shy when she got one of his letters. Neil's lips curved into a smile. His chest swelled with a deep-drawn happiness. The day was here.

Mrs. Turner had sent a note that the Turners could not come, along with a gift of £20 to be used for the ceremony and to set up the house. Muirne and Sheena had purchased enough food for a substantial wedding breakfast of cold pies, puddings, and cheeses. The dishes sat on the long table in the New Glasgow home, ready to be eaten by those who would gather there after the ceremony.

Neil led Muirne to the front of the church where Edward waited. In that splendid clapboard house of God, before her new neighbors and old friends from Pictou, he squeezed her hand on his arm. She looked at him, fairly quivering from the excitement, and with his eyes he wished her all the love she could want, before stepping aside.

She looked beautiful, no one could deny it. The silk dress was weighted with heavy lining and showed off her petite figure. The design Mam had outlined bloomed like crescent moons across her collarbone, turned into vines and flowers down her front, with a chevron of green and red joining the two. Neil snuck a glance at Mam and saw she was freely weeping already. Sheena, too, through her smile. He would do no such thing, he told himself.

Mr. Tunnithan turned out to be a pleasant, ingratiating type of man. His words barely registered, flowing over Neil until it came to Muirne's part. When she said she would honor her husband for the rest of her days, Neil did get a little choked up. His sister, out in the world now.

Edward's recitations were said with gravity and charm. Neil wondered how he could say the parts he did not believe in. *Does it mean he's lying about everything he says? No, it does not. He's doing this for Muirne.*

They kissed briefly in front of everyone and there was hooting and hollering as soon as his lips left hers. A small crowd marched the newlyweds from the church down the high street to their new home. Neil glimpsed a thin young woman next door, standing with a hip cocked, watching the procession. Jemima. His skin prickled as if a cool wind had passed over. Before he could decide whether to stop or what to say, Edward had whisked Muirne up into his arms and carried her over the threshold. Bread, salt, and wine were waiting to be ceremoniously consumed. More than twenty people crammed into the small home, and the rest hovered out back, their jaws working with fervor.

After a few minutes of being jostled through doorways, Neil found his mother installed in a soft seat watching the throng. He made sure she was all right and then drifted to a position by the wall. He listened to the chatter; people were fair excited about the musicians who would come soon.

"Always so glum?" asked a voice behind him. He turned around and saw that Jemima was leaning through the window frame. She must have gone down the side alley to peer in. Neil ducked his head in acknowledgement of her comment.

"Nay, not at all, Miss Jemima." He smiled. "Sometimes my musings are that serious, my face turns traitor, is all."

She kept her smirk. "Truly? I thought you might be sad to see your sister married before yourself."

"Nay, that doesnae bother me in the slightest. I'm very happy for her." *She is a bold one.* He glanced at the sill pointedly. *Did she have no shame?* "Have ye been in? Drunk a dram to the new couple?"

"Oh, well, no. I wasn't invited." Jemima tucked her chin, as if she was being scolded.

"What d'ye mean? Everyone's invited! Come on around, I'll—" But he was stopped mid-sentence when the young woman clambered up onto the sill, giving him a view down her dress and a flash of stocking as she kicked a leg over.

"But—" Neil spluttered. Jemima smiled and drew

herself up, straightening her plain smock dress. There was a cascade of high-noted whistles, but everyone else took her entrance in stride. Neil remained in shock. He swallowed.

"I do believe they are out dancing in the back," she said. "Wouldn't you like to join them?"

Neil glanced around, the room suddenly feeling airless and the people moving too fast.

"Come on then," she fairly shouted. She grabbed his elbow and pushed through the crowd to make way for them out back. Someone was already sawing away on a fiddle. The circle had started a general clap as three couples danced the *Duke of Perth*.

Before Neil could appeal to family or friend, he was being whirled into the middle, and his concentration was taken up trying to imitate the other men and not embarrass himself. The crowd of onlookers gave a good-natured cackle when they saw him. After a fraught round of walking and toe-pointing, someone tapped on his shoulder. Neil looked up to see a slightly older, ruddy-faced guest bow to him and whisk away Jemima. She laughed delightedly.

Neil was happy to stand on the outskirts, letting his heartbeat slow again, listening to the claps and shouts. Where was the newly married couple? Shouldn't they have had the first dance? The bonfire kept everyone warm in the spring evening, but he was beginning to feel a little too heated. His roving eyes suddenly picked up a commotion at the back door. Three people came out grinning, and then there they were: the bride and groom.

Muirne glowed. She had lost the hair pins that had kept her thick golden hair under the veil at church, and now half its length draped down the left side of her back, while the other half stayed in a knot behind her right ear. The skewed picture did nothing to hinder Neil's enjoyment of the scene. In fact, it caused his heart to swell the more. The firelight made her dress shine with a pure, soft light.

Edward's face was cooler, paler, less passionate, but pleased enough. He called to the fiddler, who started up a slower, quieter tune.

"Friends, family, countrymen—Nova Scotia Men! And all the fine ladies here to celebrate with us this day. I thank you. We thank you." He raised the goblet in his hand.

"Let us always keep faith, always share and share alike, and always be happy at such good fortune!" He indicated Muirne with his glass.

The shouts of 'Hear, hear!' came from all around.

"And tonight, let us dance!"

Edward and Muirne stepped into the circle, which now included all the folks gathered. It was dusk, but most guests were feeling an inner warmth from the whisky they'd drunk during the day's toasts. A few of the married couples stepped forward to be ready to join in after a few bars. Edward drew Muirne close and looked down at her. His face lost its gaiety and took on a tenderness that was curious to see.

Neil watched as the pair started dancing slowly in a world of their own. He had a strange feeling in his gut. Like it was flipping over. A wave of sadness and regret threatened to drain all the happiness in the moment, until he gritted his teeth.

*No. This is their moment.* He would leave Letty out of it

for tonight. Just like all his other worries, she had no place here, in his sister's new happiness. Maybe she would just continue fading away until Neil could bear to think of someone else in her place. There was a sharp twinge of pain in his spine. He unclenched his jaw and worked to breathe fully again, to be in the moment again.

He became aware of the circle around the dancers, and his eyes found his mother. Someone had carried out her chair. Her cheeks showed tear tracks in the glow of the bonfire, but her face held an inner light of its own. Neil stepped into the circle to go to her, and trod on the foot of someone who'd stepped into his path.

Jemima hissed with sudden pain in front of him.

"Miss Jemima! I'm so sorry—"

"Oh, it's nothing. Aie! All right, maybe something. Help me." She batted a hand at him, latched on to his arm, and leaned into him. He helped her limp away from the center of the dance. He took a cloth from one of the outside tables and lay it down on the grass near the edge of their property, close to the wee gully that separated her yard from theirs.

She sat with her legs to one side, massaging the top of her toes where he'd evidently caused her some pain. It was dark out and Neil faced away from the bonfire. He could see the glints of light and color reflected in Jemima's eyes. He also saw the careless state of her dress. Either it had caught when she clambered over the window sill, or it had become roughed up in the course of her dancing with others in the past hour. A shoulder seam showed threads coming loose. A bit of lace was torn from the collar. The button at her wrist was missing.

"Bit of a time you've had," he said.

She looked at him with a devilish grin. Her smile made him forget the rips and tears and missing button. She pulled a flask from a pocket in her skirt.

"Cheers," she said, and took a sip. Her eyes closed and Neil imagined kissing her. She thrust the flask toward him.

"Ta," he said, and threw it back. It didn't sear like whisky, but felt queer in his wame. He wiggled a bit, feeling it slide down like quicksilver. "What is that?"

"Just moonshine," she said. "Like that." She gestured languidly to the sky. He looked up and saw the far-out stars gleaming and pulsating.

"Powerful stuff," he said, refocusing back on Jemima. Her face swam a bit. He blinked. "The stars," he added. But she was already leaning forward into his face. He felt her hands on his hips. He scrunched up his eyes and saw his two pitiful letters addressed to Letty, and black hair, and a green kerchief. He felt like he was scrambling backwards forever, away from this girl whom he hardly knew.

When he woke, he was curled up alone on the table cloth, by the back door of the house. It was dawning grey and cold, and he was sporting the worst headache he'd ever had. He hauled himself up at the sound of the hand-bell inside, one of Muirne's wedding presents from Mrs. Conaghey. The delicious smells of sausage and griddle cakes started to settle his stomach but his head continued to pound.

He had an unsettled feeling during the early breakfast. *What happened to me? What did I do after drinking that damned moonshine of Jemima's? Where did she disappear to?* Everyone else was enjoying the feast before departing for home, but Neil took only a few distracted bites. There was no hint of Jemima, nor were there any funny looks aimed his direction. *She must have just left me out there when I couldn't take the liquor. I hope she isn't too annoyed with me.*

He started to move easier, letting go of the crippling fear of having done something irreparable. Neil helped pack their few things for the return to the ridge. Mam rode on Edward's horse, and the three children took their leave as the first few rays of sun were reaching the houses across the street.

The newlyweds were falling asleep on their feet as they thanked people and ushered them out. Neil was the last of the family to shake Edward's hand. Then he came to Muirne. She gave him a sleepy smile and hugged him. She felt like safety and security.

"*Beannachd leibh,*" he whispered.

# Chapter 35

A WEEK LATER, and the bread and wine were long gone. The salt was stored carefully in the salt pig, a gift from the Ogilvies behind McLellan Mountain. The air inside was cold, May having only just arrived, but it smelled faintly of the heather and sage from Muirne's wedding bouquet, drying in the eaves.

Muirne usually rose reluctantly, but the past week had found her awake with the pale pre-dawn light. She'd been up at this time before, but always moving quickly, purposefully, to a task. Now, she kept still and contemplated her life. There was an unreal quality to the married state, a newness that she marveled over, knowing it would slip away soon.

Edward, snoring lightly next to her, was not an early riser. She smoothed a hand down the cotton sheets, one of the gifts purchased with the money from Edward's parents, and such a luxury that Muirne felt like an angel wrapped in cloud. The same money had also procured the new horsehair and feather mattresses, goose-down pillows, four dark wooden carved chairs, and solid wood dining table.

Their clothes press was Edward's, moved from his lodgings; the same with the bed frame and the bookshelf. Neil had put together some shelves to use for kitchen goods and dishes, and Muirne had been busy stocking up on the essentials—flour, eggs, sugar, salted cod, potatoes

—that her husband expected to be part of their fare. His remarks about stocking a cold cellar had confused her, but she would be glad of an easier way to keep the butter and milk cold when the weather warmed in another couple months.

She had already burnt some of the sugar—which had smelled wonderful, until it smelt terrible. Now she knew not to let her eyes off the pot while sugar was heating. It was nothing like the honey they'd occasionally used at home in Scotland, or the maple syrup they had used a few times here in Nova Scotia; they both had a slow, syrupy mass that resisted the heat and yielded results slowly. Muirne regretted the waste of sugar immensely, even though Edward had assured her he was not angry.

She heard a hitch in his breath and felt answering butterflies in her own belly. On their wedding night, she had been tentative at first, then gave herself fully to her husband. She trusted him. She wasn't surprised by the noises and motions, having been exposed to her parents' coupling long before, but the abrupt feeling of being invaded had caught her off guard. He told her that her body would get used to it, and that it would not pinch quite so much after her maidenhead was broken. If so, it was a slow change. But she reveled in his kisses and his touch, and enjoyed them until she saw she needed to help bring him to his release. The look on his face before he collapsed over her was one of blissful adoration and she would endure much to see it every night.

Alisdair would be coming to live with them as soon as Neil confirmed the tuition schedule with the tutor. Muirne was happy for Alisdair to have this chance, and happy that it made Neil feel better about their uprooting, but she was in no hurry for him to come. She basked in this little pocket of time when it was just Edward and her. She was an angel wrapped in cloud, and the only thing her husband could concentrate on.

Edward had handed the money over to Dr. Skinner for his certificate application. It would take months to receive but it was usual to start under someone else's authority, anyway, so they did not expect any trouble. He would pay his first calls on his new clients the next day. *This may be our last sweet morning to ourselves as newlyweds. He'll be up and about early to make all his house calls.*

She sought his profile. His eyes were open, turned to her; he hid a smile but not for long. He reached for her and she gave herself up to his kisses and caresses. He did not seek to enter her, for which she was glad. A soreness lingered from their lovemaking the night before. This morning, Edward merely held her from behind, playing his fingers across the skin of her shoulder and breast. Perhaps he was savoring their last unhurried morning before work as well. A great sigh of contentment made the wisps of hair by her cheek flutter.

"My love," he said.

He pulled on her shoulder and she rolled backward.

"What shall we do on our last private day together?" he asked.

Muirne delighted in his shared feeling that this time was stolen away from the world. "Well, we are limited by the lack of a horse in where we can go," she said.

"True. Neil brings Fortuity back today. I expect he'll be politic and turn up for tea."

"Fortuity," Muirne repeated. "Such a strange word. And strange name for a horse, too."

"But it was perfect! I decided to purchase her after meeting you, so it was the perfect expression of chance deciding our futures. I'm glad I got that chance, too, and no other," he said, leaning forward to kiss her deeply.

Ed continued with the kissing until she felt his excitement start to get the better of him. She put up a hesitant hand against his chest and, after a moment of fumbling with his bedclothes, he sighed and flopped onto his back. Muirne put her arm across his chest and he made a sudden move to bite it. She jumped, he laughed, and she swatted him. He sat upright in order to grab her under knees and pull her closer. He cradled her head with one hand and stroked her thigh with the other. She stilled the urge to push down her bunched-up shift and cover her nakedness.

"It still hurts, does it?" he asked quietly.

She nodded against his chest. "But it's none so bad. And all that comes before is so nice," she answered. She felt his chest rise and fall on a sigh. The hairs tickled her chin and she blew on one.

"Well, I shall find ways to make it better for you, eh?" he said.

She raised herself to look at him. She bit her lip, wanting so much to conform to his expectations but knowing he also needed her honesty. That was what he had given her in his confession of atheism. She could give no less.

"All right, that is enough looking at me. I am going to dress now," she said, laughing, as she clambered off the mattress.

They took a leisurely breakfast, then sat outside. They took two chairs from the house to the back and sat side-by-side, gazing down the slope toward the creek, where a few fruit trees were looking ready to flower. The birds were active, flying to and fro gathering material for their nests. Muirne felt the ordinariness of the morning. Her new life. Unthinkable, until it was ordinary.

Muirne watched as the young laundress next door took down her white sheets and put up a basket full of men's shirts. Brown and white hung from the lines. They saw her reenter the house just as their door fell to with a loud bang. A moment later, they heard Alisdair running through the house and saw Neil with Fortuity coming through the alley.

"What perfect timing!" she called to him.

"Fortuity," Edward murmured to her, making her smile.

Edward led the horse back to the small paddock out back. Alisdair followed Ed, peppering him with questions, while Neil followed Muirne into the house.

"It is just as Edward predicted: you are here in time for tea," she said.

"Well, I didn't want to intrude on the newlyweds too early!"

They grinned and she set the pot of water on the boil while she gathered the flour, butter, egg, and salt for scones.

"Have you seen that girl next door lately?" he asked.

"Aye, in fact, this morning I watched her putting up the laundry. She must be doing good custom. Why do you ask?"

"Oh, no reason. You did see she came over for the wedding reception, did ye not?"

Muirne creased her brow. "I think so…she was dancing with some of the gentlemen, as I remember. I forgot to invite her specifically, but I suppose Mr. Bracethwaite brought her with him." Muirne looked at her brother. "It was a fun time, wasn't it?"

"Oh, aye. And you two were sure knackered by the end of it."

Muirne squawked, playfully shoving him in protest. "Well, we are certainly recovered by now. Edward goes out tomorrow, and everything is in place for Alisdair to start with the tutor, no?"

Ed came in then, and they nodded to each other. *One thanking the other for the use of the horse, and the other thanking the one for keeping him clean and in good form. Men are so transparent.* Muirne almost giggled. Alisdair was poking around the back of the property looking for birds' nests in the few trees. They talked of plans and schedules for a quarter of an hour more before the water boiled and the scones puffed up on the girdle. Muirne called in her brother for tea and returned to the hearth.

"How is Mam doing?" she asked as she served her husband and brothers.

"The same as when you left," Neil answered. Muirne chewed her lip as she held out against the feelings of guilt waiting to flood into her.

"I'm sorry for it," she said. "Is Sheena managing well enough?"

"Aye, Sheena's doing a braw job, and Alisdair helped me with the logs well enough. He's getting some meat on him."

"Finally!" Muirne said. Alisdair just smiled, shoving another girdle scone into his mouth.

Edward praised her scones as the steam escaped from

his mouth. The sight made a little pride burble up in her chest.

# Chapter 36

WHEN NEIL WENT to the general store the next morning, he checked if there was any mail for him, then handed his own letter to Mr. Bracethwaite. It was addressed to the Janneys at the town they'd mentioned on the mainland. He hoped they would respond in person, and soon, for his fear of the word getting out about his suit had been growing. A reprisal might take place before the man was even charged. If any violence was directed against *him*, it would kill his mother. She'd got to the end of her rope, he knew. If it wasn't him Brown lashed out at, but at someone else in his family, he didn't know if *he* could take it. It must stop here, he thought for the umpteenth time. He idled a moment at the counter.

Being as it was May, there would only be a few weeks of schooling for Alisdair before he must come back to help with harvest, but at least they would see if the tutor, Mr. Mahon, would suit. Muirne would winkle it out of Alisdair soon enough. With Alisdair settled in, and the latest request of the solicitor sent off, he should finish his trading business and head home. He felt reluctant to set off, though, and lingered.

The general store manager was fussily rearranging some papers behind the counter. Neil watched him stacking the seed catalogues, then cleaning his boots with a wire brush. Neil finally took the hint and drifted toward the door. As he passed, the big man noisily cleared his throat. Neil flinched.

"Somethin' else, sir?" Neil asked.

"I wouldn't be knowin' about that now, would I?"

"Beg pardon?"

"You ain't deaf. I'm talkin' 'bout my niece. Jemima. Word is you've got her up the pipe. Now I don't say she's all innocent, but I won't stand fer——"

"What? I've done nothing of the kind," Neil returned, heated. He'd never heard the expression but understood the man's unspoken menace.

"Oh, no? Nothing started at that wedding o' your sister's, eh?"

"No, sir, and ye shouldn't be passing along such barefaced lies. Good day," he said, and stalked out. Terror. *Had* he——? He rushed back to the Turners' residence but stopped at the front door. He felt the pull of the next door over, Jemima's door. He couldn't look. He didn't want to see her if she'd started the rumor. And who else would have known or cared?

He shook himself and went in without knocking. The newlyweds were sitting with Alisdair at the large table, all bent over something which lay in the middle of it. He was ready to rail against the talk at the grocer's when Edward unbent first, showing a pleasant surprise.

"Neil, come see what your brother has been working up here." He beckoned, but Neil couldn't ignore the bitterness that the rumor had lodged in his body. His sister would be able to read him.

He tried to give a few halfhearted congratulations to Alisdair. No sense alarming everybody. The boy chewed his lip and concentrated fiercely on the tablet on the table. Muirne drew back to meet Neil's gaze.

He saw she was blooming. He saw her straight back, the clear complexion—she no longer felt the axe against her throat, the hunger and need of scratching a living together. He couldn't rob her of that with his anger and petty problems.

He shook his head slightly. Her eyes left his face. *She'll come at me soon, but at least I'll have time to cool down, consider the consequences of this terrible fabrication. Maybe I can ask Jemima myself—no, it wouldn't be wise to talk to the girl now. It would only incite more talk.*

Had she been the one to start the rumor? Probably. The girl was so forward, so dangerously intoxicating. She'd turned his head, it was true, but he'd never be so foolish as to commit himself before considering such a match. Even after drinking from her flask, he'd bid her good night and muddled his way back to the house. *Didn't I?*

He couldn't have been so pudding-headed that he'd toss her on the ground there in front of everyone.

Later, he lay on his pile of blankets in the front bedroom, which was not yet furnished. Alisdair was still in thrall to the ability to use as much ink and paper as he wanted to write, and Muirne and Ed had stayed up to chat by the fire. Before he started wondering if the babe was his, could he even be sure that she was pregnant? Her, he could not ask. And the mother never came out of the house. The uncle had made it clear what he believed. Could you even know after a week? His mind whirled between whether it was true, what he might have done, who knew, and what he should do. Nothing seemed certain, and no one seemed appropriate to ask for help. He beat his brain for answers, anyway.

More quickly than he expected, he heard the fire being banked, the chairs being scraped back. Alisdair went out back to the privy, and Muirne slipped into his room.

"What's wrong, Neil? Tell me, quick."

"Nothing's wrong, Muirne. I'm pleased to see things here—"

"Don't lie to me. Is it the case against Mr. Brown? Or the credit with the seed-man? I can help."

"Muirne," Neil said, low and urgent. "You've yer own house to look to. Ye mun consult yer husband, mind. But it's fine, nothin' tae worry about. Just don't listen to that washer-woman next door, is all."

"Jemima?"

"Wheesht. Hush." He dropped his voice even lower. "Aye, her. She may be starting trouble, is all. I'll handle it."

"Oh." The candle she held showed wavy points of light in her dark brown eyes. She looked relieved. *Just a girl,* Neil thought. *Aye, and they can cause the biggest problems of all. But I'll not worry this one.*

"All right, then," she murmured. Alisdair came in, rubbing his hands quickly to warm them before peeling off his outer woolens and curling up with his back against Neil's side.

"Night, Muirne, Neil," he mumbled, before shutting his eyes and drifting off.

"Good night," Muirne replied, nodding at Neil before withdrawing with her candle.

Neil sat in the dark, listening to Alisdair's breathing settle, then turn into a whistle. He still had tomorrow morning to act. But what could he do? *If everyone in town wants to believe me a scoundrel, what will that do for the suit against Brown? Damnation.*

No, he'd make his way home to his mother and Sheena, who needed him as much to plough the fields under and bring in firewood as to keep the house alive with good cheer. He prayed Mam would recover her strength. Edward's evaluation of an apoplectic fit didn't give them much hope, but hope they would, nevertheless. Sheena seemed more sure of herself in her new role caring for Mam. He hoped it would lift some of the homesickness from her. It had been a year; she still had plenty of time to call this rugged place her own.

# Chapter 37

HER COURSES HAD not come. Her courses had not come!

Muirne sat in the back of the house, in the area which now held an immense porcelain sink, a cast iron 'stove' with a 'stovepipe' connected to a second chimney, and two long handsome stained shelves for pots and lids. She was preparing potatoes for dinner that night, rubbing the dirt off in water, peeling them, and throwing the skins into the soup pot where the beef already rested with its complement of herbs. The repetitive nature of the task helped her to stay calm, but she really felt as if something inside her chest was growing and growing, pushing at her throat and the backs of her eyes. Pretty soon she was hard-pressed to prevent the chuckle from escaping her lips, and a choked sort of teary laugh could be heard throughout the house.

When Alisdair returned from his lessons with Mr. Mahon for dinner at noon, he noticed it immediately. "Muirne, what's the matter?"

She saw his wee, worried face peering at her, and the pressure she had been trying to pack down came spilling out. Alisdair took the full brunt of her full-throated laughter, the tears streaming down, the high-pitched giddiness. He hesitated on the threshold to the back room, his books and satchel still in his arms. Muirne finally managed to calm herself.

"Och, Alisdair. Come here." She gave him a firm hug,

her giggles now firmly under control. "'Tis nothing. Only I think I have some good news, and I'm excited, is all. I was stewing about it on my own, and you know that does no one any good. I'm glad you've come along. No telling how long I would have been laughing to myself like a hyena." She grinned, and Alisdair's whole body sagged with relief.

"Good, then. I thought you'd lost your wits."

"No, ma wee man. Just happy. How were your lessons this morning? Here, slice off some of this." She shoved the crusty loaf of bread she'd made that morning and he sheared off two slices for each of them. She took the knife and did the same with the rich cheese kept under cloth with the eggs, in the standing cabinet also newly introduced to the back room kitchen. She grabbed a few more sticks of kindling and thrust them into the iron stove's belly to keep the soup going, then plucked a couple of the honey oat sweets she'd set to dry and brought them with her into the main part of the house.

Brother and sister held a happy session over their midday dinner.

"Mr. Mahon says as how I've got good basics but no exposure."

"Exposure?"

"Aye. He means I've not read anything, which is true. But I do know some of the Bible."

"True, though Neil has had a task getting you to concentrate on it."

Alisdair fidgeted. "I know. It just seems pointless." He crinkled his brows up at her, and she knew exactly what he was getting at.

"If you are thinking because of Edward's way of think-

ing, I'll let you forgo your Christian catechism, you'll
have—"

"Fine. I'll not do what he did. But I'll be happy to get
some other reading." He reached down to get a book out
of his bag. "Like this one."

He brandished the book. It was unseemly in its opu-
lence: a rich red binding, gold on the edges of the pages,
and a satin ribbon attached for a place marker.

"He gave it you to read?"

"Course! Didna think I'd steal it, did you?"

"Is it for you to take home while you help Neil?"

"Aye. So I don't waste away." Alisdair said it with a
rakish grin that was new for him, Muirne noted. It revealed a level of irony that he'd never exhibited before.

"Let me see that," she said. He handed it over and she
read. "*The Parish Register*. George Crabbe. Have you started it, then?"

"Only the first few pages. Mr. Mahon wrote some
comments on the front part, so's I'd be able to understand the rest better."

Muirne opened and read the beginning lines. She
could read and write, and proud of it she was, but the
sentences didn't seem to make sense. There were too
many words she didn't recognize. She handed it back.
"Well, nae doubt you'll make quick work of it, and quicker progress."

Alisdair didn't seem to notice her flustered dismissal.
She pulled him to her and kissed the side of his head
roughly.

"I'm aiming to make Mam proud," he said, looking at
the floor. "And you." Muirne's heart caught at that. He
must be feeling some of the pall around the slow progress

of the investigation, even though they tried not to speak of it in front of him.

"You will, lad." She winked and the mood lightened. She felt the weight of her own news shifting. She felt calmer, more secure in it. Her hopefulness for Alisdair spilled over into more for her own house. She sent Alisdair out to tend the orchard trees in the back, which needed pinching off, while she checked on the soup. It burbled away, so she felt safe preparing the tallow for dipping, as they would be out of candles soon.

*Even when you buy so many of the necessities, there is still so much work to do.Well, at least I won't have the bleeding to worry about laundering for a while,* she thought, laughter threatening to burst forth again.

That evening, she'd put up the candles and perfumed the air afterward with old sachets of lavender at the big homey hearth. The smell of the citrusy smoke was pleasing. It almost reminded her of home on the croft. She tried to keep the other memories at bay—the loud crackling of fire, the screams of her mother, the pain in her arms as she'd tugged to pull their loom through the doorway—but they closed in.

She nearly missed the stool as she closed her eyes and sat down abruptly. She teetered and grabbed for the sides of it, and held on with a firm grip as she remembered. Being thrown out. Into the darkness. The neighbors gone already, and Neil and Gillan far away.

She curled over on the seat, no longer smelling the lavender smoke. A low keening moan came from her throat, and she couldn't breathe normally. There was a crash off to her right and she couldn't look up, felt too ashamed. Then there were arms around her. When the memory had shuddered out and faded, she blinked. Several times. There was Edward. She smelled him before she turned her head to look: a musky scent, unmixed with the soil. There was her husband, his work bag and coat abandoned on the floor.

"Darling," he said softly. "What's the matter? Are you ill? Has something happened?"

She shook her head, and saw Alisdair standing on the other side of her, in the doorway to the back. His face looked miserable again. "I heard you but I didn't know what to do," he said. His eyes flitted to Edward's, apologizing, back to Muirne's, desperate for reassurance. Muirne pulled herself together.

"I'm sorry," she said. A hiccup escaped, and then a giggle. "I've been up and down all day. First with laughter, now with tears." She drew a deep breath, and then another. She squeezed Edward's hand on her arm. "How long have you been here?"

"Only a few minutes. A short-lived tempest. So, nothing is wrong? What happened?" He looked perplexed now, rather than pained.

"The smoke from the candles, I just—I just got scared for a moment, is all." She avoided Alisdair's eyes. When she did look up, it was at Edward. "It's past. I'm sorry for worrying you both. I have had a very pleasant day, in fact. Alisdair had a good lesson as well, I believe. And what about you? How was the round of visits today?"

A tight smile flashed onto Edward's face. "Well, I had hoped for better. There seems to be some general reserve about me, but I can't imagine what it could be." He rose and paced away from Muirne on her stool, then turned to face her. "I've been as forthright as I could in my answers about my scientific beliefs, but there seems to be another line of questioning surrounding you that I don't quite follow."

"Me?" Muirne was astonished.

"Yes. And your brother. Not you," he said, when Alisdair's chin also jerked backward in surprise. "Neil."

Muirne gazed wonderingly at both of them. Is this why Neil had been so on edge yesterday? Something about the washerwoman starting trouble. What could she have said about them? That they didn't wash their own linens? What could she possibly have said about her straight-as-an-arrow brother?

Edward shook his head back at her. "I know. I haven't the faintest either. But we'll have to get to the bottom of it, or I'll not have any patients, and therefore not much of a practice. In the meantime I'll make the rounds out Middle River way. They should be thankful enough to have anyone attending out there," he said, with a grunt. Muirne felt the burgeoning resentment in his slight change of tone.

The uncalled-for prejudice was hard to dismiss, and they ate their supper quietly. If no one trusted Edward as their doctor, either they would have to move or he would have to find a different profession. They couldn't really afford to wait on people's opinion changing, unless they asked for more money from Ed's parents, which she knew he'd be loathe to do.

*But a child on the way.* Muirne felt a chill. She thought of Neil's comment about someone starting trouble; the chill felt like a whisper of another great storm.

# PART THREE

# Chapter 38

BY THE BEGINNING of June, Alidair was back on the ridge, and a good thing, too. It had warmed quickly and the farming duties quickly ratcheted up in importance: turning the rows, pulling the weeds, staking the edges, mounding the manure. Neil supervised the start of each task set to the boy, then returned to the cabin to check on Sheena's needs for Mam. Ever since her comment that he wasn't to worry, Neil tried not to, but she was doing the work of three women, and he couldn't help it.

A few days after Alisdair's return, Neil was helping Sheena preserve some of the mushrooms she'd foraged. He wanted to prod her a little to see whether she was adjusting to their new home. They sat on stumps by the byre, soaking up the sunshine, as they cleaned the latest batch of mushrooms gathered: the bright orange and meaty chicken-of-the-woods, now that it was deemed safe to eat, and the translucent brown and shriveled wood ears. One went into a wooden bowl for the morrow's meal, while the other was strung onto a line to dry.

"I want to try dyeing the reeds different colors and braiding them into designs. Wouldn't that be pretty, Neil?"

"Aye, very pretty. Is Mrs. MacGregor to help ye with the dyes?"

"Yes."

"Ah. That sounds well." Sheena gave him a small

moue.

He made a face right back at her, and she smiled a genuine smile.

"It is nice to have Alisdair back here," she said. "It was fair lonely with just Mam and me." Her fingers brushed at tiny bits of mud clinging to the mushroom cap. "Fewer people but the same chores. Animals still need looking after. Or killing," she added.

"Your traps?"

Sheena nodded.

"I say that's a fair show of industry. What did we catch?"

"Stoat. Already gone brown, even though the snow's still on the hills."

"Did ye toss him in the smoke shed?"

She nodded again.

Neil breathed in deeply; he relished the earthy smell of the forest floor that came with the mushrooms. He fetched the heather broom and swept around the pens as he thought.

"Almost all of us here, Sheena. And I believe you may see a turn at Muirne's before too long." Neil had to hide the grin he did not want to explain. From the looks of it, there would be children in the happy Turner household soon enough. But he could wait until he was officially told.

Sheena could help Muirne with the babe and see if anyone in town pleased her eye. But he did not want to be explaining all this to his thirteen-year-old sister; she might take it out of his skin.

His good humor was quickly checked as he thought of that shifty-eyed Jemima. Alisdair had come home from schooling with the news that Edward's practice was off to a rough start. People had been asking about *him*, about Neil! So the minx was spreading rumors about him, and damaging not him but Muirne's husband's livelihood? Not to be borne.

He'd stopped in at Tommy McClelland's, a courtesy call before leaving town, as well as a last chance to see if there was any new mail. *I'm that desperate, am I?* But it was no use fighting that inclination; it was hope, simple enough. It could well die in the next year, so Neil gave it free reign. Tommy had told him of the deplorable rumors about the Wallace women: Jemima was rumored to take in gentlemen as well as laundry; the mother was too ill in bed to discipline her daughter.

Tommy counseled him to lay low; the gossip would most likely die down. Neil had felt better that someone else believed him. He decided to follow Tom's advice, and came home to deprive the gossips of their prime target. *Starve a fire of air and it can't grow, right?* But Alisdair's unwitting report of the damage put him in an impossible position. While he could not produce evidence he hadn't been with the wretched woman, *she* could most certainly produce *evidence* that she had been with *someone*, in the form of a babe. Meanwhile, Muirne and Edward would be spending all their savings on living expenses while his medical practice failed to thrive.

But he was getting in a snit dwelling on it again. Since there was nothing he could do that would not make the situation worse, he resolved to leave it be and concentrate on the new rows to plant. Rye or barley? Rye berries were good feed; he'd had some at the MacGregors' and been pleasantly surprised. Why had they not had it back on the croft? Surely it would grow there? Well. He heard Mam call from her bed.

"Time to start on the onion beds, Neil?"

"Of course, Mam. Sheena'll help me make a start."

Sheena had almost finished the bigger mushrooms, but groaned at the reminder that there were more rows to turn over, and they were in the patch of the kailyard that was the farthest away from the house. He tried to offer her a happy thought to coax her back into a good mood.

"I'll be skinning that stoat, so if you'd like his coat to do summat with—"

"Oh yes! I've an idea going... All right, I'm going." She hopped up, brushed off her skirt, and left, grabbing the long-sleeved coat she used in the field from its hook.

Alisdair came in after Neil with pails of ice and water for the kitchen. He deposited his burdens by the hearth and went to talk to Mam, so Neil quickly put the ice down the hole, layering the chips with dried grass and moss. He fit the cover over the bucket of water to keep it clean. Then he sat, enjoying the way Alisdair peppered their mother with his thoughts. Today it was a treatise on the weakness of character evident in a man who mourned for too long. As usual, Alisdair was playing both God's and Devil's advocate, chattering while he walked circles around the table, only slightly conscious of his audience.

"So Mr. Mahon says it is a lack of manly resolve that allows the man to be lost, when, having lost an object of his love, he should rather thank God for its possession in the first place. I'm not too sure about the possession part."

"Well, this tutor sounds like he's made quite an impression," said Mam. She was much more able to concentrate in the past month, but still had trouble manipulating her limbs.

"But I thought that there should be a part about womanly resolve in there too. What you've got for Father, and what Sheena's got for home—that seems right and true. Holding onto something and thanking God for it at the same time, like. Then it's not lost like the man in the story."

Neil felt frozen by Alisdair's innocent words. Mam sensed his stillness. She reached out a hand. Neil came to his mother's side and squatted.

No, they were not lost. But he still felt on the edge, not of hunger, but of losing his purpose. He'd lost his way. Nothing seemed to come out as he meant it. The murder investigation stalled, Turner's practice the victim of gossip, Mam's health...

"It's time for tea, it is," Mam said.

Neil left her alone. He took the bucket of kindling and started feeding sticks into the fire. There were some griefs that would always be with them, no matter who was brought back to stand trial.

# Chapter 39

THE GOLDEN TIME had passed quickly, as she knew it would, but Muirne did her best to make her household a happy one. It was pleasant enough with Alisdair with them, but there was still a sort of strain. The decided lack of income was frustrating but Edward tried to ease her worries. He told her to wait, that things would get better, but after another month, they still hadn't. At least she knew he was happy she was carrying his child.

She told him in May. She gave herself a few days to privately adjust to the idea, especially after the panic of the smoke incident. Then she told Edward, one evening as they sat together by the fire after supper, Alisdair having gone to bed.

He'd said nothing at first when she told him.

"What, nothing to say?" Muirne had teased, half-worried that she had misjudged the moment. Breathlessness pressed her chest as she waited for Edward to respond to her announcement.

"I should have known, shouldn't I?" he asked. He looked surprised more than anything. "Am I neglecting you?"

"No! It's only a few days since I knew. Edward, tell me you are happy."

"Of course I am happy. I have a lovely wife who can fend off my parents with one hand and..." He grinned wickedly. "Who satisfies my desires with the other."

"Edward!" She laughed at his scandalous allusion and swatted at him.

But Edward was happy. She saw it in his slow smile, his whistles when coming and going, his extra officiousness.

Those few days after the wedding had been wrapped up in layers of slanting sunlight and fire-shadows. Muirne kept them carefully in her mind, just as she kept the wedding dress carefully folded in layers of clean linen. She would wear it again for special occasions, but not just yet. Now she worked hard to manage the house, keep Alisdair focused on his studies, and get more meat on her bones, for the baby's sake. And keep Eddie happy, but that was a simple thing.

Ed had been right about their physical relations getting easier, though. That was certainly an improvement —even if everything else lost its magic, their lovemaking seemed to grow more comfortable and somehow, more meaningful. The funny thing was that it came about because he was absent so often, for such long drags of time, because he had to call on the backcountry houses to earn any money. When he came home from his first tour of the Middle River homesteads, which took some five days, Muirne experienced the same shivery sensations upon his entering the house as she had at his kisses before the wedding. Their coupling was a relief, and a height, and a glory, and she welcomed it.

But here it was, mid-August, and she sat at table feeling the weight of a worried silence she'd not yet encountered in her husband. Edward ate slowly, staring at the center of the table, his mind occupied. Muirne fairly trembled with her need to ask him how his last week of visits had gone in the hills, but she thought she knew the answer by his face.

She gave up and forced down a few spoonfuls of the stew that she had thought smelt heavenly only an hour before. She trusted her husband; she did. She was simply coming to grips with a part of him she hadn't seen. There was a crisis, aye, but he'd figure out how to weather it. And they would have their child to sweeten their home life. The tension in her back loosened a smidge at the thought of her babe.

At four months there was still no sickness yet, but she felt a weight—her belly hadn't expanded significantly yet but there was somehow a weight centered there. An unshakeable core, like the heartwood of an oak. This made her feel more solid. It helped as she waited, watching Edward's daunting expression.

"Muirne, we've two marks against us here. I was confident of working with the first of them—that is, that my atheism could be understood—or forgiven—after some work to earn the people's trust. But this second—I believe I've found the source of it."

"Yes?"

"The questions about Neil—yes. There is some talk about him and the young woman next door to us, Jemima. That she is with child and it is his."

Muirne's hand went to her belly as she exclaimed. "That is absurd! Neil would never. He's waiting for—that is—" She did not know if she should reveal Neil's secret. Edward waited for her.

"He is waiting on a girl he knew in Glasgow. I believe they have an understanding. I haven't asked him directly, but Neil would never do something like that!"

Edward's eyes bored into hers. "*We* can know that, but no one else does. And no one I know is close enough to Neil to stand character witness. Only me, I suppose. And this isn't Tatamagouche." He blew out a sharp breath. "I will call at Bracethwaite's and try to suss out what is actually known, rather than gossip. Perhaps if I do that, the rumor will melt away. God knows some of these people are ill and need seeing to!"

Muirne, who was going to thank him, suddenly smiled.

"What is it?"

"Only, God does know." She said it gently, trying to make him see the humor in his using the phrase. But Edward didn't laugh. He closed his eyes briefly in forbearance, and then fastened them on his bowl. He shoveled his spoon into his mouth. It might as well have been gruel, as much as he savored it.

The good summer weather passed quickly: first, the lambing fair; then, the vegetable garden yielding its bounty. The berry bushes sparkled with treasures, and the fruit blossoms gave way to orchard fruits. There was a lovely surprise in the post from Muirne's Uncle Kenneth in North Carolina: a rocking chair, sent by ship up the coast. It came with a letter from her aunt, who said it was one of her favorite local customs—presenting a new wife with a rocker.

Muirne was well pleased with it and Edward, though preoccupied with their situation, was happy to see her so. And as it looked like she would carry their first child without evident trouble, that was more good fortune to be grateful for. The midwife had been by to counsel Muirne on the signs to worry about. But she hadn't been ill, and Edward's regular assessments hadn't detected anything amiss. She was still learning to deal with the awkwardness of being bigger than she thought, and was embarrassed after knocking over a piece of crockery. But her body seemed to be assuming the rest of its duties without too much complaint.

Edward still wrestled—with limited success—with the people of New Glasgow. Bracethwaite had given him nothing but dark looks when he talked to him. He had explained the situation to old Dr. Skinner, who had agreed to assist him. Now, when someone sent for a doctor, they went for the old man, who sent for Ed, and they went to the house in question together. Skinner's open acceptance of the new doctor had done a little good with the people in town, but the ones in the surrounding lands were a much tougher nut to crack. Muirne's family had been marked as bad, and Edward's practice was being tarred with the same brush.

Finally, on the last Sunday in August, Muirne persuaded him to accompany her to the kirk in town. Even though it was not her own, she could do with a bit of contact with the divine at this point. Muirne was desperate to salvage their reputation. She tried to dress as befitted her station as a doctor's wife, with only the resources of a poor doctor's wife at hand. Still, the motherly glow did much to bring people forward. They walked in together, surprising not a few heads in conversation, and sat in a pew halfway to the back. Their neighbors flicked surreptitious glances at them, observing Muirne's state—which was no secret—and Edward's affable manner. She hoped their appearance would reassure folk.

Sure enough, Muirne's smiles and open manner encouraged their neighbors to greet the couple politely. Muirne made her face as expressive as she could: it was the most she could do as his ambassador of goodwill. She knew she would be exhausted by the end of this outing. She was not overly comfortable in new social situations, and even though this was church, they were strangers. The tensions zinging through the air could have been splashed in red paint. Edward joined her in one of the small knots of conversation before the service started.

"Mr. Blackstone. How do you do? I hear you are in for a splendid summer. With the roads being upgraded, I hope you have many new customers."

The man nodded at Edward from the pew in front of them and turned to face forward again.

A turn to their right showed them another neighbor family.

"The Collinses," Edward whispered. Muirne immediately remembered his account of the father that had stood stiffly by as his little boy writhed and screamed with the colic. The man had refused to listen to Edward, and stubbornly waited on Skinner's assessment. Muirne commented on the boy's comely face.

"Such a beautiful dark blue his eyes are. And so well-behaved. Has he been at school already, young as he is? How wonderful," she gushed. The mother preened.

"Do you plan to bring him to town to tutor then, after he masters the reading and writing? My wife's brother——" Edward began.

"Thank you, Ma'am. He gets his eyes from my mother——beautiful, she were."

"Of course," Muirne murmured. She smiled down at the child, hiding her dissatisfaction at the way they were treating her husband. Cutting him. It stuck in her craw that they did it in their own church. *What hypocrites.* She glanced at Edward. He no longer smiled but pursed his lips in a frown. He would come out of this better if he'd keep up the smile, or at least a gentlemanly passivity. See if it shook any apples loose from the cart.

Muirne listened intently to the readings and the sermon. When she glanced over at Edward at a particularly compelling passage, his face was flushed red and hot. His lips were pressed into a thin line. She faced forward again, hoping Edward would survive the singing and sermon without exploding in frustration. She was almost afraid to ask him what he was feeling being back in a church. Did even being present make him this furious?

After the service, Muirne tried to focus on the purpose of her visit and engage in more conversations. She thought she'd won him a few grudging acceptances, but they wouldn't know until the family called Edward for help. If it took too long, they might have hardened against him again. If only one could call down a catastrophe, as Moses in the Book. The thought of Edward with a bushy white beard and snapping black eyes made Muirne smile, which fortunately the Hexhams took as agreement with their point about the Natives needing to be put down again.

"Maybe you'll turn soldier, eh, Mr. Turner?" asked Mr. Hexham snidely.

Muirne noted the absence of his professional title of doctor.

"Perhaps, if the soldiers are in need of a medical professional, and the fighting is truly necessary. But I don't think the Mi'qmaq—"

"Aye, well, you don't live close enough. We're up east, close to Merigomish. We come down every month for service. I tell ye, they're planning something, those sly devils. Begging yer pardon, ma'am." Mr. Hexham touched his cap to Muirne. His own wife evidently did not warrant that courtesy, inured to his language as she must be.

"Do you also send down this far for a doctor? That's a long way in time of need."

"Ah no, we've a doctor up there right enough. Mr. Smithson, it is. A great gowk of a man."

Finally, Muirne and Edward detached themselves from the milling crowd, nodding as they passed the minister. The man, a curate named Pierce, stared sallowly at them as a woman of the congregation whispered in his ear. She silently watched them pass by as well. Unnerving.

The man had performed his office well enough, but Muirne could not allow this foray to become a defeat. She murmured an excuse to Edward and marched straight back to the curate.

"Good afternoon, sir. I was very impressed by your sermon. My husband was too. Won't you come and meet him? He is the town's new doctor."

Pierce took his eyes off Edward and looked at Muirne after she finished speaking.

"How do you manage to live under the roof of a *heathen*?" he spat out. "And you with your sinner of a brother. Excuse me, Mrs. Turner, I must ask that you leave with your husband, for the good of the church."

Muirne's mouth hung open in shock. She felt suddenly vulnerable, in front of all those neighbors watching. She nodded gravely to the odious man and went back to collect Edward. He ushered her out gracefully. She leaned on him heavily all the walk home.

They entered their own door, and Muirne fell into the large chair by the hearth. Edward raked the coals to get a fire going again, while Muirne stayed with her elbow on her knee, her head on her fist.

"Darling," Edward started. She turned away, still trying to master her worry. People were scorning *her* for *his* atheism and *him* for *her brother* being a scoundrel. One was a lie and the other...she'd thought she could understand.

"You are such a soldier," he said gently. "I never expected this to be taken out on you. I'm so sorry."

He finished stoking up the fire, adding kindling to bring it to a roar. Muirne looked up at him, glassy-eyed. She reached out her hand to him. He took it reverently.

"For better, for worse," she said. "Besides, MacLeans have been treated much worse." She broke eye contact and rose from the chair, moving away from the compassion in his eyes.

# Chapter 40

IN EARLY OCTOBER, Alisdair came back for lessons with Mr. Mahon. When he arrived, Muirne, now with a sizable belly, told him to put away his things and go out back. He blinked at her, surprised at her abrupt demand, a departure from her usual pattering of news, but he went. Muirne smiled as he walked out.

When he returned, his hands were full of small apples, streaked with red and yellow, that had fallen from their two trees. His eyes shone as he carefully corralled them into a bucket by the back kitchen. Muirne laughed at his childish wonder. He was as delighted as she had been, when she first saw that someone else had laid out such riches for their present enjoyment.

He crunched into one, and Muirne held up a finger.

"One only. Fetch me some more so I can make a pie tonight. I'm happy you're back, ye wee scamp. How long does Neil say ye should stay?"

"Neil says 'til St. Andrew's Day would be enough, as I'm to help him with timber carry over winter. It's nice being part of two places, it is." Muirne let the warmth of the boy's smile seep into her bones.

The position of Edward's practice had not shifted much after their churchgoing, but Muirne held out hope that people would trust her husband as a doctor, and stop all this pointless suspicion. As for the charge against her brother—well! She'd seen that girl Jemima in the street a few times over the past weeks, and cut her very purposely. It wasn't worth being civil, when your own livelihood was being threatened.

Muirne hadn't written of the accusation to Neil in her letters home, which went quickly to and fro in the fair weather. She had wanted to make it disappear before revealing the gross baseness of such a claim. But the rumor was being stubborn. People were stubborn. *Maybe Alisdair will help make a good impression too*, she thought. He crunched right through the apple, making a wry face as his teeth wrestled with the core. He worked the fruit around his tongue and spoke with his mouth full.

"Do you eat the seeds, too?"

"I suppose not, less'n you want an apple tree growin' in yer belly," she said.

Alisdair stretched back his lips in a smile that didn't show teeth, and spit them into his hand. "Nah, but I will take 'em back to plant over Sheena's patch."

"What a lovely idea! Our croft garden, shaded by a colonial apple tree."

She made the promised pie that evening, and the mood lifted a little. The baby was being restless, kicking at all hours. *Well, no, not all hours; just those ones while I'm trying to sleep*, Muirne mused wryly. *Wee beggar.*

Alisdair asked questions about what it would be like when the baby came.

"Will it have hair?"

"Some do; some don't. Mam says none of us did. You came out like a wee mushroom, your bald head the roundest I'd ever seen." Alisdair snickered at that.

"Do ye ken if it's a boy or a girl yet?"

"Nay, but I think it's a boy. From the kicking."

"Who will be here to help ye?"

"I wish Mam could but even if she was herself again, there probably wouldn't be time. By the time I know, the babe would be born before she could make it down, if everything goes the usual way."

*The usual way. Aye, and who could bloody well say what that was?* She wasn't worried, to speak of. She was married to a doctor, for goodness' sake! She should be fine. *And if I start having my pains when he's out on one of the long rounds he does because people around here won't pay him? What then?* But she put such thoughts away from her when Alisdair was about, as he was almost as quick as Neil to discern her unease.

The conversations over supper among the three of them went on routinely until St. Andrew's Day. She allowed Alisdair to remain an extra few days while the weather held clear, as he had made two friends his age in town. The boy was just asking permission to go out into the soft, virgin snow with them one early December afternoon when Muirne felt her first labor pain. And sure enough, Edward had judged one last loop of the southern territory passable before her time would come.

Muirne sent Alisdair out to get word to the ridge, but told him to come straight back after he'd passed on the short message. She was torn between needing someone to stay by her, and wanting to save her wee brother the pain of seeing her in what she knew would be a harrowing experience. Alone... Between her waves of blinding pain, she tried to reassure him by explaining that it wouldn't be as bad as it sounded. But as soon as he seemed settled, and his little face set, she would have to release his hand so as not to crush it.

*Is this the usual way? Should I send Alisdair for Dr. Skinner? How long has it been?*

Alisdair checked out the side window, judging it to be about four o' the clock.

*God, am I saying all this out loud?* "Go, go for the midwife, then, Alisdair. I need someone."

He burst out the front door like a shot.

Much sooner than she anticipated, his blonde head popped back into view, followed by the midwife, Mrs. Aggons.

"She was jus' next door, Muirne!"

The tall, pale woman nodded. "Aye, ye are both coming at the same time. She's late; you're early." She looked straight at Muirne. "I don't care about all the whispers. I'm just after delivering healthy babes, no matter whose they be. So. Let's see then." She waved Alisdair out of the bedroom and Muirne finally collapsed onto the bed after pacing around the main room for an hour in restless agony.

She didn't want to scream. But the pain kept getting worse and worse. And then unbearable, so that she held her breath, sure she would split in two. Mrs. Aggons kept telling her to take deep breaths, but she kept forgetting, or couldn't hear until too late. She fainted and was jolted back to consciousness by the midwife's *sal volatile*, time and time again. She'd never smelt the stuff before.

"It's both your first times, you know," Mrs. Aggons said some time later, when Muirne was holding onto a breath again. The information didn't enter into Muirne's head, full as it was of the pain erupting between her hip bones and up her lower back like a firebrand. The woman kept popping in and out of the room, returning with warm, wet cloths each time. The midwife spent a good quarter-hour at a time with the woman in each house, doing several rounds of back and forth before finally taking a break herself.

Later, Alisdair would tell her he watched it all from the hearth-seat, and when he couldn't stand the screaming, he went down to the very bottom of the yard, below the apple trees, where there was a small settle. He curled himself into a ball and lay on his back in the crisp leaves, rocking side to side, gazing at the leaden grey evening sky darken to black. He willed the clouds and wind to hurry Edward back, so he could fix everything.

# Chapter 41

WHEN ALISDAIR'S MESSENGER came, Sheila didn't even hear the man finish panting out his message before she flung herself from her bed. Neil hurried to help her out of her contorted flail.

"Mam, you can't go. You're not well," he said.

With his help, Sheila sat on the edge of the box bed. She held onto the wooden edge with the hand that obeyed her.

"Neil, she's my daughter."

Her heart was breaking. Her body was useless in helping her daughter give birth. She looked to her kit of dried herbs and salves on the table, bundled and made ready by Sheena at her direction. She wouldn't make it down in time. Muirne was out of her reach, unhelpable, just as she believed Sheena had been when she had her fall. It was painful to realize that she was living past her usefulness. She could no longer protect her family, no longer care for them in the way she knew how. She was stuck here, a burden. She started to cry.

"Mam, no. Please don't. We'll go. We'll all go. I'll ask the MacGregors for their horse and we'll be down the mountain in a flash."

Neil sought to comfort her. He was a good boy. But so far from understanding her fears. She looked to Sheena, who stood nearby and watched. She was growing up into a sharp young woman. She hoped she would be alive to see her find her own home as Muirne had done.

"Let me get you some of the willow-bark tea," Sheena said. With two of her children hovering, she assented. She clutched the tea cup with her good hand. Neil ran out toward their neighbors. Sheena rubbed soft circles over her back.

Sheena then began adding to Sheila's kit on the table. The new caps she had woven under Sheila's supervision. The wee jumpers she had sewn from some castaways of the Turners' linens. The miniature bed Neil had crafted by stretching bear sinew across a wood frame. Sheena packed it all carefully and wrapped it in rough linen. She flung two ropes across the bundle and tested them against her shoulders and hips.

The girl looked up and saw Sheila watching her. She bounced once with the pack on her back. "Look like it'll stay put?" she asked.

"Aye," Sheila replied. *My brave, clever girls.* She finished her willow-bark tea and felt a little bit of release in her rigid hand. "Come here to me, Sheena."

Sheena set the pack down and sat by her mother's good side. As they waited for Neil to return with the horse, Sheila put her arm around her and sang to her the old cradle song in a musical whisper.

*Baloo, baloo, my wee wee thing,*
*O saftly close thy blinkin' e'e!*
*Baloo, baloo, my wee wee thing,*
*For thou art doubly dear to me.*
*Thy daddie now is far awa',*
*A sailor laddie o'er the sea;*
*But hope ay hechts his safe return*
*To you my bonnie lamb an' me.*

The family arrived in New Glasgow the next day, as the autumnal evening light made the white stones of the road glow. They barged in the door where a silence greeted the loud bang. Sheila's eyes rolled at the implications of such a silence, but Alisdair quickly poked his head out from the bedroom. He saw who it was, and ran to his mother's arms.

"Got to be quiet, Mam. Muirne's only had a couple hours' sleep," he whispered.

"Everything all right?"

"Aye. Little one's finally asleep. Come look at her."

After assuring themselves that Muirne had not woken from the loud report of wood on wood, they crept up in rapt silence. The baby was washed and bundled, resting in one of Sheena's reed baskets on the table next to Muirne's bed.

"She's mighty reddish, but Muirne said they all start out like that, and it'll fade fast enough," Alisdair whispered to her.

"You were a lot redder than that," she replied.

"No hair," Alisdair noted, "and no teeth, neither."

"She'll get those as she grows, don't you worry. Does Muirne have a name for her yet?"

"She likes Mollie, but she wanted to wait to see if Ed agreed. He's to come back today from Middle River."

"The midwife was here, then?"

"Aye, but she was helping the woman next door at the same time. There seemed to be some sort of fuss about it."

Sheila saw Neil straighten and give Alisdair a sharp

glance.

"I don't know why everyone's been so mean to her. Even Muirne," said Alisdair.

"A fuss about a baby?" Sheila said, and clucked sadly. She passed over Neil's strange reaction and edged forward toward the basket. She stroked the baby's cheek with the back of a finger, entranced by the same texture of all babes: a little scratchy 'round the corners, angelically smooth on the curves.

"Well done, little one."


When Edward arrived home later that night, it was with a grand exclamation.

"I am a father!" he shouted, opening his arms high and wide. The welcoming party of Sheila and Alisdair, sitting together at the table, looked up first in alarm at the rumpus, then happily congratulated him.

A fretful cry went up from the bedroom, and he immediately ducked his head to play the guilty party.

"It starts," he said merrily, then crept quietly into the bedroom. They followed to observe the first meeting from the doorway.

Muirne didn't reproach him for startling the baby when he entered, but gazed on him with a tired, contented smile. "I thought you would never come, Edward. What kept you?"

"Dickinsons had a daughter ill with a rather serious throat complaint. I hurried back as soon as I could. How are you feeling, my darling girl?"

Muirne shook her head at his timing.

"You have another darling girl now: we have a daughter."

Sheila chuckled inwardly at her daughter's passing over all the hard work she'd accomplished to get to this moment. What tough stuff she was made of. She felt proud of her daughter in that minute of self-effacement.

"What do you think about Mollie for a name?" Muirne shifted her arms so the little girl faced outwards. She stopped crying and stared with inky black eyes out at him. Sheila marveled all over again at the calm face. *How like old souls they look when they first meet the world.*

"I think she likes me," Edward said, holding out a finger to trace the same curve of cheek Sheila had. A little cough, a hiccup, and Muirne turned the baby back to her chest to hold comfortably.

"A little," he amended. "Come on in, MacLeans. Look at the little wonder again. I'm sure you haven't got enough of her yet, have you, Alisdair?"

Alisdair grinned shyly and shook his head. He tiptoed in from the doorway. Sheila took a hesitant step into the small room, staying close to the wall for support. Looking at the domestic picture, she felt full of the same satisfaction she'd known birthing her own children. She felt flooded with blessings as she gazed at the bedroom scene. It was enough to still the self-pitying voice for a while.

"Muirne says the midwife was also helping with a birth next door. It made her job convenient enough, shuttling back and forth," Sheila said with good humor. "She hasn't come back yet to say how it's gone over there, but maybe we could ask."

"Uh, no," Edward said. "That won't be necessary. She was just leaving as I came home and gave me the full report. The boy is healthy. We don't need to be disturbing the mother."

Muirne pushed out her lower lip at this announcement, staring fixedly at the baby without pleasure.

Sheila looked between the two of them. "But surely it's the Christian—the *neighborly*—thing to do? After a few weeks, of course?"

Edward acknowledged her amendment with a wry smile. "Much as it may be, I would not like for it to take place. The woman has given birth to a dark-skinned baby boy. A Native father, no doubt. Which she claimed to be Neil's. Now it is safe to say she was lying." He sighed a little, then muttered, "Poor Jemima."

Sheila's pleasant haze evaporated. She was shocked by the news and had a hard time wrapping her head around the change in circumstances. There she was, pitying the wretch when she'd had the nerve to accuse Neil!

"Poor—?! Are you saying that woman has been spreading lies about my Neil?" She looked around suddenly. "Where has he gone?" Panic tautened her face.

"Neil stepped outside when we got in," Alisdair said. "Said he needed the necessary."

*All right. Calm down. We'll not have a repeat of my foolishness.* Sheila drew a breath to slow her racing heart. She felt as though she might go thrash the impudent woman next door, newly spent though she must be after giving birth. She turned to Muirne, baffled.

"You knew, and you didn't tell me?"

Muirne's eyebrows knitted together. "I wanted it to go away. I wanted to say it was no longer a problem. I didn't think Neil knew what she was saying about him. Think how hard he'd take it, after what he's gone through over Letty."

Sheila hugged one arm over the other, squinting her eyes closed, trying to see why it was always the innocent who suffered. She felt Edward's arm around her.

"What did we do?" she asked Muirne. "Why are we marked for such mischief?" Muirne had no answer for her. After a charged moment, Edward helped her into a chair out by the fire.

Edward returned to Muirne's side, sitting on a stool to watch wife and daughter in silent wonder. He leaned in to kiss Muirne's brow. Sheila watched through the doorway, feeling like a spectator to a play she no longer understood. The children were managing their own affairs. They didn't, in fact, need her. *So this is how it will go: losing little pieces of myself at a time.*

"Thank Heaven you are safe, and so is Mollie," Edward said softly. Sheila turned her face away but heard the soft smack of a kiss. Close quarters, even those of a doctor, she thought. She was glad at least they were so comfortable with each other. *But my poor Neil. Where will he find happiness?*

She heard Muirne echo Edward's words:

"Thank Heaven."

# Chapter 42

As the MacLeans meant to be all together for the eve of the new year, 1826, and as Mollie was much too young to sustain the bitter cold tramp into the mountains, they decided on Hogmanay at the Turners' home. They would all join in sharing the goodwill of the Turners with their neighbors. Bringing gifts and offering the friendly dram would help root the still-shaky foundation that bound the doctor to his new community.

The news about Jemima's dark-skinned baby had already got round. Jemima herself hadn't been seen, but Edward reported that Bracethwaite the grocer had shuffled awkwardly over when he spoke to him. The blacksmith met Muirne's eyes briefly when she placed her order for hobnails. And the seamstress who lived next door knocked on their door one afternoon to invite Muirne to tea. The signs were changing. Neil was happy to see it: the dissolution of whatever blackness his questionable conduct had wrought upon them in the town.

Neil and Sheena packed to go back to tend to the animals on the ridge, while Mam and Alisdair stayed in town for the few weeks remaining in the year. It would save Mam the arduous round trip and give Alisdair more time for his studies, which were going extremely well.

Muirne gave Neil tins of sugar, tea, and flour for the cabin's supply, substances which they would otherwise have gone without due to their cost. In the bustle around their leave-taking, Muirne slipped a small muslin bag into Neil's hand. He waited until he could open it surreptitiously and found a wooden oval frame surrounding a graceful painting of a woman's head, half turned away. The woman had black hair and a long, smooth neck.

"I saw it in the carpenter's shop and it reminded me..." Muirne whispered behind him.

Neil's Adam's apple bobbed down, then up. He turned the frame over and opened the compartment for the picture, where he found a pressed violet and a scrap of paper, which he couldn't read in the dark shadows of the hallway.

Neil closed the compartment securely and slipped it back into the muslin bag. He folded the bag over again to protect the frame, then met Muirne's eyes. In that moment, she seemed to see through his facade to the weariness and uncertainty haunting him. He squeezed her hand and dropped his gaze.

The animals were calm and everything was tidied up at the ridge for another short absence. The day before New Year's Eve, Neil made the round of their mountain neighbors, distributing the baskets of baking and preserves Sheena had made. Some of the preserves were runny, but it was the thought that counted.

Neil had to explain to the neighbors that the family would be in town for First Footing, for Heaven forbid someone tramp out in the snow to see them only to find an empty house! The MacGregors, last on the route, were, as usual, the most hospitable. Neil was still smiling and wobbly-footed by the time he reached home. When he entered the cabin, holding the doorway for a moment's support, Sheena was dressed in all her warmest clothes, clutching her colored reed baskets tied in a large plaid. She looked at him skeptically.

"You all right, Neil? Ready to go?"

"Mm-hmm," he replied in what sounded like a completely rational manner to him.

"Right. Well, could you help me settle this on my back? I've eleven made. I want to knock on doors and see if anyone has a mind to buy them for threepence, first thing tomorrow morning. That'll do, won't it? Good timing, with people having money from Hogmanay and all?"

Neil blinked and tried to clear his mind of its fuzzy icicles.

"Aye, I think you stand a fair chance of turning a profit."

"Shall we go, then?"

"Why don't we use the sled? It'll get us downhill by the river much faster," Neil said.

"Do you know how to stop it?" Sheena countered.

"Well enough. It can be driven by your weight, how you lean. I've tried it."

Sheena narrowed her eyes at her brother. "You're sure?"

With a salesman's smile, Neil convinced her. They loaded everything onto the sled and dragged it the half-mile to the river, whose surface was frozen at least two feet thick. Neil and Sheena each took a side and pushed with a leg when the slope wasn't steep enough to do the work. Sheena clutched the cargo on her right side and laughed as the wooden runners slipped along the icy path. Neil laughed right along with her; it was exhilarating.

When they ran out of river, they divided the ropes and trudged up the river bank to the road through New Glasgow. After Neil unloaded the sled, they trooped in. It had indeed got them to town much faster: it was merely nine o' the clock, but it would have been deep blackness were it not for the waning light of a two-thirds moon.

Sheena, with her baskets still in a great lump on her back, carefully collapsed in the middle of the room. She needn't have bothered; she was slight enough that she couldn't crush them. She shrugged off the rope running round her shoulders and Neil helped pull the parcel away as she scrambled back up.

"Ye'll have worked hard enough fer yer profits, won't ye now?" Neil said with a grin.

"Even with the moose hide gloves you made me— they are wonderful warm, mind—but the string bags do have their bite."

Garbled noise from the two bedrooms tumbled out to the main room. Alisdair came out from their left, rubbing his eyes and scratching his bum.

"We didn't think you'd be here until tomorrow!"

"Aye," said Edward, emerging from their right. "And I barely managed to get him to bed as it is," he said, pointing an accusatory finger at the lad. "Getting too tall, you are," he added.

Alisdair, who only came to his brother-in-law's elbow, tried to stretch a bit taller.

There was hugging and exclaiming for a good five minutes more, which included Muirne, who stood in her shift, shawl, and stockings, holding the baby out for the last of the MacLeans to see.

Sheena didn't reach out her arms to take the baby but

peered at it closely. Neil had to make an effort not to laugh.

"She looks healthy," she said. Sheena nodded a little at Mollie, then smiled at Muirne. She looked utterly unen-raptured.

*So Sheena is none sae interested yet in babies. Weel, plenty o' time for that!* Neil chuckled to himself. After the brief ruckus, they all settled down to feign sleep again, visions of First Footings playing in their heads. For this was the main celebration of winter, when all households would await a tall, dark-haired man to cross their threshold and bring good luck for the new year. He was supposed to bring a coin, salt, and whisky for the house, but the Turn-ers were stocked with plenty of rum punch in case the weather turned bitter and the First Footers ran out of drink.

# Chapter 43

SHEENA WOKE MANY times in the short time allotted for sleep that night, wondering about their fortune for the new year. *Bliannath Mhath Ur*. Happy New Year. She finally woke for good, feeling strangely suspended—light-limbed. She rose eagerly and put on her heavy layers, shucked only five or six hours before. She didn't want to start the fire going and wait for water to boil, so she would wait to break her fast until after her first round of knocking on doors. She lit a candle from the coals and placed it in a holder, then grabbed her hoard of baskets. She gathered the loops of the baskets in the complicated manner she'd practiced and stepped outside the front door.

She looked first left: messy snow sparkled in the purple dawn. She saw some chimneys belching thin tendrils of smoke, heard some sheep bleating and metal clanging farther down. It was hard to tell from where, as the wide road wound downward and turned quickly east. She looked right: no stirrings next door, less sound in general.

*Very well, then. My path is clear.* Sheena leaned forward about forty degrees to balance her load and faced left. She crunched through the snow with her still-damp moose hide slippers. She took six carefully balanced steps to get to the first door. She glanced back at the other neighbor. Neil had warned her away from one of them, and she was pretty sure it was the one on the right, but she was suddenly unsure.

She summoned a bright smile, and knocked quietly. A moment later, a woman with grey and white hair opened the door. She held her own candle up to Sheena's face. Before she could get a word out, the woman shooed her inside and shut the door.

"Don't want to let the warmth out, dearie. Now, what is it you need?"

Sheena gaped. She blinked and heaved her bundle around to show her purpose. "I've made these nice reed baskets, for folk who want to go a-visitin'. Here's one," she said, and pulled out the top one of the muddled stack. It had a wide, shallow bottom, with two sides raised and two sides flat.

"It would be good for flowers or something long like kindling. And there's this one," she said, pulling out another, this one with a small, enclosed basket and a handle dyed to a dark carmine. "Good for egg-collecting, I was thinking, but also for gifts." Sheena glanced uncertainly at her hostess, unsure of her reception.

The woman also looked a bit stupefied. "You're not here for a commission then, but to sell to *me*! Oh, Lord!" She laughed heartily, a throaty, gutsy quality that Sheena's had never heard before. She smiled, charmed by the freedom of it. "I'm so used to the last-minute fixes and fasteners that I forgot myself." She sighed and smiled at Sheena.

"I'm Prosperity, but folk call me Possie. Suits me better than the other, I think." She made a wry face. "And I'm the best seamstress in the town. I support myself since my husband died last year. Importer, he was, but none too successful, poor man. I met your sister and her husband when they came to call, but I was busy so we didn't have a proper talk yet. It is your sister next door, eh? You both have the lovely lilt of the Isles."

Sheena still felt a little bewildered, but after a few minutes of talk, became more at ease. *Why, she's just like the church ladies from home, the fishers' wives.* They had a polite chat, but Sheena, realizing her time to garner her profit was slipping away, soon made an excuse to be going.

"What about that one?" Possie pointed to a small basket on the side of the pile. It was almost entirely closed, as Sheena had dared herself to keep going on it, making it somewhat odd-looking, but useful for keeping small things hidden. "I'll take it for sixpence," Possie said with finality.

"I'll sell it for that," Sheena said, trying to sound calm but inwardly rejoicing. Doing business like this was like getting one over on the other person, but with both knowing very well what was going on. *That must be often how things work.*

She sold all of the baskets she'd made, and by nine o'clock was home feasting on breakfast, telling the story to Alisdair in front of their fire. Her brother's eyes were round as moons as she told him.

"Whatcha goin' to do with the money, Sheena?"

Sheena flashed back to the moment when Neil had asked her what she wanted. She liked the idea of weaving the plaids like her mother had on their loom back home but she wondered whether it would now be impossible to learn, with Mam so helpless as she was. She took care of her and helped her out to the privy, so she knew how little balance she had after her fall. That fall was still a unique moment—Sheena felt the whisper of ghosts whenever she recalled the sight of Mam tumbling down the trail and then vaulting forward to land, splat, on the level ground.

"Buy a new loom," she whispered. *So what if it's impossible. I don't want to lose this part of us, too.*

Muirne was talking with their mother in the back kitchen, preparing for the evening festivities, but still she kept her voice low. "For when Mam gets better, see."

Alisdair nodded. "Aw! I want to do something, too!"

They stopped whispering as Neil came in from the cold with kindling. He gave them a brief glance then proceeded to layer the wood on the fire. When he'd gone, Sheena whispered again.

"I've made thirty-six shillings today, Alisdair. We'll have that loom by May-Day!"

They grinned, thoroughly unsuccessful at hiding their glee. Neil turned his head to watch them next time he entered the room. A creeping smile transformed his face. He stuck his tongue out at Alisdair, who obligingly reciprocated.

Soon enough, the family was all congregating in the main room to celebrate the day. Muirne added spices to their big pot of punch on the fire, and Edward lugged a small keg of beer into place for the adults. Everyone got a dollop of whisky in their tea at noon. It made things lively, homely, and as their tongues loosened, their cares floated away.

# Chapter 44

THE FAMILY DOZED, crockery on the table, gifts scattered in laps and hands and on the floor. The fire was silent, a mass of glowing charcoal. Snow on the ground outside deadened any sound, and the wee house hugged its occupants like a cocoon, keeping them warm and satisfied for a time. There had been singing and dancing until around ten, when the early alcohol had started to take its toll. Neil figured the young ones would need a rest to be able to stay up the night, and closed his own eyes for a wee nap as well.

A couple hours later, they began to rouse, stretch, and peer at each other through slitted, contented eyes. A knock came on the door. Neil shot up at once.

"Not yet?" he boomed in mock dismay. Everyone straightened their clothes and positioned themselves to greet their first visitor. Mam was smiling, a little lopsidedly, as Sheena and Alisdair shimmied and jiggled with excitement.

Mam shooed Muirne forward, as mistress of the house, to do the honors. Neil motioned Edward ahead and stood behind the two of them as Muirne opened the door. In front of them stood Jemima, shivering in a brown hooded woolen cloak, her hair completely hidden in a plain, sandy-colored cap, her white neck bare.

"I've come to beg pardon, afore the new year, for the wrong I did ye."

Neil's mind went strangely blank. He felt no anger at this pale vulnerable creature at their door, even after the trouble she'd caused Edward and Muirne. They were getting on fine now, but Jemima surely was not. He remembered the way her hot breath had felt on his neck, sitting out back of the house; it was curiously connected with the queer feeling in his belly from the moonshine she'd given him. He pulled himself back into the present. He hadn't done anything wrong. Oh, but he'd wanted to.

Jemima's brown eyes pierced the darkness of the passageway to find Neil's. He felt the need to clear his throat, but stayed still. Jemima's gaze drifted slowly back to Muirne.

"I—I was in a bad way and had no one to help me, and I just panicked. I'm sorry for how all the folk treated ye—I heard about it. Feelin' it myself, now."

The three of them in the hall stayed silent. From behind them, Sheena piped up, "Is it the new year, then?"

And Alisdair, "Is he tall and dark? Darker than Da?"

Their laughter, for Gillan had been blond, echoed out into the night.

"I'm sorry to bother you," Jemima said. "I just— didn't want to have bad blood between us into the new year. Sorry," she mumbled. She turned away and stumbled into the street's darkness. Neil stayed locked in place, his throat feeling more and more strangled, and a little of the heat of resentment coming up to flush his face.

"She's not staying next door anymore?" Edward asked from behind Muirne.

"Door's been crooked for weeks. Haven't you noticed?" Muirne cocked her head to the side to reproach Edward, then looked out again.

"Where's your son?" she shouted to the retreating figure, already invisible except for the light cloth of her tightly wrapped cap, which glowed like the snow.

"With his father," a strangled voice called back.

Neil observed all this back-and-forth with mounting apprehension. Was this to be their last taste of the old year? Bitterness and resentment and putting a poor, starved creature from their door? *What does she mean, anyway, about the father? Back to the tribe? Is that where she's gone?*

Mam's voice from the main room startled them.

"Don't you think you should invite our visitor in? Close the door! We're letting all that lovely heat out."

Plainly she had no idea who was at the door. Muirne looked at Edward. Edward looked at Neil. Other voices from the main room joined Mam's as they started up a song to welcome the First Footer, choosing the last one sung before they had fallen into a drowse:

*I will twine thee a bower*
*By the clear siller fountain*
*And I'll cover it o'er*
*With the flowers of the mountain*
*I will range through the wilds*
*And the deep glens sea dreary..."*

Neil finally spoke.

"Aye, go on back in. It's not yet midnight. I'll just— go out and have a word with her. Make sure she's got somewhere to go."

Muirne flashed a look of incredulity at her brother. "No, I'll do it. No one can suspect *me*—"

"No. Muirne, stay here. I'll only be a moment."

She looked back at him. The happy voices were quickly hushed as Edward went back to tell them it was a false alarm. The silence hung upon them. Neil didn't need Muirne's permission, but he looked back at her, willing her to understand that this was his own business. He cleared his throat, finally.

"All right. But tread careful, Neil."

"Of course. Now go on."

There was a little moonlight, and some torches were out already—it must be very near midnight. He looked both ways, up and down the street. Down, he saw lights, so he turned the other way. The barest glow of blue-white movement convinced him.

"Miss Jemima," he called in a low voice after a few strides. "I'm walking in your footsteps. I can see you there, by the smithy." He couldn't see her face, but he imagined her anguish: trying to do right by them after doing wrong, feeling repulsed and rejected, having nowhere to go. It was how his family had felt leaving the croft, during their bone-chilling journey through Glencoe to find him.

When he caught up to her, they both shifted awkwardly in place with their feet, pacing down the snow. His feet in their leather boots were already turning into blocks of ice. She wore only low slippers. She wouldn't look at him, but clutched her cloak tight, gazing down, like an errant child waiting for punishment.

"I forgive you," he said softly.

She still didn't look up, but he saw her hand fly to her face, the palm wiping eyes and nose so that the tears and mucus wouldn't freeze.

"I don't deserve it," she said in a voice low with self-disgust. Then her words tumbled out in spurts and he thought she might be trying not to cry. "I just thought that I should get it off my chest—I didn't mean any harm to come to ye—before the old year is out. Superstitious cow, my mother was. I thought it might help me in the new year." Her words were sullen but her voice itself held no hope.

Neil steeled himself. "Your mother's passed away?"

She nodded, barely. "Last month. A fever."

"I'm sorry."

He didn't know this girl well enough to know if she had truly repented of her mistake but he wanted her, and himself, to be free of the burden.

"And your baby is with the Mi'qmaq at the lake?"

The shaking young woman made an extreme effort to stop her hiccups and sniffles. She drew herself up; the sullenness disappeared.

"They took him, when the rumors reached 'em that an Indian baby'd been born." She raised her eyes to his then. "The man I was with, he's gone. It's his brother who's taken Charlie. They won't tell me where the boy's father went." She cleared her throat; her manner became brusque.

"Anyway, it's midnight. Time for new blessings. New brooms for old rubbish. That's me. Go on back to your family now." She tried to smile jauntily at him, a scarecrow of her former self.

It wasn't his battle. The little heat of resentment on Muirne's behalf that had pushed him out the door was gone. He felt sad that things had turned out this way, because in other circumstances he might have got used to her rough tongue and enjoyed her company. He bid her blessings in the new year and turned back with a heavy heart. Candles were now displayed in the windows of their house. He glanced at the house next door, where no light shone, and the door hung off-kilter. Perhaps he would speak to the minister.

If it was midnight, he didn't want to knock and be the family's first caller, fair-haired as he was. He snuck around to the back by the alley, glancing through the window that Jemima had climbed through. His family was huddled together. When he came through the back, everyone jumped. He gave a weak smile.

"Now we just have to wait, eh? Got the whisky out, and the black bun and shortbread? Good."

And, ignoring the worried looks on his sister's face, he braved through another tainted First Footing.

# Chapter 45

WHEN THEY WOKE next morning, the sun was already squinting down through thick clouds. Stiff muscles creaked and heads were fuzzed with cotton. They'd had a good First Footing, after all: the big man who ran the smithy had been the one charged with walking all up and down their street, and they'd been included, which was no small thing. He'd been welcomed six times by the time he made it to the Turner-MacLean household, and big as he was, still had to be stuffed with food before swallowing the dram offered him.

The morning stillness hung on well past the faint winter light's coming. Everyone was slow, but no one would be judged for it. Neil managed to avoid the curious looks from his family but there was restraint as they quietly cleaned up scraps from the feasting and put away the bedding. He hadn't yet told anyone about the words he'd exchanged with Jemima last night, instead choosing to focus on the joyous energy of the New Year.

After everyone broke their fast by enjoying the stovies made of last night's leavings, the MacLeans started packing up to head back to the forest. Neil intended to get some more timbering done before the next big storm. While they were saying their goodbyes, Muirne made a move to get Neil's attention; she would be wanting to hear what had passed between him and Jemima. Before Neil could decide what he wanted to share, there was a loud knock at the door.

Edward went to answer it this time. There was a muted conversation, then Edward returned with a rough-looking fellow. "This is Mr. Carson," Edward said. It was the same Carson who had given Neil directions to Drexel's office in Amherst.

Neil offered his hand. "Good to see you again, Mr. Carson. What can we do for you? Blessings of the new year?" he asked.

The man looked tired, and did not smile at this remark. "I've missed out on Hogmanay this year, sir, on your account, so I'd be thankful if you didna remind me of it. I've come with news you'll not like."

"Shall we speak in here?" Neil gestured, indicating the table. Other members of the family found seats and ranged themselves around the men.

"Much obliged for a bit o' tea," said Carson. Muirne shot up and went to the back kitchen, returning with a mug of the hot beverage. Ed picked up the brown bottle of whisky, almost depleted from the night before.

"Aye, a wee tot. Thank'ee, sir," said Carson. Mug in one hand, he used the other to yank from his pack a sheaf of documents. "Will you want the whole family around to hear?" Carson squinted at Neil.

Neil nodded.

"Right. These is my investigations into the assault and murder of Gillan MacLean."

Alisdair started, but Mam reached down from her stool to take his hand in hers.

"I'm afraid that man Brown has too much influence. He scared the witness after Drexel showed his hand and sent in an investigator. Me. The witness is a clerk at Ford's

Mills. He was nervous at first, when he told me about overhearing Brown's order, but I heard him say it plain as day. When I come back with seal and paper, he was shaking, sayin' he never said nothin'. I wrote what I heard, to piece together the parties involved, but it ain't worth nothin' without the witness' signin' that there affidavit."

He paused as Neil perused the documents. It was a lot of loops and curls, blots and fragments, and Neil found it hard to concentrate after hearing the dispiriting news. He handed them to Edward after scanning the contents.

"Mr. Drexel won't be able to pursue this Brown. He sent me to give you this conclusion to the case, anyway, so you'd know what happened, and a bit of why. As for pinning it to the bastard, I'd say you're stuck."

Edward was reading the words more carefully, trying to sort out the man's chicken scratch into what might be legally binding language. Muirne spoke from the chair by the window.

"Didn't James MacLachlan consult a solicitor for us last year, who helped us with the property deeds?"

Neil nodded. "Yes, but this solicitor had the advantage of being closer and more immediately reachable. However, I think we may have come to the end of our association with Drexel. It's time to venture back to Pictou. We'll start with MacLachlan." He turned to the messenger, who had the mug tipped back vertically to get the last of his drink. "Thank you for your trouble, Mr. Carson."

Carson slammed down the mug and exhaled loudly. "Aw, yer all right. I'll be goin' home now." And he heaved his pack up and disappeared without a further word.

"Will we go home together, Neil?" Mam asked him. She looked scared. He wanted to reassure her but felt that delaying the trip to Pictou any longer would not help them.

"We'll go together——" His throat abruptly closed on the last word, and he turned away. Muirne stood and came over to him. He was remembering those final weeks, final moments, when he had felt so much guilt for splitting up his family. Gillan had gone west to the cities in the faith that the family would follow, while Neil stayed closer to Pictou Harbor, choosing to fight for the land they already had in their hand.

"We'll all go together," Mam said more firmly, reaching out her arm. Muirne clasped it. *Muirne will stay here. We'll return to the ridge. And then I must go to Pictou. I can't leave it like this, even if it does mean splitting up again.*

"Where the blaeberries grow..." Sheena's high, thin voice sang the line of the song they had sung together many times the night before. She offered Neil an unsteady smile.

"'Mang the bonnie highland heather..." Everyone finished the chorus, with sad and sheepish grins around the circle of faces.

They assembled again for goodbyes, broken up by whispers of lyrics and easing grins. Muirne let go of Neil without asking about his conversation the night before. *Thank God for that small mercy.* She did fling a look at him, though. A look of confidence and faith. As they took their leave, Neil trudged in front with the lead rope for Ed's horse, praying for St. Jude's protection.

# Chapter 46

THEY LET THEMSELVES back into the cabin, a weary group after all the high spirits. The girls went to check on the animals and rub Fortuity dry, while Neil took Alisdair out almost immediately to quarter the land that would become their fourth field. First the oat rows, then Sheena's garden patch and the potato field, then the wheat furrows. The fourth field would be barley, Neil decided. Leave the new idea for the next year.

The small, shallow-sloped dell had tall, old-growth trees of similar girth. "Must've grown up together," had been Neil's comment to Alisdair when they'd first found the grove.

*And they'll be felled together*, Neil thought as he marked out which ones to cut. They would be denuded of their branches in the following weeks by his sister and brother. Uprooting the stumps would be the work of next June.

Neil had to shout to be heard as the wind was blowing hard. "We'll leave them in place. Stack the cords neat. They'll keep fine. I'll be back before the snow even starts to melt."

"Right," the boy shouted back. He tied a strip of fabric to mark the last tree.

Neil and Alisdair set to, felling three mighty trees in six hours. The howling wind increased to whipping, icy pellets just as they started in on the final tree.

"Away home, Alisdair! I'll finish!" Neil yelled. He

caught a glimpse of Alisdair's blue eyes before he turned tail and hied home. Neil struggled to finish the last few inches that would weaken the tree enough for it to fall. With each stroke, he spurred himself into a frenzy to match the wind.

*The Law has failed. But we will not. The Janneys are like us. They'll stand up for Gillan. We will not...be...intimidated!*

The last thud reverberated up his arm painfully. He heard the loud crack, the rending of the tree's heart. He watched as it tipped, feeling a glorious vindication. *As the tree falls, so shall our enemy.*

He packed up the tools and trudged home more slowly, leaning into the wind that tried to lift him off his feet and rip off his heavy wrappings.

Neil stayed two more nights at the cabin to delay his leave-taking. Finally, he packed up the sheaf of solicitor papers in a sack with some food Sheena had put by. He embraced mother, brother, and sister. He couldn't hide his dismay at the similarity between this parting and Gillan's. His chin quivered as he looked down to where his mother sat, still in her box bed.

"I'll be back directly, after we set this right, *Mathair*."

"Of course you will," she said briskly, ignoring his serious mood.

*She chooses to hide. Perhaps she puts up a show for Sheena and Alisdair. Well, I'm done hiding.* He turned a face wet with tears to the young ones.

"You mind well," Neil said. "I expect to come back and find lots of animal hides, and all those chickens intact, you hear me?" He lifted his eyebrows at Sheena and Alisdair, who nodded vigorously.

He set off with Fortuity.

While Neil was off in Pictou, Sheena ruled the roost. She imposed an additional routine on the cabin's inmates: closing up the house and pens before dark, and keeping the fire going smartly all day. They burned through a terrible lot of wood but they did feel a bit more protected that way. Sheena went every other day to collect basket loads of the small branches from the downed trees.

A few weeks after Neil's departure, there was a very cold, very dry spell where the storms ceased. A little after dark, there was a knock at the door. Sheena looked at Alisdair, who shrugged. Knife at her side, Sheena approached the door cautiously and opened it a mere crack. Seeing it was Tom McClelland the post carrier, she let out the breath tensing her shoulders. She stepped aside to let him come in for a spell, after scanning the dark woods behind him.

Tommy brought with him a novelty: one of his recipients had put up buckets and buckets of cider from the fall apples, and had given him a large canteen of the stuff. It smelt of crisp winds and spring flowers, Sheena thought, before she took a sip. She handed it to her mother.

Mam took a sip and held the cup down close to her lap. Sheena swept it up again to prevent it being knocked over by her mother's movements.

"Thank you, Tom. It's delicious," Mam said. "A treat indeed. Have your journeys all been so profitable today?"

"Well, not too bad. People are ever so generous when the new year turns around." He ran his thumbs up and down the new set of leather braces, which Sheena dutifully complimented.

"Aye, done by Mrs. Courtney in town. She's quite talented with the leather, and gives a fair rate, being Newmand's sister. But she told me that your Muirne's baby is coming up fine. Had a visit with her, she did, coupla weeks ago."

Sheena smiled tightly. She knew she should say something nice about her niece, but—it was just a baby. She privately agreed with Alisdair's nonplussed reticence about the beauty of an infant more than she swooned at the idea of having one herself. The more marvelous thing was that her sister had created such a thing, as if from the air, and lived to tell the tale. But she knew what she was expected to say.

"Yes, Mollie is such a sweet little girl. But who is Mrs. Courtney?"

More small talk followed, the cider loosening his tongue into a confession of admiration for this Mrs. Courtney, before she pressed him for the letter he bore them.

"Here 'tis," he said, and produced a small brown envelope, creased and shiny. "Brung it out here just as soon as the ship landed, I did. The one in Pictou, not Halifax, you understand. She was mighty late, almost a month delayed by repairs in Newfoundland."

Mam's brow furrowed. "Oh?"

"Yeh. I fancy it even smells nice, but I musta imagined that bit. They keep the post in the hold with all them bales of wool and soda ash. Still," he said, sounding pleased. "Reckon Neil will be well pleased when he reads it. Where is the young'n, anyway?"

"He's away handling business, Mr. McClelland, but why do you say that?"

"Well, look. It's from a lady, much as I can make out, anyway."

Mam took the brown envelope and scrutinized the writing. She held it out for Sheena to take. It was addressed to Neil himself, not the family. When Sheena inspected it, she didn't recognize the writing, either. She couldn't say if it was a masculine or feminine hand. It simply looked—bad! As if someone was still learning the forms. It wasn't from Gillan's sister Jenny, who always paid a village scribe to write her letters. Sheena looked up at everyone staring at her.

"What? I don't know who it's from, either!"

Mam made a shooing motion for her to open it. Sheena hesitated, but the desire to know what information it held, and get that information to Neil quickly if need be, was greater than her regard for something as trifling as privacy.

*Dear Mr. MacLean,*

*Thank you for your letters. I am now abel to return one myself. I have been marrit, but am now widowed. I would like to join you if your offur still stands. I can pay my oun way. I was very sorry to lean about Mr. MacLean. Please give my best wishes to your family. I will wait for your reply.*

*Yours most sinserely,*

*Letty Cameron Ross*

Sheena read it through once silently, to make sure she understood all the words. *It's the girl! The one Neil is sweet on! She needs a reply straight away.*

She looked up; everyone was still staring. Mr. Mc-Clelland had a half-smile on his face, ready for good news. Sheena read it out and both he and Mam made noises of happy surprise.

"There! You see? My Neil has a wife waiting for him, only across the sea. Well."

"Shall I take back a reply, Mrs. MacLean?"

Sheena locked gazes with her mother. *Neil should be here for this.* She saw the thought communicate itself to her mother. A shadow crossed Mam's face. She bit her lip, then replied.

"No reply, Mr. McClelland. But as soon as Neil comes back, he'll be down in town to send one off, I'm sure!"

"Shouldn't we send it on to him at once?" Sheena asked. "It's Letty! Neil will be so happy!"

"But what if he's no longer in Pictou, dear? No, it's been several weeks; I'm expecting him back soon. I think he'll get it quicker if we just keep it fer 'im."

So saying, they thanked Mr. McClelland and invited him to stay until the morning, as it would drop to dangerously cold levels overnight. He accepted and battened down by the fire.

Sheena put the note back in its envelope and looked round their little space. She bent over Neil's small pile of clothes and personal belongings and placed the letter on the small metal box that sat by his mattress. Sheena had wondered before what Neil considered most precious to bring from home in it, but she knew for certain this letter would go well with whatever was inside.

# Chapter 47

WHEN SEVERAL MORE weeks went by without Neil appearing, Sheena started to get a squirmy feeling in her gut. Mam's face had got all pinched again, too. Sheena's anxiety took her out to the privy for long spells. Her guts were shaking with fear for her brother.

Sheena and Alisdair checked twice a week through their different paths of traps in the snow, and caught many an animal. Squirrel, rabbit, fox, weasel, and deer all went in the stewpot, their fur stripped carefully and stored for softening when Neil came back. Mam refused to entertain the possibility that he might not. She talked of the soft pillows she might sew, or the fur shawl Sheena might piece together someday.

Sheena and Alisdair together had managed quite a bit of the hewing work. After a week of laboring, one main trunk lay neatly stripped of its branches, which lay in piles of small and large kindling. After two more weeks, three more trees were broken down to their trunks. Sheena looked back at the end of each work session to appreciate the transformation of the landscape. *All by the sweat and toil of our two pairs of arms.*

The next week was lost completely due to heavy snows, and the three of them huddled together inside, glad of their store of dried mushrooms and meat and the ready supply of milk and eggs. They got back to chopping at the beginning of February, after digging out the giant trees from under several feet of snow. Sheena had never felt so happy at the opportunity to swing her axe.

One evening after supper, Sheena watched while Alisdair flipped one of the coins in her hoard for a game. He marked a paper he had for each flip. *His tutor's idea, no doubt. Fiddling with mathematics. Fat lot of good it will do us here.* If only Neil would come back, and Letty arrive to join him, their settlement could be so much more lively.

They'd had no word from Neil, and her mother's decision to delay sending him the news about Letty sat ill with Sheena. Where could he be? Certainly not at Pictou, or he would have sent word. He must have gone haring off after another fact, or witness, or document, that only he could find. A wry quirk of her mouth. Neil certainly considered himself their hero. Now Sheena didn't say they could do without him, but sometimes...*sometimes I wish he and Muirne didn't conduct themselves so much like parents.*

With a sigh, Sheena went to check on the chickens and sheep in the pen behind the house. The lamb from last spring, a male, shook where it stood. The ewe was curled up sensibly next to him, her head turned toward Sheena.

Sheena said her prayers with Alisdair that night, feeling the absence of anybody she might turn to for help. *I take back what I say about them acting like parents. I wish they were here.*

A storm of sleet kept them inside the cabin for another two days. Sheena went out with Alisdair and struggled to size and lug the next day's firewood up the hill. The food reserves they'd laid by were thinning. They would soon be in the dip between late winter and early spring, when nothing was growing, and they'd have to kill one of the hens or their lamb to keep body and soul together.

When they returned with the firewood on the sled, they met Eliza MacGregor on the hill near the cabin. She hailed them and they walked the last bit of road together before knocking the snow from their snowshoes. Mrs. MacGregor had been in to visit before, but looked around carefully at the interior of the cabin, as if noticing that something had changed. Alisdair excused himself to put the sled away and stack the wood.

Mam was at her prayers, which seemed longer and more desperate each day. She sat up in bed, eyes closed, one hand clasped in the other in her lap. Sheena sat at the table and started to knot fistfuls of rushes to dry in the rafters. Mrs. MacGregor pulled a stool from the table toward Mam's bed to converse more easily, and the scraping noise interrupted Mam's litany.

"Eliza! Welcome—what a surprise. Everything all right?"

"Oh, aye, I just thought as you might like some of the new colors I've been grinding."

"Oh, to be sure," Mam said. She seemed tense. Sheena wondered if there was an ulterior motive to the visit. Surely this was early for a pleasure call?

The two women shared news for a bit. Mam took some of the rushes and began patting them dry. Sheena saw her mother assume a pleasant aspect, and knew that she had relaxed a couple pegs, due to the easygoing presence of their favorite neighbor.

"Magistrate's absent, ye know."

Hands stilled.

"Aye. They told me that magistrate's absence had summat to do with your case, too."

Sheena's mind clicked through possibilities. Had Neil gone out with the magistrate? Where would they go? To Mr. Brown's locality, of course: Ford's Mills. What news had they got that provoked such a move? And why hadn't he written?

"That is news to us, Mrs. MacGregor. I thought Neil and the solicitor were waiting on a message from Sandy in Pictou. He's the witness," Sheena said. Mam cleared her throat.

"Perhaps they've just received his reply. Maybe this means that it'll be wrapped up soon," Mrs. MacGregor said. She patted Mam's hand, but Mam was working her mouth without any words coming out. Sheena put down her rush bundles to come and soothe her mother, sitting beside her and putting an arm around her.

Mrs. MacGregor drew back her hand slowly and peered at Sheena. "That could be the case. Are ye all right, dear? Are you managing all right?"

Sheena didn't need to look around the room to know what had disturbed their neighbor. Everything tied down for a storm, everything wedged shut and hidden away: They were already preparing to hide from the news of something happening to Neil.

"Oh aye," Mam replied, mistaking the question's destination. Her lips had stopped jerking and she was in control again. "Sheena's not so young anymore— fourteen, she is, and a good little mother hen. She and Alisdair have been working at the new timber. Everything's proceeding as it should. We will need Neil back before April if we want to get the wood down to the mill on time, though."

Sheena didn't respond to Mrs. MacGregor's question. She didn't want to open up the subject of how she was managing.

"Oh, my boys'll help ya if it comes to that. But it's still a ways off, dear Sheila. Now, I saw the dress you gussied up for Muirne. Real beautiful it were—but are you working on Sheena's yet? You know she'll go off earlier here to wed."

She didn't blush now. Talk of marriage had started with Neil and trickled into others' discourse, but Sheena didn't have time to talk of that, either. Of course, her mother couldn't do any fine sewing anymore, but Sheena didn't know if Mrs. MacGregor knew it. She might be humoring her mother. And Mam was going right along with it. The two women spoke of plans and relatives, trading news of local folk and long-ago stories of the homeland. Sheena finished bundling her basket of rushes and went to hang them in the byre, away from the animals' reach. When she was finishing up a few minutes later, she saw Mrs. MacGregor come out the front door. She went to bid their neighbor good day, then went back into the house. Mam looked replenished, sure of herself again.

Alisdair came in and they broke the news to him: Neil was now thought to be out west, in Lower Canada, with New Glasgow's magistrate.

Alisdair's eyes got big, and his hands stopped chafing themselves in front of the fire as he heard this. Sheena kept her hands busy picking the odd burr out of their fur rug. She ached to be held, but sensed it was her mother who needed to be reassured most at this moment.

"It won't be like with Gillan," Mam was saying to Alisdair. "We're established here now, and Neil will come back. And we'll be ready to welcome him, whether he succeeds in this Mr. Brown business or not, am I understood?"

Two quick replies of 'Yes'm' followed. A united front.

Sheena leaned into the open door frame and looked out.

"Clouds are drawing in, Mam," Sheena said quietly.

The sky showed an iron grey, and the wind could be seen flattening the treetops in waves. The forest cover bent hither and thither.

"I think we'll prepare for another storm," Mam said. "Alisdair, the fish from the smoking shack. Sheena, the potatoes, as many as you can find ready, quickly now."

The roof, the food supply, water enough for several days, wood enough for the same. Within a couple hours, the house was in redoubt, robustly facing the new eastern challenge.

"I'm proud of you, children. We'll do all right with you both handy." She smiled, and Sheena served the bannocks and buttermilk before going on to chores. The storm waited until dark before it began howling.

# Chapter 48

ACROSS THE FUNDY channel, an icy rain pelted the tempo-rary courthouse in Moncton. The official courthouse for the region had been swept away by flood the previous year, and was still being rebuilt. This hastily-built struc-ture reminded Neil more of a kirk than a court. Not that Neil had much experience of a court.

His heart was in his throat as he waited silently for the local judge, a man named Chipman, to stop his pon-tificating. *Speaking of the kirk*, Neil thought wryly, his mouth twitching. Dozens of the town's residents were assembled in the public gallery, despite the weather. Neil waited with the Janneys on the wooden benches nearest the door. His solicitor was up front with the barrister, both crusty men with the impatience of their profession; the solicitor had taken his documents and shooed him away while the barrister had done much the same to the solicitor.

But the focus of his attention waited in the docket. Seeing the man who was responsible for killing his stepfa-ther made Neil's heart feel prickly with heat. He an-swered Amos Janney's description: a well-padded man of middle age, dark hair curling around his ears, and an air of self-importance. Neil couldn't see the face of the accused, but the back of the man's curly-haired head was tilted back, his arms folded across himself. *Just try to protect yourself*. The image of his stepfather's eyes, searching for his from his swollen, bleeding face, flashed before him and he blinked.

With the Janneys' word on Brown's statement, Sandy Wilson's sworn affidavit on how the attack had taken place, and Neil's testimony on Gillan's condition when he arrived, they'd sped toward the jurisdiction where Brown could be prosecuted and acted with surprising swiftness. Neil had jumped at the chance, finally feeling the exhilaration of action after so many months of waiting and toil.

Neil wasn't allowed to be present for the arrest. He thought about visiting Brown in jail to see the man for himself but decided to wait. He shouldn't be counting his chickens before they hatched.

This was the moment he'd bring back to his mother. And write down for Alisdair, to read when he was older and could appreciate the wheels of justice rolling in their favor for once.

He listened as Chipman concluded his remarks: foreign-sounding legal speech, but no matter; the barristers then pleaded their case, from tables facing the judge. The hearing took less than an hour. The judge lightly tapped his little hammer, and everyone standing waited for him to exit before they started to shuffle out themselves. A bailiff came from the side wall and stood next to Mr. Brown, blocking his exit. The sneering scoundrel turned slowly to look at the bailiff, then held his hands out. His indignant pose yielded the tiniest bit to grudging acceptance. Shackles were attached to his wrists. *Aye, he's finally taking the situation seriously*, Neil thought. *Too late to undo now, ye bastard.* Brown's eyes swept the small space, skipping over Neil, glaring at Sandy, then flipping back to Neil.

Neil drew himself up, frowning. *I hate this man for taking away our da. But I won't crow over it as he did.* Brown's facial expression distorted when he saw Neil's grim expression; he shouted and cursed across the open space.

"Damned knave, that's what ye are! Blackening my name with no proof! You'll regret this!"

Neil stood firm, watching as he was led away, feeling the fearsome energy drain from his body. When Brown was gone from sight, he sat jerkily down. The solicitor with whom he'd traveled drifted to the back where they sat.

"Congratulations, Mr. MacLean. It was more than I'd expected, and eminently fair," he said. "Sixteen months in His Majesty's prison will probably break a proud, stiff man like that—"

The man's tone sounded vaguely regretful. *Wait—how long?* Neil jolted out of his torpor.

"Sixteen *months,* ye say?"

"Yes, you heard him pronounce on the counts, did you not? Acting in Conspiracy and Premeditated Assault were both sustained."

"You did not charge him with murder?"

"Well, no. We would not have won that case, Mr. MacLean. He was not the assailant, and yer father did not die immediately."

The solicitor's manner turned prim; he'd been offended. "This was the best we could hope for, I assure you. Now, good day." He lifted his case of briefs and papers and left without a backward glance.

The torpor returned; Neil sat on that bench for a long time. There were no other cases being heard until the afternoon. The place remained quietly calm against the background buzz of a few people coming and going.

Neil did not know how to return with this news. He'd thought they'd hang him. He wanted to return home and tell them all how the man was a complete coward and begged for mercy before the noose broke his neck. Maybe how it hadn't broken cleanly and he'd struggled for hours before dying, even.

His spirits sank. *Sixteen months?* All the guilt from Gillan's death eating at his courage for so long, only to end up with this? Now that the errand of justice was done, and done so badly, how could he go back home? The bastard would be out of jail in little more than a year. And after marking his face so pointedly, Neil would lay odds that he would seek him out for vengeance.

Would he have to watch his every step, awaiting the blow to come? Or would they take away his property in prison, so that he no longer had the means to compel others to do his bloody work? If it was down to a square fight, Neil thought he could take him. Thickset the man might be, but Neil was growing into his height, and the long hours on their farm were hardening his frame. But he doubted a fair fight would be what this wealthy oaf would arrange.

A new pain bloomed when he thought of how his mother would take such news. His guilt paled compared to hers, as she was the reason Brown had an onus against Gillan in the first place. The old love triangle. *Stupid man. You can't dictate love.* His courage deserted him and took his warmth with it.

His back was bowed. His head hung low, almost between his knees, as if he was going to be sick. For a moment, he let himself think of Letty, and a hard ball formed in his throat. How could he ever again ask her to come and be his wife with this sort of threat looming over them all? His failures crowded in on him and loosened the ties around his heart that had kept him hoping.

Neil took a shaky breath. No one was in the room to see him. He dashed tears away and grabbed his pack of gear, stepping awkwardly sideways the length of the row until he reached the end. He turned instinctively to cross himself facing what would normally be the sacristy, but saw only the high bank where the judge's desk stood.

*Man's justice, standing in for God's*, he thought bitterly. Neither had helped them with this case. God. He thought of what he'd told Alisdair a few months ago, about trying to avoid the bad folk and trust to God's will. No, he didn't trust anymore, but he did still believe.

His eyes slid to the packed-earth floor. He could not yet take Ed's view of the world. No, he couldna do it. It still felt too risky. He'd have to be much more certain of himself before he would abandon God.

# Chapter 49

As HE WAS traveling home, his head abuzz with agony and trepidation, Neil walked slower and slower until the sun was setting on him. He used that as a pitiful excuse to delay his entry into town, making camp several miles off in the hills. The rich mulch smell rose around him. The green blades pushing up around the bases of trees and the snow dissolving to mud in trafficked places all stirred an awareness of how long he'd been away: another cut to his duty. He'd not even sent word.

He scrubbed his face hard as he hunched over the small fire, lit in his dugout of cold earth which at least kept him dry. He brought no liquor with him—had no experience of the great oblivion that was rum in those parts—but he longed for something to wipe away all his cares and worries, even temporarily. He no longer felt the strength to fight everything alone, even for his family: the weather, the townsfolk, the auld enemies, the tough trees and hard earth. For this one night, he would allow himself to feel pitiful.

He huddled close to the fire, circled with stones, and fell asleep as soon as it fell full dark. He awoke with a start from a dream of jumping into placid dark water, gasping like a fish. After a moment to realize his wakeful state, Neil sensed a presence behind him in the dark. He slowed his breathing. The woods were quiet. The air was still. There was no lightening in the mist from a warming sun. It must be full night still. The presence felt to Neil like a hovering predator—something massive and menacing waiting in the shadows. A bear? Too quiet. A wolf? No howling.

He shifted to lay hold of the knife which lay just outside the plaid he was sleeping in. He grasped it and turned a fraction onto his back, exposing more of his front to the cold air. The feeling of being watched vanished. Neil lifted his head and listened intently for any sign of movement.

He lay back down, still clutching the knife over himself. *I will not lie here and cower. I will not be afraid of whoever is stalking me.* He threw back the blanket and scrambled to his feet, whipping his knife into a wide arc as he pivoted, eyes darting through the darkness.

"Who is it?" he yelled. "Man or beast, show yourself!"

But no one, and nothing, stepped forward. Neil was sweating, shaking, gritting his teeth. He slowly quartered the little dell, turning and looking, until he was back facing his pit of ashes and pile of gear.

"I know you're there!" he shouted again. His voice was frantic, torn between high-pitched worry and rough aggression. *I know you're out there, haunting my steps. I will break you; you will not finish me off like you did Gillan.* But Brown was in jail this night. Who could be following him? Whose malevolent presence had he felt? Whom was he addressing?

After many interminable minutes, Neil's arm grew tired. The presence was gone. He'd missed his chance to confront whatever was thwarting his path in life. With a cry, he slashed at a nearby tree. The large knife made the bark fly. On a second pass it gouged the bole of the pine tree, and stuck. Neil paused for half a second then kicked at its base, alternating feet, spending his rage sending snow and mud and rotting leaves into the air.

He grabbed at the knife handle, yanking it free and sank into a squat. He clutched the knife with both hands, watching it vibrate with his tension. The edge of the knife reflected the tiny bit of light from the moon. He started hearing noises: hissing, snuffling noises. Then he couldn't breathe; his nose wasn't working right. He was crying. He blew his nose angrily and a blot came out like a bullet.

No one was here. It was just Neil. Wishing for a demon in this new world that he could destroy. A euphoria came over him and his muscles went slack. He felt no disappointment anymore, just fatigue. Like he'd been fighting the same enemy his whole life.

When he woke again in the dawn, he was several paces away from the firepit. The knife lay near his shoulder. He shook his head and shivered, feeling the discomfort of old aches. He looked around: no disturbed ground that he could tell, except where he had turned in a widening gyre, threatening the air.

*What* was *it?* Not a townsperson, this far from the settlement. He banished it from his mind and packed up, drinking the last of the water from his canteen and smacking his lips. He would have to go to the well on his sister's street.

He shuffled down the street mid-morning. The sun was hidden by clouds, but it was dry enough for him to be thankful. When he had that thought, he banished it resentfully. *I'll not be thanking Ye today.*

He filled the canteen and approached Muirne's door.

There was a young woman there. He took her in at a glance: the good stuff dress, the two carpetbags on the ground, the head held high. And yet there was trepidation in her pinched shoulders. Perhaps she was there for a doctor. Had she knocked yet? It seemed not. What was she waiting for?

With dark thoughts of Jemima and her wiles, Neil stopped a few feet away from the door. The pale sun cast his shadow weakly across the space between them. She looked up sharply. The face turned to Neil was the one he'd been dreaming about nigh on three years. He dropped his pack on the ground.

"Letty?"

Her eyes got wide, and she drew herself back, but then firmly replanted her feet. "Hello, Neil," she said stiffly. "Ye are well?"

"Well? I——" Neil stopped. He couldn't even begin to think how she'd come to be there. He was in such a fog of wonder he almost didn't believe she was real. "What on earth are you doing here?"

"I sent a letter." A hesitant pride was in her voice, whose source he couldn't imagine. "Did ye not get my letter?"

"No, but——I've been away for some months." She looked down, nodded at the ground. Neil tried to imagine what she had said in her note. She had come here, to his sister's door, looking well and prosperous. Had she come in answer to his invitation? After three years? Right when he was giving up hope? Neil swallowed. *Mustn't jump to conclusions.* He shook his head roughly.

"I'm sorry, of course won't you come in? I'm just returning myself——" Miserable news, now this shock to his system—"We'll have some tea and hear what you've come about." Neil tried to remain calm, show some courtesy, and not attack Letty with his wild curiosity. When he met her eyes again, though, he saw doubt. She hesitated then turned to enter the door he pushed open.

He grabbed their three bags and followed her in. In the dark passageway, he became aware of her scent. He'd kissed this woman when she was yet a girl, and suddenly the memory flooded his senses: what she'd smelled like —buttermilk and beer and dried flowers—and what the skin of her cheek had felt like—the softest suede. She no longer carried herself like a girl.

She took off her small bonnet, and he saw the blue-black hair he remembered, pulled back in a severe bun at the nape of her neck. That hair he'd seen draped down her back, when he'd woken her on his urgent flight to find his family in Glencoe. Before his thoughts ran away with him, he cleared his throat and spoke.

"Just a few steps in and you'll see a place to sit. I'll fetch Muirne. She'll be in back with the baby."

She advanced slowly toward the crackle of the large fire in the hearth. Neil set down the bags and skirted around his guest to check the bedroom: no one. He went through to the narrow back kitchen, and saw Muirne waiting for him, sitting on a stool with the baby strapped to her chest as she worked a piece of dough on a rough board on her lap.

"Have you brought someone in with ye, Neil? Who is it?"

His eyes bulged with the incredulity of his news. "It's Letty. Cameron. From Glasgow."

His sister's eyes mirrored the shock in his own. She

stood abruptly, knocking the board forward, the dough almost sliding to the floor, before she swooped to pick it up with motherly reflexes. She placed it and the board high on a cupboard, dusted off her hands, and glanced down at the babe: asleep. She followed Neil back to the living room. Letty had sat down at the table but stood to meet them. There was an awkward, stunned pause.

"Won't you sit down," Muirne said, indicating the seat Letty had just leapt up from.

"Thank you, Miss—I hear you've been married?"

The evidence of the marriage turned her head slightly, but did not wake up.

"Yes, I'm Mrs. Turner now. And you are—"

Letty interrupted before she had to formulate the awkward question. "Mrs. Ross. I've been married and widowed since we last met," she said. Neil's body had frozen over for an instant, then sagged into breath again.

"And my father is dead. He left me the saloon. I've sold it."

Muirne nodded, joining her at the table. Neil remained standing—hovering really—behind Muirne, casting brief glances at the woman he'd been torturing himself over for three years. But what was he to do? He must have this letter. Was it up at the ridge? Had it been lost? Could he ask her now what her situation was? But Muirne was already doing so, far more subtly than he cold have done.

"Did you have a fair voyage? I mean, are you only just arrived?"

"Aye. Yesterday. I lodged at a boardinghouse in Pictou last night, and hired a man to ferry me across this morning."

"And how did you know to find me here, instead of getting lost in the wilderness?"

There was a smile in Muirne's voice, an invitation to confide, an understanding. Neil noticed it, and was grateful to her for it. He knew Muirne had thought damned poorly of Letty when she'd cut them off and sent no word. But Neil had always figured—hoped, really—that it had been at her father's instruction. Her showing up as they were taking sail to Canada had proved him right, he thought. It had been a cruel, if unintended, confirmation. But Muirne was at her most gracious now. He struggled to appear calm and follow the conversation.

Neil's awkwardness vanished as he listened to the tale Letty told. She was already losing the hesitation she'd had.

"I stayed with a Mrs. Conne—Coningsby?"

"Conaghey?"

"Aye, that's it. And I asked after your family. She was rather protective at first, but when I told her my business —" She fluttered her gaze to Neil, which made his heart beat thunderously. "She told me where I could find you here in town. I was planning to send word to you up the mountain, if need be."

"So you've come for a visit?" He deliberately tried to sound bright and unaffected. He certainly sounded like a dolt. He wouldn't jump to the conclusion that she still wanted to be with him after three obviously tumultuous years for both of them.

"I've come—well, to see if the offer you made still stands." She straightened in her seat, looking Neil square in the face. Her tense calm no doubt hid as much of a whirling maelstrom as his did.

"Letty, I—"

Her control held, but her anxious voice betrayed her. "And there's no need to take me on if it's not your choice. I've left Scotland for myself as well. I'm not—I won't be stranded here, if you've made other plans. I've got a bit of money—"

"Letty." She stopped spluttering. "You would make me very happy if you'd be my wife."

Her face opened up. A wide smile. The breaking of that icy formality. She was his own sweet, charming, captivating barmaid again.

She stood. He came to her side, placed his hands gently on each shoulder, and pulled her fiercely into the circle of his arms. His lips found the hair along her temple and he kissed it, over and over.

# Chapter 50

Muirne had barely recovered from her shock at seeing Letty Cameron standing in her doorway when she realized that Neil couldn't get a grip on himself. She took control of the situation and easily maneuvered the conversation to get to the heart of the matter. *They've both come so far, now they've just got to get out of their own way.*

When Neil gave what she supposed was his proposal, Muirne turned away, knowing they would embrace. After giving them a moment of privacy, she turned back. She saw Neil with his eyes closed, his cheek against the top of Letty's dark head. A peculiar pain pulsed in Muirne's breast. *It is bittersweet to gain the object of your love after so much loss; that's a lesson I learned as well.*

She cast another glance over Letty. The girl had definitely come up in the world since the last time she'd seen her in Glasgow. Either the sale of the saloon or the husband who had died had left her with the money for passage and then some.

She seemed more staid, perhaps, but with plenty of that cheeky spirit floating behind her rosy cheek. Muirne figured that playfulness would serve Neil well, him with his long serious bouts and wanting to fill both Gillan's and their father Alec's shoes. Muirne summoned a smile and cleared her throat.

"Well, so?"

The pair broke apart, each smiling and laughed at

each other's expressions. They still didn't look away from each other's gaze. *I was most certainly not this pudding-headed.* She felt a little exasperated at their intimate, silent communication, but then relented. It had been quite a long time apart, and quite a long chance that they would find each other again. She spoke softly.

"Would you be needing to stay the night with us, Mrs. Ross?"

That interrupted their tête-à-tête. A little of Letty's womanly self-possession came back as she turned to Muirne.

"If it would not be too much trouble, I'd be very grateful."

"No trouble at all," Neil responded. "I'll make up a bed on Alisdair's cot in there after supper." He indicated the second bedroom, where his brother stayed for lessons during school terms. Letty nodded.

"Can you come back to the cabin with me tomorrow? It's a single day's journey if we step lively," Neil said.

Letty looked undecided for a moment, then assented. "I suppose that is the first place to go. Will anyone be coming up with us?"

"If you can wait a day or two, Ed will be here," Muirne said. "We can all go."

"Do we need to—should we send ahead to let your mother know?" Letty asked delicately. This produced a bark of laughter from Neil.

"If they have the letter, they'll know already. I'm the one you surprised like a bolt from the blue!" He grinned.

Edward came home the next evening and heard the tale of Letty's arrival. He agreed to accompany them back up the mountain in two days. Neil spent the day showing her the wee town, walking up and down the lanes in the cold spring sunshine. Muirne had to reserve her judgement again about being pudding-headed, but she hoped he was acquainting his future wife with the situation—the multiple situations—facing the family. If he was, it didn't look like Letty minded a sick mother and a murdered family member. *Well, ye're very welcome, then,* Muirne thought with a laugh.

Two mornings later, Neil, Letty, Edward, and Muirne, with Mollie on her back, made their way up the now-familiar forest path. Letty's luggage was pulled on a travois by Fortuity, making them look like quite the grand party. Neil was murmuring again to Letty. Muirne caught a few words—*fall, effort, judge*—and breathed a sigh of relief. He was the elder but with boys it was hard to say when they first began to use their common sense.

They were toiling up the simple dirt road to their cabin when Sheena spied the party and let out a shout.

"It's Neil!" she called, as his blond head topped the rise first. When Muirne and the horse and Ed and a stranger followed a moment after, however, Sheena's expression went from jubilant to wary to anxious. They reached the cabin clearing and Sheena was waiting close to the door, muddy from her knees down. She took a few steps forward to meet them as they straggled into the yard.

"We've been waiting on you, Neil. What's happened? Why has everyone come? Is the house—?"

"No, the house is fine. Is Mam inside?" He spoke quickly, lightly.

"Aye, and Alisdair out in the field below. Shall I call him?"

"No need." Neil curled in his lower lip and let forth a loud, high-pitched whistle. "He'll be up in a minute. Let's go in."

Neil gestured with his arms for everyone to precede him toward the door. Muirne flashed a grin at Sheena as she hugged her sister so she wouldn't worry. They heard Alisdair's huffing and puffing behind them.

"Neil! You're back! Guess what—" he stopped mid-sentence as Neil put up his hand.

"Come on in, Alisdair. There are people to meet."

# Chapter 51

NEIL USHERED THEM all in. Letty was here! She was *here*. He could hear Sheena chattering and Alisdair squeaking his consternation at seeing everyone assembled, and then, he caught sight of his mother.

Mam stood in front of the hearth, near the dark doorway to the byre. She clutched the doorjamb with both hands to keep her balance. She wore a rapturous expression. What had she been expecting? He hardly knew. She made eye contact with him and he saw the tears brimming in her eyes. Happy tears. She was glad he was back, that was it. The memory of the news he had to deliver rushed back: the roar of thunder that he had been ignoring for two days. He ducked his head.

Mam struggled into the room, and Edward went to hold her arm and buttress her side. She waved her good arm toward Neil's pallet. Everyone was silent as she and Edward tentatively stepped toward it. She whispered something to him and he bent to pull a paper out of Neil's metal box. Neil wrinkled his brow. *That paper—a letter—it must be—* Ed handed it to Mam and everyone waited in respectful silence.

Mam turned to look at Letty fully, and Letty straightened. Mam put out her good arm and Letty advanced the few steps to clutch her hand. Mam handed her letter back to her and patted her hand. "Go on," she said. "Give it to him yourself."

Letty gave her cheek a quick kiss before turning to Neil. She opened the letter and handed it to him with its four points splayed out. He looked at the writing, painstaking and amateurish, and looked at Letty, whose eyes were like twin cauldrons of black flame. She was excited, proud, bashful. The words did no justice to the determination and desire in that dear face.

"You wrote this?"

She nodded emphatically once. "I so wanted to be able to return one of your letters. It took me the better part of a year to get the alphabet and some spelling basics. I had to learn—in secret, a bit."

"Well, I'm sure I'm fair impressed!" He smiled at the general oohing and awwing that came from his family. His smile didn't quite reach his eyes. "But there's some news."

His warm humor was suddenly dashed with cold water as emotions flooded through him. Letty come to him, only after he'd basically followed a wild goose chase to failure. He turned toward his mother, leaving off his light tone.

"I think I know what your news is, Neil," said his mother waggishly. Bursts of laughter from Alisdair and an excited gasp from Sheena.

"No. I mean I have something to say about the suit against Mr. Brown."

It was as if a finger of frost had touched them. Letty was the only one left wondering.

"I had just come back to town when I met up with Letty—Mrs. Ross," he said, nodding in Letty's direction. "The case is concluded. I found a solicitor in Pictou recommended by MacLachlan. Almost as soon as I had engaged him, he got the news of an arrest in Ford's Mill—

some other assault charge which meant they would accept the testimony of our witnesses. So. The solicitor or
barrister decided the best strategy for conviction was to
try Brown for conspiracy and assault instead of murder.
We won. He's received sixteen months' time in prison."

A silence fell. Neil's heavy face told them to wait for
more.

"He couldn't be tied directly to Gillan's murder—the
assault—so that was the most they could do. But he
marked me, in the courtroom. I—I fear I shouldn't have
made myself known to him. I'm afraid he will come here,
be emboldened—" Neil's eyes flashed to Letty. "I've
made us more vulnerable, instead of finding justice for
Da. I've failed twice over. I'm sorry, Mam. I—"

"Stop it!" Muirne wore a fierce, terrifying look: knitted brows, open mouth, pointing finger. "You *found* the
devil, Neil. Now we know. There is at least that to put to
rest. As for punishing the man, you know that's God's
work. Leave it to Him."

Muirne's words did not remove any sense of his burden. But he yearned still to be free of it so he could reach
out and take hold of the happiness—*his happiness!*—that
stood in that room. They were all watching Neil. He
looked to his mother. Mam took a halting half-step away
from Edward, her hand wringing the end of her apron.
She stilled its shaking, straightening her arms at her sides
and sending her chin aloft.

"It is certainly not your responsibility to be law and
order around here, Neil. You've done what you can. We
can't bring Gillan back. But we can put him to rest. That
is enough. Now is the time to enjoy the peace you've
won."

A moment passed and Neil nodded. Mam turned to Letty.

"Letty, welcome to our home. I am happy you've come to stay. Neil should be, too. I'm thinking we should build another cozy house 'cross the way, don't you think, Muirne?"

Muirne's eyebrows went up, then she scrambled to follow her mother's lead with a mock-innocent grin. Neil would have rolled his eyes if his heart hadn't been so full of gratitude for their mischief. "Why yes, I think another cabin in the clearing might help with the wind—"

"And be a perfect place to welcome visitors," Edward chimed in.

"Surely not. A whole house for the two of us?" Neil asked.

Mollie chose that moment to start burbling again.

"Oh. Ah." Neil said, to general laughter. "Well, perhaps we should make a start on a new structure…"


The days lengthened, and the work expanded to fill all the hours of sunlight, and more. Still, there was time for Neil to sit by the fire in the evenings and muse on how he could have done better in his pursuit of Brown. His regret set up house within him, layering over and filling in the chinks of his guilt from having stayed while Gillan left. Now, he ruminated on how to be ready for an attack, for come it would, he was sure, in sixteen months or so. At least the judge had punished the man with fines as well, so there wouldn't be extra funds to hire an assassin while he was in jail.

After the kirk in town had posted the banns, he and

Letty were married on a June afternoon. He moved the byre farther back toward the drop of the hill and built an addition to the cabin for Letty and himself. This took four weeks of grading, stone-gathering, and log-selecting, after which they got the help of the MacGregors' sons to attach larger logs for a new roof for the whole structure.

There was talk of getting all the neighbors together to help build a whole new cabin, but that was a project for another summer. Neil contented himself with the farming and the construction of a new porch for their front door. He pictured coming up the rise to the cabin clearing after a day's work to see his mother at one doorway and his wife at the other, talking the day away. He grinned as he imagined Letty's very different ideal of domestic bliss.

But at night, Neil let go of worries over the crops and future threats. Letty said good night to his family members and came to join him in their bed. He was the happiest he could remember. He told her tales of his island home. He listened to her anecdotes about customers at the tavern and her more somber tales of marriage to a cold old codger who had eventually obliged her by dying of pneumonia.

Letty told him how proud she was of his steadfastness at work, his cleverness with new tasks, and her kind words helped to draw the venom of his other disappointments, though these did not disappear completely. Most of all she liked his quiet excitement when he got a new idea and told her about it. After her cold old codger, Letty seemed to want to love him all the more enthusiastically. It was a new flood of sensations for Neil, these pleasures of the body, and he was happy to experience them on the edge of the wilderness, hidden from the rest of the world.

After the midsummer wedding, the MacLeans argued good-naturedly about how to situate the second cabin. Supplies were purchased, crops tended, and animals guided to the sweet summer forage. The family regularly hosted the neighbors' ceilidh of a Saturday night. Neil made plans for a hay field, this one a little farther from the cabin, to feed their growing number of animals over winter. He sweated in the sun, he schemed for greater security, and he kept a weather eye on the path down to the rest of the world.

# Chapter 52

WITH HER HUSBAND, daughter, and household to manage in town, Muirne didn't see her family on the ridge as often as before. They exchanged regular missives, some written and delivered by Tommy, some verbal and borne by Edward on his longer rounds. Muirne spent an awful lot of time talking to Mollie, making sure she knew what a wonderful baby she was. How adoring her father was. What a wonderful life she would lead, free and clear of the terror of the landlords back home.

With her husband becoming a popular guest in homes around town, Muirne learned how to strike the right note of reserve required when she attended dinners with him. She told the tale of how they met only about a hundred times. She didn't warm to the finer ladies at these dinners, nor did she really relax while visiting her mother-in-law.

The lady had visited a month after Mollie arrived, without her husband. He was at sea again, she said. Muirne wondered if he would always be at sea when it came to relations with his son. It settled into a pattern of two yearly visits from Matilda: one on the baby's birthday and one when her husband went on his long summer voyage, sailing to Australia and back. Every visit demanded a performance, a keeping of the peace, an effort for Edward's sake. Muirne ached at the end of a long meal, groaning not with the weight of the rich food—although there was that—but with the soreness in her back from holding herself so stiffly.

It was new, and not unlooked-for, but it pleased Muirne immensely when she saw that Edward understood her. He sat her upon his lap late at night, caressing the base of her skull with his palm, and she felt—gentled. Eased from the pair of pincers pressing her head, and relaxed. She treasured this stolen time, just as she marveled at the way she was able to love little Mollie.

The respect of the shopkeepers didn't thrill her quite as much after a few years' time. She went to the town kirk once a month, Edward choosing to make his rounds in the countryside more and more often during these times. She wended her way back with Mollie from each of these outings. She tried not to think of Jemima as she passed the door next to theirs, but it was impossible.

The door hung more and more askew until September, when it finally fell inward. She noticed it one day as she passed with her day's purchases. She peeked her head in and felt a cool gust down her spine as she saw the cobwebs, the moss, the puddles. Not a stick of furniture left. What had happened to Jemima's mother? She hesitated to ask Mr. Bracethwaite what had become of his sister when his niece's reputation lay in tatters. Muirne had not seen her neighbor once since the birth.

Hard as she tried not to let it, her gaze would dart to that doorway for the year after Mollie's birth, and whatever she was thinking of would be swept out of her mind. It was hard to identify all of the emotions individually: there was anger, outrage, bitterness. But there was also pity, and buried very deep down, compassion. Jemima had been desperate and alone. Who knows what had happened for the child to be conceived? Not she.

As the next autumn cooled the air, and the snow started to fill in the nooks and crannies, Muirne wondered one evening whether Neil had ever gone to see if Jemima was at the lake settlement, and how she was faring. *Likely not*, she thought. *Not with he and Letty bein' as happy as a pair of bluetits up on the ridge.*

She stopped to really consider what had become of Jemima and her baby. Her thimble arrested itself mid-air and she lost track of where her needle should have come up as she remembered that cold, dark night. Jemima had said on the night of First Footing that the baby boy had been taken away to be with its father. Did she live with the man's family? How did the Mi'qmaq do these things? Her curiosity was growing as she thought about it, the thimble feeling out the needle's place again.

"Everything all right, Muirne?" The firelight played across her husband's face as he watched her from his writing desk.

"Yes, Edward. How are the accounts looking?"

"Very good. We are doing very well, at the conspiring of just about everyone we know." His eyebrows relaxed as he gave her a half-smile. "But you were stopped suddenly just now. Was there not a dramatic discovery just being made?"

"Oh, don't tease me. My mind drifts, you know. I was only thinking—well, do you ever visit the lake settlement to give care to the Mi'qmaq, Eddie?"

"Quite regularly. The gentleman from Merigomish and I take turns each month to visit. Why?"

"Oh, because I thought—oh, no reason." Her fingers flashed more urgently in the thick layers of cotton. "Do any ladies of the kirk visit them? Only, we used to have ladies visit with baskets of dry goods once a year, back home."

"That's a nice thought. Were you thinking of organizing a charity outing from the kirk? I would think an escort in order. It is quite a journey, even on horseback. That particular route is quite grueling, up and around those hills. I have to rest the horse when I've got any extra supplies. And in snow—well, you'd have to pick the right day."

"Mmm," she mumbled in reply, all the while formulating a plan that was half-curiosity, half-charity. It would also assuage her increasingly demanding conscience.

After a week of calls around the neighborhood, she embarked for the lake with two carriages of three ladies each. They brought medicines, pats of butter and lard, and thick woolen blankets in baskets. They also brought Peter, the errand boy of the general store, who was known to the Mi'qmaq of the lake settlement from his message-bearing visits. He was a self-possessed twelve-year-old, and would be both a male presence and an envoy recognizable by tribal members.

Muirne arrived with the party of ladies and oversaw the greeting and unloading process with half her attention focused on her peripheral vision. They were outside, as the village had no communal building. She stood at the head of their column of ladies, in the open space between the half-dozen large tents. A stiff wind blew at their backs. Past the last hut was the slow sweep down to the lake, where large, dark pebbles and rocks replaced the thinly packed soil.

She swept the small crowd of black-haired, stalwart

faces for a glimpse of a dirty blond head, but she did not see Jemima in the group. She was surprised there were so few families living here. Were there more still squatting among the settlements? Why had they not seen any on their ridge?

A clumpy line of toddling babies fanned out among the crowd that had gathered to investigate the fuss being made by the white women. Muirne searched each little face for a hint of Jemima's lineage, but could find no child unlike the others in nose or chin or hair color. Her vision blurred a moment; the disappointment was overwhelming. She only wished to see them safe, know that they were not abandoned. She turned her head to the side to dab at her eyes with her handkerchief.

That's when she saw the two solitary figures, down by the lake, beyond the edge of the village. One stood in profile, dress and shawl a light grey smudge against the dark shine of the shore rock. The other squatted low at the water's edge, wrapped in the same canvas-colored smock that the village children sported. The standing figure had a cloth wrapped 'round her head, but the swatch of dark blond fringe at the front was unmistakable.

Muirne's hand went to her belly; she clenched it to a fist as the fizz of emotions welled out of her. It *was* Jemima. And her boy, whatever name she'd given him. The woman's stance was forced casual, as if she knew she was turning her back on everyone. She was completely focused on the innocent way the boy was bending down and breaking up the ice, looking, grabbing, showing his mother. *So Jemima has made up her own world, with a healthy child at the center.*

Jemima pulled her shawl closer around herself then put out a hand to lead the boy away. She labored up the hill toward the group of women, whose voices Muirne only then started to hear again. She swung around to appear attentive, the next minute waiting for the tug at her sleeve that would be one or the other of the pair importuning her attention. She hoped she could muster a generous smile when she turned to meet them.

But no tug came. When Muirne finally turned back, there was nothing but footprints in the snow, leading away from the lake, toward the other side of the village. *They must have avoided me. Small wonder.* She squinted at where the footprints led and saw the two figures across the lake. Jemima stood, waiting for her attention. When Muirne stood watching, she lifted up her arms and shook them triumphantly. Then she turned, and they vanished between two huts.

Muirne focused again on her pretext for the visit, attending to what the elderly Mi'qmaq man was saying. She only half-registered the placid, interested smiles on the faces of the five other ladies as she felt deeply shaken inside. *What was the meaning of that? Did she shake her fists at me? Was that a threat? Or a protest of strength, when I seemed to be pitying her? Why did she not come speak to me, as she's done before?*

She returned late that evening, picking up Mollie from Possie next door, who'd been happy to watch her during the day. She patted the small bulge of her second pregnancy as she sat and started peeling potatoes. Muirne felt oddly bereft of Jemima's presence, as if an opposing force toward which she had oriented herself was now gone. *It's as I told Neil; meting out the real punishment is God's work. Perhaps best I didn't talk to her.*

But the way Jemima had disappeared disturbed Muirne. On the way home, she chatted to Peter in the carriage. He regretted to say that he knew almost nothing about the white woman who lived among the Mi'qmaq settlement. He found the other residents at the lake much more interesting.

Muirne stayed up late that night, far after she had lulled Mollie to sleep in the rocking chair. That presence that had vanished—was she not glad it was gone? Had it not felt like a weight? She looked down at Mollie's face in shadow, splotchy and plump. *Be at rest, Father. Gillan. Jemima. Be at peace.*

Edward found her asleep in the rocking chair when he returned past midnight. When he woke her with a cold nose in her ear, she bolted up, then eased back down, smiling.

"It'll be fine," she murmured, before letting her eyelids drift downward again.

Glossary of Select Terms for *The Grasping Root*

*Beannachd leibh:* (Gaelic) blessings with you, a form of good-bye (Ch. 34)

*Bliannath Mhath Ur:* (Gaelic) happy new year (Ch. 43)

*Boneys:* an early 19th-century derogatory English term for the French military (https://www.geriwalton.com/21-nick-names-of-napoleon/)

*Box bed:* a type of wooden bed built into a recess, attached to the panelling or roof timbers, or freestanding. It could have panels that opened or curtains to be drawn across for warmth and privacy. (http://www.oldandinteresting.com/box-beds.aspx)

*Byre:* (chiefly British) A barn, especially one used for keeping cattle in

*cas-chrom:* (Gaelic: 'crooked foot') a type of digging implement which looked like a shovel but with a wooden step for the foot instead of a blade

*Ceilidh:* a gathering of people for the purpose of visiting, celebrating, singing, dancing, eating, and drinking. They are still very popular in Scotland.

*Creel:* a wicker basket. Large creels were used to carry peat from the field or seaweed from the beach to the fields for fertilizer.

*Croft:* a small plot of arable land farmed by tenants for a large landowner. Croft farming used to be the norm all over Scotland, but today it is a rare occupation.

*Duke of Perth:* a Scottish Country Dance performed to the reel of the same name

*feileadh beag:* an abbreviated version of the feileadh mhor, or great kilt, where the top half of the plaid was cut off and the bottom half permanently pleated, so that it was easier to put on and take off (http://www.tartansauthority.com/highland-dress/ancient/)

*First Footing:* the New Year holiday as it is observed by Scots and some northern English people. It consists of someone entering the house soon after midnight. In order for the residents to have good luck in the new year, the first visitor should be a tall, dark-haired male. He is also expected to bring symbolic gifts such as bread, salt, and whisky.

*Glencoe:* a deep, impressive valley in the northwest of Scotland. It is known for the massacre that took place there in 1692, in which the Campbells reputedly hosted the McDonalds in their house, then tried to kill them on a government order. The two families were traditional enemies, and this event was part of a large struggle for the government of Scotland.

*gowk:* Scot & Northern English, dialect for a foolish or stupid person (http://www.dictionary.com/browse/gowk)

*Hogmanay:* the celebration of New Year in Scotland. There are various traditions that make up the holiday, including Norse and Gaelic roots. It was much more celebrated in the past than Christmas Day.

*keening: a* sharp, wailing sound. It is how a person might express grief at a funeral, and it was actually a profession for women who mourned at strangers' funerals in Scotland and Ireland.

*kelp-burning:* During the Napoleonic Wars, Great Britain had no source of barilla, an alkaline powder made in Spain, which was used in the glass and soap industries. For about thirty years, kelp was the domestic source of alkaline ash for those industries, with the result that it became very profitable for a short amount of time, then collapsed when the wars were over. (www.biomara.org and www.highlandclearances.co.uk)

*ken:* know or recognize someone or something

*kirk:* Scots dialect for church, used when speaking of the Church of Scotland. It is a loan word from Old Norse.

*Michaelmas:* the feast of St Michael for the Western Christian Church. Important feast days such as this one were used as calendar markers because everyone celebrated them and they helped mark the seasons and tasks of the year. Michaelmas is on September 29, and marks the end of harvest. (Ch. 29)

*mo fheadhainn ghaolach:* Gaelic for 'my dear ones' (Ch. 13)

*plaid:* refers to the large section of tartan or plain woolen cloth worn by men around the lower body and folded up and over the shoulder or head as well. Today it is used for formal dress, but it used to be more of an everyday garment.

*sal volatile:* smelling salts, either in liquid or crystalline form, a compound made with ammonia to arouse consciousness

(https://en.wikipedia.org/wiki/Smelling_salts)

*Seceders:* a group that seceded from the established Church of Scotland. There were numerous secessions in the 18<sup>th</sup> century due to the turbulent political climate and the way in which the church and state power structures intertwined. Sometimes known as Dissenters, or Covenanters, after the 17<sup>th</sup> century Secession movement.

*St. Andrew's Day:* November 30, when the patron saint of Scotland is celebrated.

*smoor:* to smother or suffocate a peat fire, in order to keep it controlled overnight and be able to rouse it again in the morning. There was often a prayer said when the fire was smoored at night. (http://www.dsl.ac.uk/entry/snd/smuir)

*travois:* (Canadian French) a historical frame structure used by indigenous peoples to drag loads over land (https://en.wikipedia.org/wiki/Travois)

*wame:* (Scottish and Northern England dialect) the belly, abdomen, or womb

*Did you enjoy this book?*

*Please consider posting a review.*

Reviews like yours help this book find its way into the hands of new, grateful readers. This helps self-published authors gain readers online and through word-of-mouth networks.

Reviews are much appreciated at Amazon.com, Goodreads.com, or any other review sites. Or spread the news through your own networks on Facebook and Twitter!

You are welcome to visit my author website for blog posts, events, news, and giveaways:

www.margaretpinard.com

Good books should be shared!

My eternal thanks for your time, attention, and encouragement.

*-Margaret Pinard*

# Acknowledgements

This book proved a particularly difficult nut to crack. I could not have delved into the heart of the story as deeply without the support of the diverse cast of characters that populate my writing life. To the following people go my heartfelt thanks:

To the Portland writing community, including my GSD partners in crime, the Guttery critique group, fellow WDSers, and my editor, Claire Rudy Foster.

To the specialist knowledge wielders that supplied endless answers to research questions, including the Northwest Slighe nan Gaidheal family, writers met through the Historical Novel Society, and the good folk at Wikipedia.

To my friends, coworkers, and bosses who rallied support in times of scarcity instead of giving a hard eye roll, especially my Early Readers and Sarah Brown, Kindra Mohr, Monica Barnard, Jess Berlow, Rooske de Joode, Melia Dicker, Leigh Suga, and Kim McClain.

To my mother, my biggest fan, as well as my dad, sisters, cousins, and aunts who support their off-the-beaten-path relative. And finally:

To all those who send Christmas cards,

To all those who come out for karaoke,

To all those who have journeyed to Renaissance Fair,

To all those who leave reviews!

# About the Author

MARGARET PINARD is a writer, bookseller, singer, cat-owner, language-lover, and tea-drinker living in Portland, Oregon. Her first documented inspiration for writing fiction was *Newsies*. After a cringeworthy attempt to pass as 'normal,' she was inspired again to write for her very survival by the *Outlander* novels. She now leads a madcap existence pursuing what she loves.

You can connect with Margaret on her website, Facebook, & Twitter:

www.margaretpinard.com
www.facebook.com/wetastelifetwice
www.twitter.com/tastelifetwice

Made in the USA
Coppell, TX
11 April 2021

53552133R00204